ITALIAN
DREAMS

ITALIAN
DREAMS

□

Elizabeth Howe

STRAND
PUBLISHING

Acknowledgements

The author thanks the Victoria & Albert Museum Reading
Room staff; The London Transport Museum; and recommends
readers interested in railway poster art visit the large collection
held at the National Railway Museum, York. Special thanks are
due Leonardo Bercovici for encouragement and criticism; Adriana
La Gumina Crockford for Italian grammar; Malvina Tribe for
editorial endeavour; and family and friends for their support.

The cover art is by Clare J. Rushmer.

A CIP catalogue record for this book is available from the British Library

ISBN 0 9524344 1 5 (Casebound) ❀ ISBN 0 9524344 0 7 (Paperback)

Printed in Cornwall by Hartnolls Limited

Strand Publishing
The Strand, Lucy's Beach
Flushing, Cornwall
TR11 5TY

Author's Note

This is a work of fiction. With the exception of actual historic figures (Mussolini, Guzzoni) and incidents (Italian invasion of Albania) mentioned, all names, locales, events, characters, and conversations are products of the author's imagination.
Any resemblance to persons living or dead is purely coincidental.

Chapter 1

Like the touch of cold fingers against the nape of her neck it was happening again.

Maureen closed her eyes, shook her head, and slipped her arm into John's. When her fingertips contacted the fabric of her husband's sleeve, the sense of otherness and half-memory drifted away. She opened her eyes and looked around. Inside huge carved doors, swung wide for this evening's festive occasion, they stood before three shallow steps that led into an elegant room.

After the rapid pace John had maintained ascending the wide curved staircase of the *palazzo*, Maureen had been relieved to pause and catch her breath. Now she tried to dispel the strange feeling that she was somewhere else, or someone else.

The XVIIth Century Palazzo d'Orinici, off the Via Giulia, lay in what once had been the ancient heart of Rome. It looked severe and forbidding from the taxi, but inside, and especially here on the second floor which overlooked the River Tiber, she was dazzled by the effect. The faded grandeur of the Italian Renaissance was displayed in all its richness of design, materials and imagination.

Across the salon Maureen could see Rome's skyline, framed like a series of painted vistas by the tall windows. Low on the horizon, the September sun drenched the russet-tiled rooftops, the ornamental facades and the fretted domes with gold. Evening trailed ribbons of amethyst, lapis and ruby in the golden light.

Beneath high gilded ceilings and ornate chandeliers people strolled about or stood in groups talking. They looked cool and fresh despite the lingering heat of the day. Their movements added shifting pools of colour around the rose marble pedestalled urns, which overflowed with flowers.

Waiters bearing silver trays glided expertly among the eighty or more guests already assembled. The practitioners and researchers from diverse fields and countries who would be taking part in the forthcoming 1975 International Medical Conference were accompanied tonight by spouses and friends. In a far off corner, seated near dark green marbled walls, a string quintet could just be glimpsed and heard. Respighi's "The Fountains of Rome," was a melodic surround to the murmur of conversation.

"There they are - I've spotted them," John said. "All the way down to the right."

His voice brought her back into focus. At least he hadn't noticed any of her strange interludes today. Not that he was ever much aware of what she might be experiencing. Because of his busy general practice in a small London clinic, that was understood and accepted. Many of his evenings along with some weekends had to be sacrificed to his work. Anyway, she couldn't have tried to explain to anyone what had been happening since they'd arrived in Rome.

The disturbing sensations had begun right after

vacating the taxi from the airport outside the Hotel Apollino, and again when walking into a sunlit square nearby. She had seemed to be stepping out of herself, caught up with some other existence. But this time an added dimension had momentarily frightened her - the sense of 'knowing something'. As though she had a memory of this place, an elusive echo of another life.

It had nothing to do with the normal excitement of a ten-day holiday in a city she had always dreamed of visiting. During her childhood something similar had occurred.

John was now propelling her forward down the steps and into the room.

"Let's find out how the Grants are bearing up to it all at the Excelsior. They must be suffocated in pomp and circumstance. And luxury, the lucky fools."

Their own entirely comfortable but more intimate lodging had been reserved back in April when they had first planned to attend. Laura and Michael Grant, met on this morning's plane from London, told them theirs had been a last-minute decision.

As they approached the attractive couple who were about the same age as themselves, mid-to-late thirties, Laura assumed a theatrical pose.

"You haven't gone out and done it already, have you?"

"Done what?" Maureen was immediately cheered by the proximity to people again.

"Gone shopping, of course - why else are we here?"

"No, I haven't shopped. There hasn't been time yet."

"Well that dress is gorgeous. It looks designed just for you."

Maureen smiled at Laura's graceful compliment and moved to stand alongside her, for Michael and John were already immersed in their own conversation. The simple leaf-green silk chiffon that fell to handkerchief points at the knees flattered her chestnut-coloured hair and green eyes.

"And I'm not sure I can go now. Last week I blew most of my spending money on this - at a sale in Mayfair."

Laura laughed. "Then your punishment, my girl, will be to accompany me, when I bargain Rome's best couturier into the basement." Her smile grew wicked. "Or the bedroom, if that's what it takes."

"I'd love to come along - bargaining lessons are just what I need. And I've heard the workmanship here is so good."

She had liked this woman the moment they met, and began to look forward to the evening ahead. Although both were raising two children, Maureen found it refreshing that Laura wasn't overly preoccupied with them; and she seemed totally devoid of that irksome addiction some English women had for the cleverly cutting remark. It was especially noticeable among London wives of professional men.

Their husbands too had found a common interest discovering that each had a general practice. After learning the Grants lived near Greenwich, barely ten miles from Chelsea, she was confident they would continue to keep in touch after their return to London.

Maureen was admiring Laura's appearance tonight which revealed taste and a dash of flair. Glossy black curls had been swept up into a chignon and dramatized her vivacious blue eyes and ivory complexion. The black taffeta dress had a froth of embroidered white lace around the low curved neckline.

It gave her the look of an impish courtesan.

As they stood talking another couple joined their foursome, soon followed by two more people. The last arrivals were known to the Grants, so Michael performed the introductions. He was just finishing, and Maureen had half-turned to accept a glass of white wine from the waiter's tray, when her glance was caught and held.

Halfway across the room a man was standing quite still, staring at her.

Maureen managed to complete the act of taking the glass, but she hesitated before bringing it to her lips. When she raised her eyes again she saw the man had started to walk towards her. The expression on his face was one of acute surprise, almost disbelief. She felt transfixed by his look as he advanced. Then he was there, standing in front of her.

"Marinella . . . non è possible . . . non può esser vero, tu."

Everyone within their group stopped speaking and stared. Maureen felt a stillness settle over her, an easy quietness that made it unnecessary to respond or even avoid his eyes. Some part of her mind had registered that they were dark brown and gentle, if troubled right now. It was impossible and yet it seemed that he knew her. Then, for a brief second, she felt a flash of response, even though she was certain she had never met him before.

John cleared his throat and said in a tight, formal tone,"I'm afraid my wife doesn't speak Italian."

For a long moment the stranger continued gazing at Maureen, then he turned to look at John.

"Excuse me. Please. I thought . . ."

He extended his hand in a gesture that looked more British than Italian.

"I am Cesare Bracci - Dottore. Your wife, Signore, she . . . she looks so much like someone I know . . . that I once knew." He turned his glance back to Maureen.

"My deepest apologies, Signora. It was . . . that you resemble very much an old friend of my family."

John, who had accepted Bracci's extended hand in a brief but firm handshake, said, "John Standish. And, this is my wife - Maureen Standish."

Maureen, aware that John was being stuffy and British, still wondered why her attention was so drawn to this stranger before her.

"But my wife is English," John went on, managing to sound even more stuffy. "Well, that is, we both are of course. And - since this is our first visit to Italy . . . " He paused, then continued, "Unless your friend is English too, that's rather an odd mistake to make."

"No, no! Now I see, it is an error. It was . . . a lapse of memory only. Forgive me, please."

His face relaxed into a charming smile as his glance swept around to each of them in turn.

"Is there not some expression too, in your language? Something that says, 'one is brushed by a ghost from the past'?"

Like a stab, the phrase reminded Maureen of the feeling as she entered this room. That touch of cold stillness, the sensation she had become someone else for an instant. And now here was this man, who seemed to be linked to that other world she had almost, but not quite entered.

Somehow the conversation had resumed in a normal manner again and Michael Grant was introducing everyone to the newcomer. Maureen heard him say he remembered seeing Bracci's name

on the roster of Italian hosts and participants of the
conference, in a field different from his own. After a
few more minutes, Cesare Bracci excused himself from
their company, with another graceful apology to John
and a small bow to Maureen. She watched as he
disappeared into the shifting clusters of people now
filling the salon.

One of the older men started teasing John about
the weakness of Italians for a pretty face, causing his
plump, plain wife to direct a stony look toward him.
The conversational pace picked up as talk returned to
medical matters and the agenda for the days ahead.

Maureen took a sip of wine and found the crisp
taste refreshing, and normal. Close beside her ear she
heard Laura giggle. She turned to look at her.

"S-o   good-looking. If I were his wife I'd insist
he limit his medical practice to Geriatrics Only !" Her
look sobered and her eyes on Maureen's face had a
searching quality.

"Curious. It was quite uncanny there for a
minute, you know."

"What do you mean - why?"

"Well . . . he really did look shocked to see you
here." A smile reappeared. "You wouldn't conceal an
exciting double-life from a pal, would you?"

At least Laura's sense of humour was a support
right now. Maureen tried to make her response sound
casual.

"The only strange part was, I didn't understand
a word he was saying, but I thought. . ." She stopped,
then hastily added, "But then Italian's an easy
language."

Confused that she had said this when the only
other language she spoke was French, she made to
move away and attempted to catch John's attention.

"Do you think we could persuade them to escort us, to that wonderful-looking banquet table over there?"

"Hell, yes! My sentiments exactly, I'm starving. From here it looks like a work of art, but my stomach has no shame."

Chapter 2

If judged by the now dedicated interaction between the participants and the rising volume of conversation, the reception was a success. The string quintet had decided not to compete for a while and had taken a well-deserved musicians' rest.

Maureen found an opportunity to slip away and spend a few quiet minutes by herself. She had accompanied John on his methodical progress around the room to find people he knew and to introduce himself to others. He was now immersed in serious discussion with a man whom she recalled was on the board of the British Medical Association.

The Grants had long since been absorbed among a crush of people at the other end of the salon and before they parted Laura had promised to call her in the morning. She started to walk over to one of the tall windows.

"Signora." A waiter intercepted her and she took a glass from the tray.

"Grazie."

"Prego."

She smiled to herself as he moved away and

proceeded to where she could gaze out on the darkened roofs. The illuminated dome of St. Peter's glowed in the night sky and she thought of all she had ever read about *'La Citta Eterna'*, The Eternal City.

From whichever portal entered, whatever part that is first assayed, Rome captures a visitor's heart. There is a joyous impression of familiarity and permanence, and once the famous structures of antiquity have been explored, their outlines re-membered from school textbooks, travellers are apt to linger in hallow-eyed wonder before each cobble-stoned alley and ochre-umber-carmine-sienna painted building, before every ornate facade and the many churches and fountains. Though one is a stranger in a strange land and unsure of one's bearings, the soul of the city does not seem strange.

Her own introduction to Rome had been a more ominous jolt of familiarity. But she must put that aside. She had anticipated this trip ever since John decided he could at last manage to attend his first conference abroad. They had travelled in France, and in Switzerland and Austria, but Italy had remained unvisited till now. While she was still single and pursuing her art studies, she had spent two summers on the continent, but she had never been able to stretch funds or time to come here.

Her mother had agreed to care for eleven-year-old Sara and ten-year-old Mark at their London home while they were gone. Now that Grace Lyle was a widow she could sometimes be persuaded to leave her small cottage and beloved garden, in the quiet Essex village where she had always lived. Mother and daughter had grown more tolerant and understanding of each other in recent years, but while she was growing-up there had been many conflicts. She had viewed her parents as narrow, too complacent and overly cautious. They in turn had resented her desire to expand her horizons, to explore and seek out challenges.

Maureen almost let the wineglass slip from her fingers. As thoughts raced backwards connecting with others from the past, her memory suddenly retrieved the forgotten connection, the special key to all those trance-like states she had known as a child, similar to the ones she had experienced today.

It had been a railway poster. One particular brightly-coloured scene of some foreign place, that had hung in the waiting-room of the Lingford Oaks station. Each time she had walked over to stand in front of it she underwent a scary, yet fascinating, transformation. The picture seemed to have an impelling force, to induce magical, trance-like dream states, and because she told no one it became her secret. A private world, the way to escape from everything and everyone around her.

Before she had a chance to explore the memory in detail, she was abruptly returned to the present. Reflecting back towards her from the darkened window, like a mirror, she saw that she wasn't alone any more.

A man stood behind her in shadowed outline. Without immediately turning she knew at once who it was. She also knew that this was something she had been expecting, and a part of her might have been hoping it would happen. She slowly turned around to face him.

"I give you my word, I am now seeing only you, Mrs. Standish."

His contrite smile made the mature forty-ish looking face seem boyish, although the dark wavey hair was becoming flecked with grey.

Maureen smiled. "Well, that's quite all right, Dottore Bracci. It is said that 'everyone has a double'."

"That is so. And it must be true."

He reached out, took the wineglass from her hand and placed it on a small table near the windows. The action startled her.

"If we accept that the statement is valid, I will now produce the evidence to prove it. You shall see with your own eyes."

Maureen stood looking at him, intrigued but suddenly wary.

"Where we are now," he went on, "this Palazzo, you understand," - his arm described a broad inclusive arc - "was once the home of the Catalbi family. And Marinella Catalbi's portrait is in a room very near to this one. There . . . well, you will be able to see the reason for my surprise."

For a moment she experienced a feeling of dread, but it was followed by a faint twinge of curiosity.

"I . . . I really don't think that I can do that right now. You see - "

"It will take but a few minutes only." His smile became quizzical. "Do you believe you will be missed?"

He seemed to be daring her, challenging her. "Then you can explain to your husband that, in fact, you do bear a very striking likeness to someone else. *Venga Signora.*"

She hesitated but had moved a fraction away from the window. He started to turn away, and she followed. Together they threaded their way between the other guests. After the steps had been mounted and they went out through the doorway, Cesare Bracci lightly held her elbow, leading her to the left along a broad corridor. There were double doors on either side and at one set he stopped, turned a handle, and opened one in a pair.

He drew her forward before him as they entered a long gallery. Polished wooden floors stretched away in three directions. He pressed a switch and the room sprang to life under bright chandeliers and triple wall sconces.

Paintings hung from all the surfaces of the walls. It was a true gallery of art and seemed to contain representations of every traditional subject. Given time she might even have been able to name the periods and styles. There were also a few gaps where the blue fabric wall-covering showed as darker hued squares and oblongs. Obviously some paintings had been removed over the years and not replaced.

She watched as Cesare Bracci slowly paced away from her down the length of the room with his hands clasped behind his back. At a midway point he stopped and looked up towards a picture. She waited and then began to move toward where he stood, conscious as she did so of the silence, broken only by the faint tap-tap of her sandals against the wooden parquet floor tiles.

At least once in life almost everyone hears of their marked physical resemblance to another. The claim is easily dismissed, a passing illusion. For no one else can share our own unique appearance; even identical twins show slight, but essential differences.

When Maureen lifted her head to look up into the intelligent jade green eyes of Marinella Fiorenza d'Orinici Catalbi . . . she saw herself. Herself reflected back so exactly, she might have sat for the portrait. The same classical facial contours, the generous mouth and full lips that the artist had captured with a little smile beginning, the bronze glints on loose waves of coppery chestnut hair. All was the same image that she saw each morning in her mirror; even the style of Marinella's hair was her own, parted on the left with a wave that curved in at the right eyebrow, then falling just above the shoulders.

Cesare's voice behind her was low and held a new inflection of wonder. "When you entered that room, when first I saw you . . . I had the same shock that you now have. Truly, it is amazing."

Maureen remained still, unable to respond. The overwhelming feeling of shock included the attempt to reject what her eyes confirmed. She looked away and brought a hand up, brushing it across her eyes. Then finding it impossible to resist, she looked up again, and with an effort she forced herself to take in other details.

Posed against a balconied window that depicted a formal garden scene beyond, the slim young woman in the painting was dressed in a gown of white silk. It might have been a long evening dress perhaps, she couldn't tell, for the figure proceeded down the canvas only to the hipline. An unstructured bias cut to the fabric and the delicate shoulder straps had been a fashionable style of the late 1930's. Maureen recalled pattern books and illustrated magazines from the period. She noted that the dress bore that inimitable simplicity, a sort of artless construction, that only the top designers can achieve. It fell loose around the curves of the body beneath and lent an effect of well-bred sensuality.

A single strand of pearls around Marinella's neck glimmered like the fabric of the garment. There

was no ring on her wedding finger, but on the hand
that held a white silk scarf a large emerald encircled
with diamonds had been captured in sparkling detail.

Without removing her eyes from the image
before her, Maureen finally managed to speak, her
voice as hushed as Bracci's had been.

"How old is . . . Marinella Catalbi . . . now?"

He didn't answer right away and Maureen
thought there was a slight reluctance in him to reply.

"She would have been . . . oh . . . perhaps fifty,
fifty-one. But of course, she is dead." She wondered if
the remembrance might still be painful.

"She died during the war . . . sometime in 1943."

There was a long silence while they both
continued to stand and look. At last Maureen moved
and turned to face him. With her back to the portrait,
still seeing in her mind's eye the imprint of herself
that should not be there, she looked at Cesare.

"You . . . knew her very well?"

"Yes. I knew her well. While I was growing-up
I would see her often. Later . . . oh, not after she was
nineteen, twenty perhaps."

Maureen studied his face closely. "And you
were - in love with her?"

At once Cesare's face relaxed into its former
expression, his smile a broad one, which put attractive
wrinkles around the warm brown eyes.

"No, no, no! Not that at all. We were . . . just
children, who grew up around the same time." His
eyes developed a faraway look.

"You see, there were a few families who met
socially in those days. We often dined, played together, had parties. My father was one of the Catalbi
family doctors, a friend of Marinella's father. He saw
some of her family enter the world . . . and leave it."

Maureen regarded him for a moment or two longer. With an attempt to regain an air of normality, she said, "There is an unusual similarity, I agree, and yes . . . it is a shock for me too. But you must realize that I was born in England. My parents are English - ."

A smile lit his face. "I know. I know. Your husband was . . . very precise on that subject."

He waited a moment. "And yet, you see that you look exactly like an Italian woman I once knew." And after another pause, "A very beautiful woman."

The smile was leaving his face and something different appeared in his glance - an intense appraisal of this English woman who stood before him. She felt that his thoughts were no longer on the dead Marinella. Something more personal seemed to involve just the two of them who faced each other, in this lonely gallery.

Maureen looked down at the floor. She had to break this new . . . bond that seemed to have occurred.

"May I see the other family portraits, please?"

His response let a few seconds elapse. "But of course."

He moved away from her and walked farther down the gallery. When he lifted his arm to indicate a larger portrait, she watched the curve of his hand as it extended from the white shirtcuff, where a gold domed cufflink caught the light.

"This is Marinella's mother, the Contessa d'Orinici Catalbi. The palazzo was her family home, which is why it is so named." He turned his head. "And Marinella's two brothers are up here. Over there is an aunt, the Contessa's sister."

He swung around. "And on this wall opposite, all of the other Catalbis, I believe."

Maureen moved closer to look at them and he said, "But it is only with Marinella that you will see that same likeness."

With the Contessa's portrait, of an aloof be-jewelled aristocratic woman, Maureen could discern the same general colouring as the girl in the first painting, and also one of the brothers. They had no effect on her of a likeness to herself, and their features were more rounded, the eyes a more greyish green. After studying the paintings on the opposite wall it was apparent the dark eyes and hair of Marinella's father - Lorenzo Eduardo Catalbi, the plaque informed - were a predominant family feature, for several generations.

A wave of tiredness dropped over her like a heavy curtain and with it an intense urge to leave this room, all these images of people she had nothing to do with. A vague stir of panic began to rise. The eyes in all of the family portraits seemed to be watching her, as if waiting.

"I must leave now - I should rejoin my husband." She had said it too fast. " . . . Thank you, Doctor Bracci. This has been an . . . unusual evening. One certainly doesn't expect to come to a foreign country and find - ."

"That you look like one of the 'foreigners'?" he finished for her. His tone carried a slight edge.

"Surely Italy is not so 'foreign,' Signora. For centuries many of your distinguished countrymen have not found it so."

Easily chastened, Maureen received his ironic look steadily. The mute apology in her eyes was expressed in her voice.

"I'm sorry, now you must forgive me. That did sound rude." Her voice lost its clipped precision. "I . . .

I really did appreciate your . . . taking the time to show me . . . and it's just that I'm feeling tired, and . . . a bit overwhelmed."

As if his natural good manners were in question, an instant look of contrition appeared. "Please, I was simply teasing you."

He put out a hand and began to guide her back toward the doors of the gallery.

"Here am I, a doctor, who should be aware that you travelled today, met so many people at this reception, and the different climate - it was enough."

A faint grin reappeared. "And then a total stranger - a 'foreigner' too - " he looked down to gauge her reaction, "insists that you see your own likeness."

Maureen was able to muster up a smile of her own by then. They had reached the door and she thought of the other room beyond it. Lots of ordinary people, Laura and her sense of humour, the glass of wine - that had been taken away from her.

They proceeded down the hall toward the salon and ahead of them she saw that a few people were now walking away toward the staircase, a signal that the reception was winding down for some of the guests at least.

After reaching the entrance at last they both stopped. Maureen politely extended her hand to Bracci and he received it into both of his.

"Well, then. Thank you, again," she said. "I will now say goodnight."

A soft glow reflected off pilasters and cornices to shed an ambience around them. From the salon, she became conscious of music, floating up over the steady hum that still emanated from the room. She recognized a romantic theme from a Puccini opera, and it began to penetrate the mask of formality she was trying to keep in place. The slow, paced, emotive middle passage of *Recondita armonia*.

'Tosca' was just too much to have to cope with - here, in this magnificent setting, and right now - with this man who had disrupted the everyday normal order of her life.

He still retained her hand as he met her eyes. "We shall be meeting again, and I look forward to that - do please call me Cesare. And remember . . . it is only you I see now. *Buona notte,* Maureen."

Chapter 3

Sunlight was etched in multiple narrow bands through the wooden shutters onto the flowered curtains drawn across the window. Maureen came awake by degrees.

Sounds of bustle and activity, human and mechanical, rose up to the bedroom from the street below. The morning air carried a faint and delicious aroma. Freshly baked bread and coffee.

She looked around the room and made a quick orientation to the new surroundings. The night's sleep had been complete, uninterrupted by any dreams, and she felt rested. With a long, luxurious stretch she considered the day that was just beginning, the tour of the city she would soon make. Laura would be going too and the thought made her smile. Day one of the holiday. Yesterday really shouldn't count.

From the bathroom that adjoined their bedroom she could hear John. In a few minutes he emerged and straightened his tie, tucking the ends into the waistband of his trousers. Maureen always thought it an endearingly youthful habit.

"Ah - you're finally awake. Good morning,

darling. Thought I'd let you sleep on since your ladies'
tour doesn't leave for another hour or two."

He talked as he went over to the armoire that
served as their closet. Its polished surface had an aged
patina on the cracked wooden panels.

"But I have to be off. The first meeting begins
promptly at nine." He pulled his jacket from a hanger
inside. "At *Il Conservatore,* a short walk from here."

"Thank you, dear." Maureen rolled onto her
side and propped herself up on an elbow. "I smell
lovely edible smells coming from somewhere. We
missed a proper dinner last night."

"Yes . . . well, I think they only serve a light
breakfast downstairs - probably in that room off the
lobby. There's no room service, I'm afraid. Not in a
small hotel like ours." He had already reached the
door.

"So you'd better get down there soon if you
want something!"

Maureen looked over at him with a tolerant
smile. "Couldn't you put something on a tray and
bring it up here? Bring yours too - it will only be rolls
and coffee." She pointed toward the window.
"There's a table and two chairs, and a balcony. And
we are on holiday, John."

He stood at the door with his hand on the knob
and a small frown of concentration. "Oh, I don't think
so. Anyway, I've got to eat and run."

"But you know you'll only be coming back to
the room afterwards to wash your hands and go to the
loo before you leave."

John considered the logic of her statement for
another second, then seemed to give up. "You're right
I suppose. Okay. I'll see what I can do." Then he was
out of the door and off at his usual speed.

Maureen stretched once more and got up. Pulling on her robe she went over to the windows and swung the curtains wide. She opened the doors to the balcony and stepped out, into the brilliant sunshine.

Below were a group of shops that faced the hotel across the narrow road. They were all open and seemed busy with customers . Last night they had been blank and featureless, locked shut with garage-type shutters. A man swept the pavement in front of one and talked to a woman as he worked. Motor scooters were manoeuvring through from each direction and there were vocal exchanges between riders and walkers. A car made rapid progress down the street as people ambled across its path. They carried shopping bags, loaves of bread.

To Maureen the street had an atmosphere of being self-involved, like a village that went about its own business, indifferent to the city beyond. She warmed to the uncomplicated air of camaraderie she could observe from the balcony.

She could still recall the events of yesterday and last night, and knew she would eventually want to re-examine them. But right now she felt rested and content and determined to enjoy the carefree day ahead of her. There were no mysteries under this glorious sunlight.

John announced his return with a couple of light kicks to the door. She ran across to open it and he entered with both hands supporting a tray and with pieces of paper clenched between his teeth. Putting the tray on the table he folded the papers and stuffed them into a folder.

"Just meeting schedules - changes in the order of presentations, I imagine. The conference committee must have had a courier out early and delivered them to each of the hotels."

He looked down at the fresh fruit, crusty rolls and preserves that she unloaded onto the table. Two large jugs steamed with hot milk and coffee. He sat down in the chair across from her and a companionable silence ensued as they spread butter and honey, speared melon and strawberries, and munched and sipped their way through the meal.

Sweeping up the last crumbs from the table onto her plate, Maureen looked across at John with a satisfied air.

"Ancora cafeè e latte, Signor Dottore?" Her voice was low-pitched and slower than usual. She caught his look of surprise before he realized she was clowning.

"Grazie, Dottoressa, nope, *niente* for me. And now I've got to run."

Before leaving he gave Maureen a quick kiss on the cheek as he grabbed his jacket and the folder.

"Have fun at the Forum and you ladies watch your handbags - I'll catch up with the sights later in the week."

The telephone rang as she dressed. Tucking the receiver under her chin she fastened the linen slacks. Laura's voice was as cheerful as the sunlight streaming into the room.

"Are you still on for The Grand Tour . . . or did something more exciting come along, Maureen?"

"Of course I am, I'm just getting ready."

Before leaving the *palazzo* last night she learned that Laura had looked for her while she had been gone. Avoiding any explanation for her absence she had detected a faint question in Laura's gaze before they said good night. She wanted time and distance. And she hadn't decided whether to confide in her yet.

Perhaps later after they returned home, on a cold day over drinks when they remembered their time in sunny Rome.

"It's going to be a hot day Laura. Be sure to wear something comfortable."

"We're to be collected from our hotels in rotation so save a seat for me with you if you're picked-up first."

"All right."

Laura chuckled. "And do try to avoid a certain Mrs. Andrews. Last night she had me wondering if she would lead the tour! Pompous old biddy."

❀

Under the perpetual blue umbrella of the sky from which the sun blazed down, everyone enjoyed the carefree luxury of a guided tour, in a city that could not fail to delight.

An easy rapport cemented Laura and Maureen's friendship as they explored mutual interests. Both preferred cut flowers, Tom Stoppard's plays, and liked opera so long as it wasn't Wagner; they deplored the arrival of supermarkets, the way teenagers were allowed to dress today, and the inability of the Liberal Party to reach power. They still loved Noel Coward, preferred Daphne du Maurier to Doris Lessing, and dance tunes of the Fifties. Neither could wait to visit the United States.

Their indefatigable Italian guide instructed volumes of history, sprinkled with humorous legends and stories; and they drove through more piazzas and vias dei, della, da, than they would ever remember; past portals, palaces, pillars, churches, statues and ancient walls.

They walked all around the Pantheon, to the top of the Colosseum, through the grass-grown remains of the Forum and down steps at the Curia to consider the black marble grave of mythical Romulus who had founded the whole amazing city.

Under a vine-covered arbour they lunched on linguini al tonno, insalata di gamberetti and iced vino bianco from Latium. Laura counted off seven nodding heads to Maureen after they re-boarded the coach for the next destination.

It finally happened at the Palazzo Venezia.

One minute Maureen had been walking down a hallway, past open doors to left and right, and the next she felt Laura's arm around her shoulders and heard anxious questions as she struggled back to the present. Once again she had been lost within a void with no adequate reason why, but a feeling that . . .

"Hey - Maureen, are you really all right? Do you want to sit down somewhere, have a drink of water?"

". . . What?" Maureen looked ahead of her down the hall and saw the last of their group disappear around a corner.

"You stopped for so long. And the way you looked into that room . . . I thought you were going to faint and were going for a chair. Or planning to steal a Fascist souvenir off the desk."

A hint of concern behind her easy banter made Maureen try to rally herself while she thought. A sudden temptation to confide in Laura was followed by an impulse of caution. Not yet.

"I just - I don't know . . . but . . . "

"Well let's get out of here, that's quite enough of the past," Laura stated.

They began to walk away and Laura continued to talk, which saved her the necessity to reply.

"That museum was interesting, but Mussolini certainly isn't my favourite historical character. And though the Caesars, singly and collectively, were probably worse - they've been dead a lot longer. Even I can forgive and forget after two thousand years."

So much sightseeing and the heat were easy excuses, to add to the wear from being part of a group all day - a lot of fun, they agreed, but only in small doses.

It was after six before the coach dropped Maureen back to her hotel and she was too weary to dwell on it. She looked at the entrance and anticipated its welcome dark interior, careful to avoid a glance at the building beside it. A long soak in a bath of tepid water was her next goal.

In the cool lobby she stopped to select two postcards for the children: an ornate fountain for Sara, with one of Rome's ubiquitous cats poised at the edge; and a bright coloured aerial view of the Vatican City for Mark. She added a third, of the Forum, so her mother would not feel left out.

When she paid for them and retrieved the room key from the Concierge, he passed her a hand-written message. With typical brevity John informed her they would join the Mendells for dinner this evening, at eight. Maureen climbed the stairs in optimistic anticipation of the evening diversion.

Showered and with wet hair wrapped in a towel - reminded that *C* for *caldo* meant hot and *F* for *freddo* meant cold - she filled the tub and tossed in lavender-scented bathsalts.

She lay back and watched the surface of the

water   catch shadow and light from the tiles and fixtures, then closed her eyes. Perhaps she was over-sensitive to this city. Their guide today had them half-believing every stone carried the past on its surface for all to see, or for those who wanted to see. History as a perpetual backdrop to the present, distorted outlines seen in a reflecting pool, as a television screen is glimpsed in a shop window as one passes by. Was that the way Virginia Woolf was moved by Greece, when she described her first visit in 'A Room of One's Own'?

Yesterday she had looked up at the building beside the hotel as she got out of the taxi. A surge of recognition, return, some prior 'familiar' attachment had isolated her. She had been puzzled at John's irritation and her arm being briskly shaken in his grip. His face had an impatient frown on it. The taxi driver had stared at her too, though with more sympathy in his expression. Their travel bags were at their feet and John was waiting for her to produce the lire banknotes to pay the fare. During travels he insisted she handle foreign currencies.

"*Duemila, Signora,* - two thousand, *per favore,*" the driver repeated and she peeled off the bills. No problem with computing the tip: she had added three more notes, a perhaps too generous twenty-percent.

She let the memory slip away, soothed by the scented water, content to hold onto any acceptable rationalization for a while, however tenuous it was. Ahead lay the cheerful thought of dinner, with another couple whose undoubted eagerness to relate their own experiences would submerge her own. To-night she would make sure she finished all her wine. At least restaurants could be counted on to provide a mundane environment. Ghosts didn't seem to bother about gustatory exploits of the past, thank God.

As they crossed the Tiber over the Palatino bridge, Ellen and Felix Mendell provided a thumbnail history of the ancient quarter for Maureen and John. The restaurant, "Porto Scalbi", was in the Trastevere.

This diversion of their attention was calming as their taxi challenged everything in its path with unnerving bursts of speed. The journey was accompanied with jubilant bulletins from the driver on his triumphs, who so far had left no obvious fatalities in his wake.

" . . . where sailors lived up to the Middle Ages," Felix said, "and then it became the artisan's and tradesmen's quarter - a bit like London's East End used to be."

Once they left the bridge for the west side of the river Maureen could see that the area was shabbier. It looked different from the city they had just left. The taxi whisked them through a confusing rabbit warren of narrow grey streets and piazzas. Maybe in daylight it had a better appearance. The night seemed to emphasize its faintly sinister air. At least there were a lot of people around who seemed happy enough to be there, but whether they were residents or visiting too, she couldn't tell.

She had hoped for an evening where she could forget physical surroundings for a few hours and the effects they could spring when least expected.

A few minutes later her wish was granted. The restaurant, once they had stepped inside the plain grey entrance, had a smart modern decor and the atmosphere was bright and sophisticated. It was obviously popular with Romans and the voices around them, a lively melange of words and phrases, were becoming familiar to her.

The Mendells, who were in their sixties, had been frequent travellers to Italy throughout the years. Admirers of the country, the culture, and its people, they entertained the younger couple with amusing remembrances.

The large and complex menu took some time to negotiate with no explanations of the dishes in English provided. Maureen was attuned to John's diffidence at having to accept the older man's assistance. This was done by way of discreet interchange and questions of merit with Ellen, whose role had a seasoned aplomb to it. She was glad for him when their waiter arrived to take charge and describe the main dishes, in perfect English and a cheerful manner.

That taken care of, John's efforts to plunge into discussion about conference happenings was gently rebuffed by Felix Mendell after a few minutes. With charm and tact, he suggested they concentrate on other topics tonight for the benefit of their wives. At once Ellen deftly asked John to explain Chelsea Football Team's chances in the season ahead, and how the new League rules would be applied.

Maureen relaxed, enjoying the older couple's genial company. Wine was brought, tasted by their host, and the first course arrived in style. The restaurant was designed as a series of adjoining rooms, and through an arch she could see a small combo who were playing a popular tune. There was a minuscule dance floor too but it must have been early yet, the other diners were ignoring it.

Conversation lapsed for a moment and John,

who might have been running short of small talk, brought up the incident of the reception at the *palazzo* last night, and Cesare Bracci's confrontation with Maureen. He described it in a humorous way but made it sound a ludicrous thing at a professional gathering.

Felix Mendell smiled across the table at Maureen. "That doesn't sound such an odd mistake to me, John."

"Ah, you agree then that he was just being a typical Italian," John said, and shot a smug look at Maureen. She cringed inside at his blatant disdain of the culture their hosts had extolled.

"Not at all. Your wife could easily be mistaken for an Italian - especially here in Rome. She looks like one of the famous 'Roman Reds'. I noticed that when we met."

Maureen stared at Felix, surprise and curiosity on her face, which made Ellen smile.

"What, or who, are the 'Roman Reds'?" she asked.

"It is a particular type of colouring that has persisted from antiquity, my dear."

He drank some of his wine and continued. "A shade of hair very much like yours, occasionally lighter. Green eyes, sometimes hazel or blue. Some well-known beauties have possessed it."

Ellen glanced fondly at Felix. "He's always had an eye for good looks, Maureen."

"And no one knows for sure whether it was a legacy passed down from the Etruscans, the invading Celts - or some other tribe."

Ellen winked at her. "If he gets started he'll recite historical data for hours."

Felix paused. His eyes had a reflective cast.

"Bracci, you say? Now why does that name sound familiar to me . . ?" He sat thinking for a while and the waiter brought more plates to their table, exchanging them for the ones there.

". . . ah yes - now I've got it. That's very interesting, Ellen. You know it's quite possible I once knew that young man's father. I shall have to seek him out and inquire."

Later, after the last wine had been poured and Maureen studied the rich red colour, she looked up to see that several couples were now dancing. The band was playing 'El Amor' and she touched John's arm.

"Could we have a dance, dear?"

"Oh come on, Maureen - you can't expect me to dance after a meal like that. Not here."

"But - just one."

Felix laughed. "Why not, John, you're still a youngster, go ahead. Ellen and I will enjoy watching, and remembering when we were still able to."

As they got up and walked by a table, Maureen intercepted a quick glance in her direction. The man who looked up might have been older than Felix and his dark brown eyes had a smile in them.

She moved towards John on the dance floor - and slid into Cesare's arms. Her imagination dancing with the man who had held her hand, had looked at her.

With a guilty start and a subtle warmth inside that she was sure was colouring her cheeks, she gave a mental shake and concentrated on John as they slowly turned in unison to the romantic melody. Out of the sides of her eyes she studied him - the agreeable features, his blue eyes and sandy hair that was just like Sara's. His complexion had a freshness that was distinctive of many Englishmen and often lent a youthful look well into maturity.

Her husband of thirteen years. Why on earth was she indulging in silly fantasies?

She was proud of his dedication to his work, his competence. They shared similar values, even though their personalities were different; and were equally devoted to the children.

They were compatible and he loved her. She accepted that any stronger emotion, which might be called passion, was for his work. But their physical interaction was still frequent and warmly satisfying. That it could be grouped with a cosy fire on a cold evening, or a ritual set of tennis, was natural surely. Every happily married couple must feel the same after years spent together.

She simply needed to develop new interests. The children were growing-up and the hectic early days of establishing John's practice had passed. Certainly she was happy, so avoid silly fantasies, she scolded.

The evening ended with a stroll through the cobbled streets and squares of the Trastevere before hailing a taxi. There were too many people around for Maureen to feel nervous, but there was still something dark and sad in the shadows for her. It had nothing to do with the ancient tales, humorous even when gruesome, that the Mendells related as they went.

When they reached the hotel she had dismissed it and only retained a warm memory of her second evening in Rome.

Chapter 4

That night Maureen dreamt. She was a child again, and at the station in Lingford Oaks.

From the waiting-room door she could see the poster and began to walk towards it. She stood before it, waiting. Like an invisible mist the trance-like stillness began to envelop her within its own separate atmosphere.

She watched as each vivid detail of the artist's flowing brushwork started to change, gather dimension. The painted surfaces turned into rough textured stones and the scene came alive. There was shifting light as people moved on the verge of the scene.

The sound of a faint, plaintive melody permeated the air at the edge of her consciousness. Still within the dream state she knew the music was Italian. She was walking forward now, moving closer and closer to the painting. And she walked through the frame . . .

In the small square she stood beside the cafe of the painting, its tables and chairs arrayed along the sidewalk, the steps of the church just beyond. And of

course - she was in Rome. At last, after the long years
of waiting, she had arrived, where she was always
meant to be.

But in the dream she was not a child any more.
And suddenly, over the sound of the sad melody she
heard a man's voice. In anguish he called to her.

"Marinella . . . *Marinella!*"

Maureen awoke with a start, knowing she had
cried out, both of her hands grasping the sheet. Fully
awake now, her head throbbed and she felt moist with
perspiration.   Beside her in the bed John, still fast
asleep, changed his position and then resettled.

To steady herself she looked around the room.
It was still dark but an edge of light around the
windows indicated dawn had broken. On the night-
stand beside the bed her travel clock showed luminous
figures, five-thirty. With a deep breath she forced
herself to sink back against the pillows.

The memory of the dream lingered and its
element of sadness washed over her again. The
colours and the sunlight in the square had served to
accentuate the heartbreak in the voice that called
'Marinella'. It had been a young man's voice she was
sure.

Maureen felt that in some way she was
supposed to know why and how the dream events
were important to her. That the poster from her
childhood was linked to everything that had happened
since she arrived.

She sighed and tried to reason away the effects
that had left her with a dreary lassitude. Most dreams
were simply jumbled reprises of the day, of several
days. Her brain could have paraded old memories
and added them to the catalogue of recent events, com-
bining them into a bizarre and ingenious sequence.

The red wine last night had been rich and she remembered she drank two large glasses of it.

There were other things, however, she couldn't easily reason away. The odd sensations that kept recurring, her feelings about this city . . . and that portrait in the gallery. These were real, not dreams.

Only one thing was clear to her now, that the poster seen in childhood was of Rome. And although there had been other posters in the waiting room only that one had attracted her. Then she had grown up, moved away from Lingford Oaks, and forgotten about it. Until now.   Tired from the dream and the mental energy expended in trying to explain it, the possible meanings that escaped her, Maureen closed her eyes to lie in a troubled, drowsy half-sleep.

They had both gone downstairs to eat breakfast that morning, in the room where individual tables accommodated several other guests besides themselves.

"What have you girls got planned for today, Maureen? "

"Nothing's planned . . . I think I'd just like to relax and then perhaps walk around on my own."

Maureen had brought her coffee cup back to the room and after John left she picked up the map of Rome she had purchased yesterday and went out onto the balcony to sit. The sun and the cheerful street below were the same but her carefree outlook of yesterday had vanished. Whatever improbable reasons there might be for these feelings they had become too insistent to ignore.

A vague idea had taken shape during breakfast.   To try to find an actual location that matched the poster. Whatever that might achieve or whether it would lay the insidious ghosts to rest she had no idea. But if she meant to resolve anything perhaps it began there.

Unfolding the map to study it, she first found the locale of the hotel and with her finger traced a wide circle around it. As she covered the north-west arc she stopped at the words Palazzo d'Orinici. Lifting her head she sat for a moment. A small square, a little piazza, was what she sought - and there were so many.

Going back into the bedroom she picked up the pencil from the top of the bureau. With a light impression she outlined the circle, then drew a straight line between the hotel and the palace. A frown of concentration on her brow, she pored over the areas around the straight line.

There were at least four lesser squares around the immediate vicinity of the palazzo, and two more near the hotel. The distance between the two points didn't seem too far to cover on foot. The exercise would be good for her and might banish the grey mood. If the search proved fruitless, at least she would be seeing more of Rome - which was why she was here. But first she would telephone Laura.

"Oh God, not more sightseeing - "

Maureen lost her frown at Laura's down-to-earth tone. "Not really, I'm just going to wander around alone for a while this morning."

"Wander away, dear girl. I plan to stay right where I am for a few hours - in bed." Laura sounded sleepy but affable as ever.

"I thought, perhaps this afternoon, we could have tea together."

"As soon as you've had enough come and join me here."

"All right, around three." Maureen considered telling her then about everything. It was a more persuasive thought today.

"We'll examine all the wonderful shoe stores on the Via Veneto," Laura was saying. "Then there is that lovely cafe/bar place outside the hotel. You know, Doney's."

Maureen had to smile. She could imagine the audacious comments Laura would make on the passing scene.

"So long as you realize the days of La Dolce Vita are over and - "

"Well we'll just have to see if we can start them all up again, won't we?" Laura retorted.

Feeling more buoyed when she put the telephone down Maureen collected the cards she had written to the children and left the room. Downstairs she bought stamps from the concierge and then went outside.

The shops had warranted her attention since she arrived, so she crossed the road to look at the small array in the jeweller's window and she could see him at work in the back. A shoe repairer's had handmade shoes for sale, and in the stationery store there were some marbled papers that she might buy later for gifts. There was a small pharmacy and a grocer's with fruits and vegetables and the bakery from where their morning rolls must come, which had little cakes and confections in the window.

Before reaching the corner she stood and then turned to look back toward the hotel. She forced herself to take in the building beside it. There were four rows of windows in its sienna-coloured walls and as she continued to look a little prickling sensation ran up her arms. Yet the building appeared to be nothing more remarkable than offices, a lot of large bookracks to be seen in the windows. It could be some government agency or perhaps a law office. There didn't appear to be any prominent lettering to indicate its purpose. With a mild shake of her head she turned away.

After another glance at her map she headed off to the corner and dodged the traffic to cross over the wider boulevard that intersected it.

It was noon by the time she had passed through three of the squares she had marked on the map and the heat rose from the dark cobblestones. With the sun directly overhead only taller buildings provided shade and at each street she came to she crossed to the side with the deepest shadow.

The initial purpose of her journey began to yield to curiosity about some of the buildings she passed and at one church she ventured inside. A service was underway although just four or five people occupied the front pews in front of the priest. She stood at the back and tried to be unobtrusive as the serene ritual proceeded in cadenced rhythm and pace. Glancing at the candles, the decorated walls and the coloured religious figures, she absorbed the murmured responses to the priest's voice and his slow motions before the altar.

Mesmerized, she had to resist an impulse to sink down into one of the nearby pews and remain there. It was cool and invitingly peaceful but another awareness flickered - that she had been here before. Turning away she went outside and only paused to read the name, Santa Cecilia, before moving on down the road.

The vast oblong-shaped square she encountered a few minutes later was an immediate distraction and with delight she recognized the Piazza Navona. It had been one of the early sites of yesterday's guided tour, but their group had only viewed it from the bus.

She walked past the first fountain to the second one of the three that the square contained and stood by the marble steps near the water's edge to open the guidebook she had purchased yesterday.

'The Fountain of the Four Rivers', she read as she walked slowly around the giant figures, 'had been created by Gian Lorenzo Bernini to represent the Danube, Ganges, Nile and Plate rivers'.

They supported a not too incongruous Egyptian obelisk, she thought, remembering how many she had seen on yesterday's tour. With happy interest she sat down on the marble steps to leaf through more pages of her guidebook.

She raised her head to look at the friendly crowd that jostled around the marvellous baroque setting. They haggled with the sidewalk artists and ate ice cream bought from cart vendors.

So far no area even resembled the place she sought and the poster scene was probably an artistic composite rather than a real location. Her morning mood had lifted and it was easy to become a part of the exuberant vitality around her.

In lighter spirits she resolved to play typical tourist now and appreciate everything around her, and then join Laura. She would make a droll story of it all and let that woman's practical approach to life scatter the phantoms. Putting the book and the map away, Maureen got up off the step and set out for the opposite end of the square.

The nonchalance that had put a revived swing in her step continued as she rounded the corner and walked along a narrow lane to where it opened out into a wider space. The area she entered was almost as busy with people as where she had just left. Then she stopped.

There it was. The same sidewalk restaurant as the one in her dream and the original subject of the poster. Where in the painting the artist had copied only the last four letters - 'ico's' - on the white awning, the full word - 'Federico's' - now curled across in slanted blue script. White tables and chairs were spread along the pavement outside. Just beyond was the small church with steps that led up to the familiar facade.

Maureen knew that the little square could be entered from any of three corners for at the edge of her vision people were doing just that. But she had entered from this corner and her perspective was from the exact angle the artist had painted his picture.

She felt unsteady and as if she might faint. The restaurant chairs were closest and of necessity she took the three or four hesitant steps to reach the first.

A waiter appeared at her side. "*Buon giorno, Signora! Cosa desidera?*"

Maureen gazed up at him and watched his expression acquire a look of concern.

"A glass of water . . . *Acqua, per favore.*"

"Of course, *Signora.*" His voice was sympathetic. "With perhaps *limone?*"

She nodded and he vanished into the dark doorway out of the sunlight. He soon reappeared with two glasses which he carefully placed before her and then quickly left again.

She brought the glass of water to her lips and

the waves of giddiness subsided as she attempted to adjust her thoughts and recover her poise.

There was the need to put it all into proper focus and consider it normal if curious, odd but not irrational, and even a strange coincidence. For if she didn't, then the growing unease that now permeated her outlook would not only destroy her composure, but her entire holiday. And John's too, which would add guilt to her growing list of problems. It was unlike her to distort and imagine things. So a process of rationalization began.

She thought to herself, I set out this morning in order to find something, and I found it, so hooray for clever me. And what have I discovered? That a long time ago an unknown artist painted a picture of a real place. And as a child I was attracted to it. Well, all right, abnormally attracted - but children, childhood, can be peculiar sometimes. The painting was intended to portray the charm of Rome, for tourists. The artist succeeded for a bit longer than he imagined - because here I am. Nothing extraordinary there. That I was able to locate the source of the painting is fairly easy to explain too. Rome is not a very large city.

Maureen started to falter when she realized that more than thirty years, closer to forty at least, had elapsed since the painting had been executed. A rather savage war had occurred in the interim. This was 1975 and yet the square looked exactly the same. The same restaurant, the same blue and white awning. Was it possible . . . and could 'Federico' himself still be alive?

Not totally aware that a touch of hysteria tagged her thoughts, she started to laugh. Surely not the same trees and plants - was Rome called Eternal because city ordinances decreed nothing ever be changed? The spark of levity subsided but calmed her. Maureen

Standish you are a fool, she scolded herself, and a dramatizing one at that.

The lemonade was nice and sharp and between sips she looked about her. There was music playing somewhere, but only a popular ballad that was heard everywhere these days. And it came from a radio, not played on a solo instrument as in her dream.

She studied the buildings in the square, the flower stands and shops, a small cafe and people walking. In the diagonal corner to where she sat a figure had entered the square and the quick strides caught her attention. The smart tailoring and good looks would make him stand out in any setting of course. It was his distinctive familiar features she was unprepared for, and it threatened to undo what remained of her lately won poise.

Her stare was fixated so she saw the flash of astonishment pass across his features as he recognized her, which changed to a broad smile as he approached and reached the table where she sat.

Cesare Bracci could not have explained to himself why he had arbitrarily, and on a whim, decided to visit 'Federico's' for lunch today. When he set out he had been heading for another restaurant closer to his office, until the thought of coming here appealed to him.

"But this is wonderful - what a pleasant surprise. Are you alone, Maureen?"

He pulled out the chair across the table from her and sat down.

From biological necessity perhaps, as well as social imperative, women are apt to respond quickly when normality is demanded of them. Maureen garnered what was left of her resources.

"I was sightseeing . . . before I join a friend." She

flashed what she hoped was a bright smile.

"And that Bernini fountain back there . . . it was fascinating. I . . . I thought lemonade was a good idea. It's really hot in September, isn't it?"

She bent her head and started to shuffle items around in her purse.

Although she knew she was chattering, aimless and fast, she didn't want to stop now she had begun.

"This restaurant . . . it isn't close to the conference place, is it?   Surely they have lunches there. That's where John seems to eat."

He leaned forward with his arms on the table and looked at her.

"Oh yes. Indeed they do."

He was still looking as she saw his smile begin to fade.

"But I plan to miss quite a lot of the meetings. And the lunches . . . they are really just another excuse for other meetings. We Italians take our meals more seriously."

"Oh," she said abruptly.

Maureen looked down and gave the contents of her glass serious attention. When she looked up again, Cesare was still regarding her with the beginning of doubt.

"You seem to be . . . so serious today. You are not enjoying Rome?"

"No. . . Yes. . . I love it. It's just . . ."

Wildly she stared around, and her hands were twisting the handkerchief she retrieved from her purse.

In a gentle voice he said, "Please. Tell me - is there something wrong, Maureen?"

At that moment the waiter reappeared and handed a menu to Cesare.   The tables around them were now starting to acquire patrons.

"You will join me for lunch."

He had said it with a brief glance at her that seemed to indicate automatic compliance on her part. But she was in no mood to contradict him, even though she had opened her mouth to protest.

Already in rapid Italian he had ordered and returned the menu to the waiter, who swung away from the table as smartly as he had arrived.

"Why are you eating here today?"

She had blurted it out and his shocked look forced her to correct the curt question.

"I mean . . . I'm sorry, that did sound rude of me. But what I meant to say was . . . is this an old restaurant? Has it . . . has it been here a long time?"

He unfolded a napkin with a dextrous flick of his wrist as the waiter returned to place wine glasses on the table. The bottle of greenish-white wine had droplets of condensation on its chilled surface. Cesare's look was intense before he replied.

"'Federico's' is a restaurant that has been here since long before I was born, I think."

The waiter poured the wine into the glasses, and Cesare engaged him in a rapid back and forth that was accompanied with gestures on the waiter's part and laughter from both of them. When he departed Cesare turned back to Maureen.

"He says, about seventy years."

"Oh," Maureen said.

"And I often dine here. It has been popular with my friends for many years. The same family own and operate it - but in Rome that is not unusual. Many places remain in the same family for generations."

He looked at her more curiously now.

"But why do you ask? Is there - does this place have some special significance for you?"

He had been amazed to see her at 'Federico's'. Of all the many places she could have chosen, only this one was connected to so much of the past, and to Marinella. It had been like another trick of the eye for him, as when she had first entered the salon.

Maureen sat and looked at him. Of all the questions he might have asked and the way he had phrased it, this one made it impossible for her to keep acting the casual tourist. Her glance slid away, but when she started to speak her voice was slow.

"Yes, I think it does."

In a calm, logical sequence she described the strange experiences that had swept over her since she arrived; the incident of the dream and the details of the picture remembered from her childhood. Her decision this morning to try to find a square that matched the picture, and on finding it, the attempt to explain the unexplainable.

The relief of telling let her express the fear that troubled her sanity - the past had seeped into the present, and in some way she was linked to it. The face of Marinella swam into her focus, which she had tried to suppress until now.

She stopped, unable to think of anything more to add. To her own ears it sounded like some wild tale that a child might have fantasized.

Cesare waited until he was sure she had finished. Then he reached across the small space of the table and placed a hand over those clasped in front of her on the chequered cloth.

"All of what you have experienced may not be imagination, Maureen."

He hesitated to look away.   While she had

talked he too had recalled the past. This had been where Marinella and her friends had always gathered. But he had no intention of revealing that to the troubled woman before him.

"Life has strange occurrences for everyone . . . and unusual coincidences. I am sure modern psychiatry can explain some of them, with a lot of words that sound rational. I think that to identify pictures or stories read in books with real places or music, for example, is common when we are young. Children's minds are creative and wonderfully random."

After a pause he continued. " But sometimes, and very rarely, there are different events or coincidences, which we cannot easily explain. Not by logic or by science."

He smiled. " And that is why mysticism never dies out."

"We use all the names we have invented - *extra-sensory-perception, telepathy, ancestral memory, destiny, fate,* what-you-will - but we cannot explain it. And perhaps we shouldn't try."

Maureen began to respond, but he quickly held up his hand.

"No. For the moment let it stand. Let us assume it exists."

Then as the waiter returned to them bearing a tray of dishes, he said, "Right now we are going to eat! And while we eat we will talk of other things. When we return to this mystery, we will attempt to decipher it , because we are fed."

His patient smile of understanding caused her to smile too.

Maureen picked up her fork and looked down at

the plate in front of her. Steam rose from the golden pieces of pasta that floated in a fragrant sauce. Her stomach at least was behaving normally and demanded to be satisfied. She realized she was hungry.

Chapter 5

They were finishing the tiny cups of espresso coffee before Cesare returned to the subject of Maureen's dream. The meal and their conversation about books, films and current events had restored her to the simple pleasures of life.

"Oh, let's just forget it for now."

During the meal she had occasionally glanced around the square and because she sat like any other native of the city, blended into the scene, her qualms had ebbed. There was still the sense of somewhere known and remembered, but the poster would be reason enough for that. Her own mental shadows made it oppressive and now she wanted to leave and ignore the reason that had brought her to the square.

"Are you not just delaying the inevitable, Maureen?" His question was firm but gentle.

"But the day is half over now and I have to meet a friend at the 'Excelsior' soon. You must have other things to do."

"I have nothing important to do for several hours. Would you like to see one of my favourite places, where I sometimes go to think? It isn't far from here and there is a wonderful view of the city."

She was aware of two moods that conflicted. The desire not to bring it all up again; and the ease she felt in being with him. It was a rare luxury to sit with a man and talk about everything, anything, with his undivided attention and no presumption of her opinions and attitudes.

"I probably saw it yesterday. The tour we took was pretty thorough. Only the Vatican City left to do, and that's scheduled for tomorrow."

"Which you should not miss, of course. Where I have in mind is just up there."

He pointed behind her with one hand while he finished his coffee with the other.

"It is the Villa Borghese."

He caught the wary look in her eyes and thought he deduced the reason for it.

"It is not a house. In our language the word 'villa' means an estate. The English call it The Borghese Gardens and they love it for the trees and the walks and the lakes. We Romans say 'I polmoni della citta', it is the 'lungs' of the city."

Maureen toyed with the cup in its saucer. A walk in the park together was different to sharing lunch at a busy restaurant. They were both mature people, of course, and sophisticated. He more so perhaps. When the conference ended they would never meet again. Unless he visited London sometime. And even if she might have been attracted to him at one time . . .

She was careful with her choice of words.

"Thank you, Cesare, that sounds pleasant. Lunch was most enjoyable, and I appreciated your company."

Cesare raised one eyebrow and half-smiled to

himself as he left his chair and came around the table to pull out hers. What a very correct and careful woman she was. Not at all like our Marinella in that aspect, oh no!

❧

Maureen was enchanted by the elevated view as they walked along the path at the southern edge of the large parkland that overlooked the city.

"It's like being on a balcony."

To be away from all the buildings below had removed some of the doubts and the strange oppressiveness she felt in the city.

"Yes. And you see, down there - that is the Excelsior Hotel where you will be going later."

As they strolled, Cesare pointed out some of the other key landmarks that she had visited on the tour. Now they turned off onto a pathway between the trees and walked past flower beds and statues and leafy groves. When they came to an open-sided rotunda with marble benches circling the interior, Cesare took out a handkerchief and brushed off a section. In relaxed silence they sat and looked at the green parkland around them.

"Tell me about where you live, Maureen. I have been to London, but only one time."

Deflected for a while from the original purpose of their discussion, Maureen found it easy to respond. She talked about her life and the children and John's work, each of his questions gradually leading her back to her past.

"Was it sometimes hard to be an only child? You did not like to live in the countryside?"

She described the simple background of Grace and Jack Lyle in Lingford Oaks, their small market garden and flower nursery. The difficult years as she grew up and their dismay when she wanted to study art in the city. Her need to distance herself from their rural life, and not join them in their moderately profitable small business.

The recollections faded and she became bored with the self-focus his questions had encouraged. Across her thoughts was the possibility she had also bored him too.

"This is silly - there isn't any meaning in all of this. You must just write me off as one more foolish and impressionable Englishwoman, overwhelmed by Rome."

"No, you are not a foolish woman, Maureen."

Cesare looked ahead of him with a pensive cast to his face, and then turned to her with a half smile.

"And it is *Firenze* - Florence - where tourists become overwhelmed, not Rome."

"Well it doesn't matter. I should be going now."

"I know, but please tell me again, this name of the place where you were born?"

She laughed. He had asked in such a serious manner she was sure the name sounded strange to his Italian ears.

"It is called Lingford Oaks," and then spelled it out. "The word 'ford' is Anglo-Saxon for a river crossing, and the small river there is called The Ling. The oaks are obvious, although not much of the original forest is left. Believe me, it's a very unimportant place."

His face stayed impassive and his voice remained sober as before.

"There is something in your story that is . . . perhaps important, perhaps not. Something that I have remembered." He paused. "A little thread . . . in the tapestry of coincidence."

Maureen waited and became impatient as the silence grew. She bit back the desire to ask what on earth it could be, certainly not that obscure village in Essex. That only had to do with the poster, not her likeness to the portrait, the silly dream, her feelings about Rome, or anything else.

At last he turned to face her. "But first I must . . I would like to make some inquiries before I say what it is."

Maureen got up in a swift movement. Vexed, not only with Cesare but with herself, she suddenly felt foolish. She brushed her skirt off as she got up and walked out of the rotunda. Over her shoulder she said, "Well that's quite enough nonsense. And don't waste time trying to invent something out of nothing."

He got up from the seat as she began to walk away. "Maureen. *Maureen!*"

She whirled around. The shocked expression on her face surprised him and he went forward to where she stood. He put his hands on her shoulders and looked into her face.

"What is it - why do you look at me this way?" She took a deep breath and tried to read his eyes for some devious intent.

"Your voice . . . it was like the voice in the dream."

What she said puzzled him and he drew her forward and held her. The scent of her hair was lovely and he pressed his face against it.

"That was not my voice you heard in your dream." Then he thought about her description of it earlier and frowned. Maureen lifted her head away from him and he looked down at her.

"But you heard an Italian voice. And both names, Marinella, Maureen, they have the same consonants, m - r - n."

With his fingers he gently brushed the wave of hair back from her forehead.

"Your brain played a trick on you. I understand. But why did you rush away? You were angry I did not tell you what I thought? I will tell you . . . but after . . . I must make sure."

He waited and Maureen sighed as she put both hands on his chest and with a light touch pushed herself away.

"Right now I probably need that old remedy you doctors always rely upon."

Cesare looked blank. "Two aspirins, a glass of water, and no excitement." She started to smile as she watched him consider it.

"This whole subject is crazy. What is happening now . . . because of it . . . well, I'm leaving."

As she turned to go his features took on an expression of mock indignation.

"What? It is something wrong that I touch you, try to comfort you?" He followed her as she walked away and spread his arms in front of him with the palms face up. "Here we have met again today, found interest and pleasure in talking together."

Maureen stopped and concentrated on a clump of blue flowers beside the path. When she lifted her head to look back at him a smile spread across her face and danced in her eyes. His air of feigned innocence was delightful.

"I'm a married woman, Cesare. And . . . I don't desire any changes or complications."

"So? You are married. What of that?" he said. "Have we not now become friends, and are friends not able to meet and talk, and to comfort each other?"

Maureen stopped smiling and thought about it as she continued to walk along the path. When she replied it was with a sardonic tone of voice.

"Yes, we are friends. Of course. But perhaps that's another fantasy - I seem to be given to them lately."

He smiled and then walked across to join her. Taking her arm he slipped it into his.

"Eh! Maureen. Did we not agree life is full of surprises, little mysteries? So can we not agree to wait and see - and who knows what will come our way?"

He bent his head forward to look down into her face, an impish smile on his features.

". . .Yes?" He pulled her arm in close so she was against him as they walked. "Now we are 'good friends' and will do important research together - on human phenomena. Yes?"

She burst into laughter as she looked at him and he began to laugh too. Unable to maintain her own air of mock dignity, his flirtatious sense of fun released a need to respond. Despite all the drama and overtone of the day, she knew she had not felt so much alive in years.

In the same companionable fashion, their arms linked, they continued to walk through the park toward the gates. At the lower road after they rounded the incline at the corner she withdrew her arm. A taxi advanced in their direction and Cesare hailed it. When he opened the door she expected he would follow too after he helped her in. Instead he closed the door behind her and leaned in to the driver's window. After a few words of command and some notes from his wallet he then turned to her.

"*Arrivederla*, Maureen. I will call you soon." He touched two fingers to his pursed lips as the taxi moved away.

Laura kicked her sandals off and eased back into the lounge chair. They sat in the inner courtyard of the hotel with a tray of tea on the table between them. Laura decided it was a prudent alternative to Doney's, after she had taken a good look at Maureen.

The question that was on her lips had not been asked. Before she could utter it Maureen had already begun her story and with few interruptions on her part she listened, each segment and added detail commanding more attention than the preceding one.

"Absolutely fascinating," Laura said when Maureen had finished. She sat and regarded the other woman for several minutes.

Propped up in a similar chaise Maureen picked up her teacup. After her arrival forty minutes ago it had been a relief to unburden herself even though the recitation, for the second time today, sounded as insane as before.

"Honestly, Mo, it all sounds like a severe bout of deja vu . . . or reincarnation . . . or something-or-other." Laura selected another biscuit off the plate.

Maureen had nodded acceptance of her new nickname - Laura claimed it was too hot for poly-syllables - and rather liked it. Cesare's faint stress that gave her name another vowel sounded too close to that other name now.

"It's the best mystery story I've heard in a long time. And I really enjoyed the romantic bit at the end," Laura said.

Maureen looked at her. "Oh stop it - that isn't what - "

"Hey, I've always said handsome Italians were put on God's good earth to give old ladies something to smile about from their rocking chairs." She grinned across the table.

"But seriously," she continued, "there has to be a reason for all this. And what we have to do is think of what it can be."

"Well I'm ready to believe anything. Maybe I'm paranoid, and need to visit a psychiatrist?"

Laura gulped on her tea. "Not that - a seer perhaps, a psychiatrist, never!"

Maureen helped herself to more tea from the pot and leaned back. She looked up at one of the palm trees beside the lounges and thought how serene and normal it all was here.

"Well, I've just thought of something. We could start with the poster." Maureen looked at her dubiously.

"How can we? I mean, it disappeared years ago."

"But maybe it didn't . . . there was this piece in the 'Sunday Times' Art section a few weeks ago about an exhibition of Railway Poster Art." Laura paused to take another biscuit while Maureen waited.

"I hadn't thought about posters as 'art' before. But some of the ones they showed were quite lovely."

Maureen thought about it, avoiding any comment about what the word 'art' included.

"You mean I should try to find that particular poster. But . . . always supposing I could . . . how would it help?"

Laura bit into the biscuit as she considered her suggestion. "Well, first you would discover who painted it, I suppose. And then - I don't know, but it's a start."

"Well . . . "

Her interest was engaged as she considered what it would be like to see the actual poster again. The prospect didn't bother her.

"Come on. We could try to exorcize your ghost. I'd love to help you look for it. And you have to admit it's a start."

Laura had also thought of the portrait of Marinella in the gallery but she was cautious not to mention that yet.

"I suppose so."

"Good. You know you've really hooked me now, Mo. An honest-to-God mystery."

It was at that point they were interrupted when one of the hotel stewards approached Laura and handed her a piece of paper. She quickly read its contents.

"That's lovely. Michael called. He says he and John are going to take us out to dinner tonight and we're to be ready by seven-thirty."

Maureen started to get out of the chaise.

"That means I'd better get back to my hotel, have a bath and change my clothes. Laura - you won't say anything about all this, will you?"

With an exaggerated parody of amazement Laura looked up at her.

"Me! The model of shy reserve and discretion?"

She gracefully eased herself out of the garden chair, gathered her sandals up in one smooth motion and walked over to where Maureen stood. She put her free arm around her shoulders.

"Silly girl, of course not. This is strictly between us. But what you need right now is a jolly evening on the town with 'your own folk'. Just try to forget about it all for a while. Now, scoot!"

Chapter 6

By walking, Cesare had avoided two of the four monstrous traffic jams the city suffered each business day, and at a brisk pace he turned off the Via Aureliana into the Viale Jacopo to enter the glass doors of the Clinica di Ematologia.

A modern building set between older office structures, the clinic also practised modern working hours aligned to those of Northern Europe. A two-hour midday break, the professional staff took three, precluded that time-honoured Mediterranean custom of a five-hour siesta during the hot months of summer. For the young 'mod' clerical workers this meant evenings were free at an earlier hour, which pleased them. Only sometimes would the older married ones wonder if their spouses still slumbered in solitude.

Cesare waited for the lift to take him up to his office and laboratory on the third floor, his thoughts still preoccupied with Maureen, and especially with the name of the village in England where she told him she had been born. It had culled another memory out of the past. He must have been about sixteen.

When he returned to the house one evening his mother gave him a letter from England to read. Letters from his father were a rare event because Luigi Bracci was never away from home long enough to have to write, so it was something to be shared with him, and with Caterina too.

His father had inscribed the name at the head of the page preceding the salutation, *"Mia Cara Dora."* Silently he had pronounced it to himself before reading on. English was a necessary requirement before science classes at medical school and the abrupt word-endings of the language were a challenge.

That was the same year his mother had become thin and less active than before. Her laughing excuse to friends had been that she wanted to remain fashionable and *snella.* But by the next Spring she was buried, from undetected uterine cancer. For a long time he had nurtured a silent hatred of his father, *Il Dottore.* The society doctor who had not prevented it from happening, who was unable to cure it when he knew, and could not save her. It was several years before Cesare understood how such a thing could happen, and how also 'the cobbler's children go unshod'.

Later still he had perceived that his mother's death while he was still an adolescent could have influenced his reluctance to marry. He doubted now that he ever would.

Yet Isabella continued to be an enduring interest for him. Formally separated from her husband, and with a ten-year daughter, the relationship had lasted for more than two years he realized. Longer than previous affairs, which became fewer and of briefer duration the older he got.

The lift slid to a halt and his thoughts now strayed to the sensation he felt when he held Maureen against him, the scent of her hair and the warmth of her skin through the thin cotton dress. She had commanded his attention since the moment he saw her at the palace, of course. Not only was she the living replica of Marinella Catalbi but . . . something else. Attractive to be sure, the slim figure and the way the green dress floated around her as she walked, and such a worried expression on her lovely features. But something else, a sense that she - belonged.

The amazing resemblance to that arrogant playgirl of the past had soon readjusted for him. Maureen was a quite different woman, and one that he would have devoted much time to attract to him. And to possess. Who knows, perhaps later even . . . It was sad she had to be married to such a self-important young man.

He passed through the room where several people sat at desks and one rose to hand him several papers with notes attached. In his office he read them through, added a few penned comments to one, and made a telephone call. He collected two files off the top of his desk and went outside again to confer with his secretary.

He headed out of the door and prepared to return along the hallway from where he had come. Then he paused and looked back down the corridor to where the records library was located at the far end. Lost in speculation for a few minutes he finally gave a brief shrug and continued on his way to the lifts.

That evening when Cesare returned to the large old building that contained his apartment it was after seven. Yet another of Rome's many palazzos that had been converted into apartments it was both spacious and elegant. The creative blend of old with new, in equipment, furnishing, and decor, created an effect of simple luxury.

"*Come va?*" he called out, his ritual greeting to Clara.

In the lounge he threw down his jacket and some files and walked over to the chrome and glass bar in the corner. A measure of *Punt e Mes* was poured into a crystal tumbler followed by a liberal splash from the bottle of Pellegrino. From the bowl of ice and dish of lemon set out as usual, he added a slice and two cubes. Swirling the glass in his hand he drank.

"*Posso entrare ?*" Clara said with her ritual response.

She slowly shuffled over to the couch and picked up his jacket to drape it carefully over her arm, and bent to straighten the files on the low travertine table.

Cesare turned to smile at the aged woman who had been an integral part of his life for so many years. The rough voice, which still carried a faint dialect, and her unsmiling face, which strangers might think surly, reflected her peasant origins in far-off Lombardy.

When Cesare's mother died she had arrived in their household to care for the respected Il Dottore Bracci and his children. A Catalbi gift, she continued to present herself daily at the Palazzo d'Orinici for a few hours, until the last member of that family had gone. To a holier existence she trusted and prayed.

The end of the Catalbi line coincided, more or less, with the end of the war. Two episodes of misfortune she consigned to the past, the old days had gone forever. She wondered at times if the old ways had not been better.   Harsh and rigid, they had traditions that all recognized, and in the main abided by. All forgotten now. Modern times were strange and wild and no one knew where they were.

Her life in the city had begun when she was thirteen and put into service with the Orinici-Catalbis at the big Palazzo. They were one of the last living repositories of Roman social history - one that would have made a hefty tome - although it would not have occurred to her to regard it that way, much less to think it important.

Clara had known all about their lives, their public and their secret lives, as intimately as some of the old dead ones had known her body while she was still a lissome teen of a servant. They had claimed it as they chose until she became skilled in the ways to out-fox them, and until new girls arrived to stand in her stead.

"Tonight I am staying in, Clara," Cesare told her, "and I will eat anything you prepare."

Her manner conveyed neither bother, pleasure, nor interest when she turned to leave and then he said, "But before you go back to your television . . . "

Clara was immediately aware that Cesare wore a little air about him tonight that was new. He has met a woman, she thought. Good! At least that other painted fleshpot with the sullen brat will soon be *tutto finito*.

Her devotion to Cesare was as fierce as it was to his father Luigi, and to her blessed Caterina. When the old dottore went off to live at the coast, a still unhealthy mosquito-ridden place in her opinion despite *Il Duce* and his good works, she had been content to take charge of the younger dottore's life. To have had some children around would have been nice; but then too, she didn't have to please another woman around the house. She was getting old, and she saw his sister Caterina's precious darlings from time to time.

Cesare put the glass down. "Clara, I want you to try and recall something. Do you remember when my father . . . "

The Grants' and Standishes' evening was fun and developed as chance and inclination led them.

After a visit to share a drink with another conference participant at his hotel, which was located near the Coliseum, Michael and John coaxed the women to accompany them for a quick look at that impressive edifice before eating.

"No, you two dash over there on your own. We did it yesterday," Laura said.

"Ah, where's your sense of adventure?" Michael cajoled. "It's like Mecca, a required pilgrimage. Then we can concentrate on other sites later in the week."

"Pilgrimage is right - you'll need to hire a taxi just to get across the road with all that traffic."

"Ah come on - it's still light. They won't mow us down with two women. Italians are quite sporting about that."

Laura shook her head. "Mo and I will have a glass of wine in the bar and wait for you."

"And we're wearing heels tonight, Michael," Maureen said.

"Be fair," added John. "Since you've already been there you can tell us the highlights and give us an abbreviated tour."

"Oh all right." Laura relented. "Come on, Mo, we should stay together I suppose."

Later they were able to find the restaurant that the colleague had recommended which was a modest *rosticceria*. Filled with a lively young crowd, many of them tourists like themselves, it offered a silhouette view of the Coliseum's tiered galleries from its third story windows.

In high good humour Michael and John, who were able to indulge in several more beers than usual on a weeknight, discussed conference personalities and proceedings, while Maureen and Laura enjoyed the human scene and interaction around them.

"Shall we go shopping after we finish the tour of the Vatican tomorrow?" said Laura.

"All right, we could explore the Via del Corso."

An elderly waiter replenished their dishes at the table and Maureen's reaction was automatic.

"*Basta, grazie.*"

He at once became voluble in a spate of Italian.

"It must be your copycat accent that does it, Maureen," Michael said.

John laughed. "It's crazy - everyone thinks she's an Italian!"

Laura looked at her. "Perhaps you should now think about learning the language, Mo."

Maureen studied the plate in front of her while she examined Laura's words and wondered if this was an ingenuous reference to their afternoon con-versation.

"I mean these worthless types are bound to get us lost if we go driving together over the weekend."

Maureen decided her comment had been innocent. "Well let's both do it. Starting tomorrow."

As they waited to pay the bill a young Italian girl walked by and accidentally bumped into Maureen. With a hasty apology she stared when Maureen answered her in English.

"*Non capisco*? *Scusi* - I think you are Italian," she said with a laugh and left.

Laura regarded the woman beside her for a long moment but said nothing.

Back at the hotel, John waited as she walked across the room and got into bed beside him. With a smile he reached out to her.

"Come over here to me, you little Italian piece."

Their lovemaking was warm and agreeable as ever. For Maureen there was a comfort in the familiar return to all that was normal in her life. She cuddled against him.

"Rome seems to have made you more sensuous than usual," he muttered sleepily.

Which was when she recalled her physical response to the feel of Cesare's arms about her while they stood in the park.

Before John fell asleep he said, "Isn't it nice to be alone for a while and know the children aren't down the hall."

Maureen rolled over onto her pillow and thought about that, and for the first time ever she considered what an ultimate and binding contract motherhood imposed on women. Beloved and important as Sara and Mark were to her, they also represented an inescapable rein that directed all her actions in life. Then she drifted off into dreamless sleep.

Chapter 7

The Vatican City tour not only lived up to the descriptive prose in Maureen and Laura's conference pamphlets, it exceeded their expectations.

"That was lovely, I had no idea the famous St. Peter's Church would feel so intimate. Is it simply the architecture, or the force of two thousand years of faith?" Laura mused.

As the ladies of their group emerged into the immense square on the western side of the river they all appeared to wear benign expressions. The Mother Church of Christendom had wrought its subtle spell again, and the milling crowd of tourists that day, for a brief while at least, had been embraced into one family, whatever their religious persuasion.

Maureen looked about her. "I know what you mean. And I'm not sure. You expect it to be over-whelming, but it isn't."

They stood and talked with other women for a few more minutes before walking away together down the Via della Conciliazione and the Paoli bridge.

"Let's find somewhere to eat first, Mo."

At a trattoria they practised ordering in Italian.

After some hasty page-flicks of the dictionaries they had each armed themselves with and a whispered try-out that had them laughing, their efforts were rewarded with smiles of encouragement. With a culture founded on mercantile enterprise, the Italian patience and charm toward linguistic laggards is renowned. For two attractive women with the desire to express themselves correctly, the response was warm and genuine.

Laura had waited for an appropriate moment to pose her suggestion, and when Maureen brought up Cesare Bracci's name, as she guessed she might, the moment arrived.

"Since we're in the general area, Mo, and have to walk that way, why don't we both try to see that portrait before we go shopping."

Maureen looked at her and the pause before her reply was long enough to make Laura wonder if she had been premature.

"I suppose we could. Well, why not? I've wondered if I didn't imagine it after all!"

Ten minutes later their attempt to enter the Palazzo d'Orinici was dashed by an elderly porter at the main entrance. Accompanied with vigorous head shakes and arm waving he finally managed to convey to them that the palace was not open to casual visitors. Their limited Italian phrases deserted them and they started to turn away when a woman appeared. She walked across the foyer with a book in her hands. A glance at the porter by the open door brought her over to them.

When she determined they had already visited the Palace on Sunday evening and were indeed wives of two attendees of the *Dottori Nella Conferenza*, she thought for a moment with a frown then looked at her wristwatch.

"If you could return here, *venerdì* , Friday, in two days you understand, at exactly noon, I can perhaps let you visit. For just a little time." She smiled at them in a conciliatory manner. "It is really not allowed, of course, but . . ." She gave a little shrug.

They thanked her and turned to walk back down the steps.

"Well Mo, either she hasn't seen the portrait, or you and Cesare were both having delusions that night."

Maureen wasn't sure whether she felt relieved or disappointed. But she had felt a curiosity to see the painting again, with Laura beside her.

"Now just between the two of us, did you two share a funny-looking cigarette behind the curtains first?"

She swung her bag at Laura's retreating figure and they both ran down the rest of the steps in laughter.

It was John who dropped the little bombshell when he returned to the hotel that evening. From the tiny bar downstairs they had brought their drinks, of Campari and soda, back up to the room.

From the balcony they listened to the sonorous toll of a church bell as the sky moved through the orange spectrum into a range of lavender blue. John had left the conference earlier today and it was now just after five o'clock.

He had held back until Maureen finished her description of the morning tour at St. Peter's. After tossing the last of a handful of peanuts into his mouth, scooped from the dish in the bar downstairs, his face wore a smug look as he delivered his news.

"Oh - before I forget - you know that Bracci
fellow we met the other night? He's invited us over to
his home for cocktails this evening."

Reaching into his back trouser pocket he
brought out a white business card with pencilled
writing on the back.

"I'm not sure how we get there from here, but
we can always take a cab I suppose."

Putting his drink aside he withdrew his wallet,
put the card inside, and replaced it in his pocket.

Maureen was sure her features retained the
same expression but his announcement had caused a
little thrill. She studied John's face.

"How did that come about , isn't it rather short
notice?" She waited. "And do we have to go?"

John gave her a silly grin. "Well. And I
thought you'd enjoy meeting your Latin swain again."

She swung away from him to look out over the
balcony, her elbows on the railing. Her posture conveyed how tiresome she thought his attitude, but
inside she acknowledged that an excitement had
coursed through her, and a tremor of uncertainty. She
turned to face John again as he explained.

"I suppose it's Felix Mendell who is the reason
for the invitation. I was with him when we ran into
Bracci, and the subject of his father came up. Felix and
Elaine are going, and another young Italian who is a
gynaecologist, I think. Bracci the Younger is in clinical
blood pathology."

"Weren't the Grants invited too?"

Maureen was suddenly aware that she wanted
Laura with her, but exactly why she didn't know.
Hardly to bolster her confidence. She had never felt
the need to rely on anyone, either socially or

personally. Why did she imagine this was anything more than a polite inclusion to a hasty social gesture?

John took a last swig from his glass.

"No they weren't, but that doesn't matter does it? We're going to see a lot of them on this trip and we don't have to spend every night in their company."

He looked at Maureen's unenthusiastic face. "Oh come on, Maureen! It will at least be interesting to see someone's home while we're in Rome, and we'll never get a better chance than this."

"Well . . . I suppose so. What time do we have to be there?"

She had already wondered whether the slim black cocktail dress she had brought along would be appropriate or not.

"Not until seven-thirty. We can eat a meal later at that restaurant we saw around the corner from us."

She nodded and turned away again.

"Shall we call home and see how your mother is coping with the kids before we leave? Will they be home from school yet?"

They were the last to arrive because it took longer to find a taxi and they had to walk some way before a free one came by. Maureen was relieved when it appeared. Her black silk pumps were new and she could feel the cobblestones through the thin soles.

In fascinated silence they rode up in a private lift and stepped out into a small vestibule. There was a lighted button beside a set of tall carved doors which after a moment or two John pressed.

Cesare answered the door chime himself and with a formal greeting, in which Maureen could detect no special emphasis of word or glance, he ushered them inside and along a broad hallway into a lounge.

The late arrival meant they were able to greet everyone at once and gravitate to the couple they already knew. Maureen stole a glance around her at the decor and wondered why she had been so foolish as to think the evening involved her in any way.

She noted the affluent style of Cesare's residence, an interesting blend of ultra-modern with several classical pieces in the high-ceilinged room. The overall scheme of white, beige and tan, had strong colours used as a counterpoint. He lived well it seemed, either through family inheritance or because of his single status, and she could not fault his taste. The paintings on the wall intrigued her but she was unable to examine them as she would have liked.

It was a while before Maureen absorbed the fact that the stylish woman, Isabella Ferrari, was not accompanied by the other Italian man. He was the 'young gynaecologist' of John's description, and the German couple were also conference participants.

Isabella must be Cesare's personal guest, a close friend, or perhaps she was his lover. Then why had she not accompanied him Sunday evening at the *Palazzo,* or had she? Was it possible Isabella also knew Cesare had escorted her to the portrait gallery that evening? And had he discussed with her the strange likeness to Marinella Catalbi and even the subject of their luncheon together yesterday?

Maureen experienced conflict, and a quick surge of indifference formed a protective barrier to hide behind. The other impulse was pure ego and made her react as if to a challenge. With her head held high, and a full smile that gave a flash to her eyes, she aligned her body in conscious symmetry.

But sometime later the realization that she was being watched made her forget how she carried herself. The maid, whom she had heard Cesare address as Clara when she had entered with hot hors d'oeuvres, now stood across the room. Empty glasses had been collected on a tray in front of her and she was staring.

When their eyes met she saw an odd reflection of pain in the old lady's stoic inspection. Puzzled, she watched as Clara finally looked away and shuffled out of the room.

Maureen turned back to concentrate on Frau Stern's description of her recent experiences in Pisa and Florence, and then Isabella came up to engage her in conversation.

"Which hotel are you staying at, Signora Standish, and are you being treated well? I sometimes think that Italy will never catch up to other cities in Europe. Even your small hotels are so good!"

The affable and considerate air that Isabella exuded made it difficult for Maureen to retain any antipathy toward this attractive woman. Yet she knew that her initial feeling had been one of jealousy.

The Mendells were first to announce they would have to leave and this at once evoked concurrent aims to depart by others. As each began to move around to bid their respective goodbyes, Maureen glanced across the room.

Cesare was looking at the doorway where Clara stood, and although he was faced away from her she sensed that some silent question had passed between the two of them. As she watched, the old woman inclined her head to him. It was a slight movement but acknowledged something he sought of her.

Maureen turned to shake the hand of Herr Stern and then found that Cesare was before her. His eyes now had the same intense expression she remembered from yesterday. It seemed that everyone else had either moved into the hall, or were headed that way, including John.

"Maureen, please leave tomorrow morning free." Though spoken quietly his words had a serious tone. "I shall telephone your hotel. Nine-thirty? Perhaps we have an answer."

He flashed a quick smile but without waiting for any reply she might have made, extended his hand to take her arm and lead her from the room.

After all the guests had left and the front door had been closed, Clara heard Cesare summon her back to the lounge. She stopped loading glasses into the dishwasher and stood for a moment in the bright modern kitchen with her dark thoughts.

When she returned he was alone in the room. Isabella would be off in the bedroom repainting her silly face she assumed.

"So, Clara. What do you think? Is that not a real possibility?"

At the mirror behind the bar he straightened the knot of his tie and smoothed both hands over his hair. When he turned around his eyes held her own with an uncompromising question in them. In a few more minutes he would leave to dine with Isabella, but not before she answered him.

Clara slowly nodded her head up and down. Her memories had brought sad speculations. Back at the Palazzo d'Orinici, before the war had really got started, and after that shameless little terror had returned. It had been eleven months since she had run off with young Gabriele Tuornovici to Switzerland. But she had returned without him, of course, and was once again into her old ways, with the parties and the late nights.

Clara remembered how she had been upstairs to check that all the bedrooms were prepared for the evening, and had passed the open door of the bathroom as Marinella stepped from her bath. Uncaring in the presence of familiar servants she had not been aware of her, and Clara had seen the lithe young body she had known since childhood. That night as the girl reached for the towel . . .there were the slight but tell tale signs that only an experienced woman, or a doctor, would have noticed.

"Cesare, you must go to speak with your father. I think that maybe he can tell you what is the answer to your question."

And with that longer than usual sequence of words, Clara turned and shuffled back to the kitchen.

Chapter 8

Fog which had covered the riverine coast during the night was dispersing in wispy tendrils. Cypresses, plane trees and palms, that dotted the flat terrain of the ruined city, still wore gauzy white skirts in motion, while their tops were in the morning sunlight.

Ostia had been a much larger area than was immediately apparent to the casual visitor. Part of it now lay under the runways of the Fiumicino Airport. Remains of tessellated floors, paved roads, foundation walls and the occasional standing columns belied the importance that the ancient city had once attained. It was hard to visualize that it had once boasted many five-storied apartment houses, the *insulae* that served a population of fifty-thousand people in the Second Century, A.D. Today it was little more than a village.

Ostia Antica, the site most visited by tourists, failed to indicate the vast extent of the ancient town, still only partially excavated. At the mouth of the Tiber River, a mere forty-minute drive from the city today, it was once the principal port of Rome - the locale for the great granary warehouses that fed the city and the important naval staging area for the Punic Wars.

Then it had simply been abandoned by degrees after Rome fell a century later. No concerted destruction, no invasions, no catastrophic finale. Just fading and dying slowly - as most of us do - Luigi Bracci mused as he turned away from the window in the kitchen of the country house which overlooked the farthest edge of the ruins.

He was a lion of a man still, large-framed and stockily built. A mane of grey hair, broad olive-hued features and piercing black eyes could still be arresting and turn the glances of ladies when he went out on rare social occasions. A head that was favoured by ancient sculptors when they strove to portray the noble image of that race of Mediterranean men who had descended from the gods.

He had risen early today as always. The hours of dawn were spent reading the notes made the day before, enjoying the stillness of this house set in its ancient landscape. While he ground the beans for coffee and assiduously prepared a meal for Orso, the raffish looking cat regarded him with liquid amber eyes in its immense striped head. His master usually engaged in a one-sided dialogue about Orso's nocturnal adventures. But this morning he was silent.

In just a few hours more they would arrive, and Luigi marvelled again at how the buried past could suddenly present itself after so many years, trailing its tawdry secrets of indiscretion and treachery and pain. The gods were an unkind lot of bastards. But he had always known that. Just as he had always suspected his son had a life that came a little too easily, protected from the grittier aspects of life and removed from contact with ordinary people, inside the clinical purity of a laboratory. Haematology - how precise and scientific - how sanitized and aloof from the raw blood and misery of a general physician's daily rounds.

Old Clara's telephone call two days ago had prepared him for the nature of Cesare's request yesterday. But he still didn't know how much he would tell them, or even whether to reveal the true story. Well, never the complete story, of course. He would always avoid that. Ego wasn't given to man without a purpose; it was the gods' compensation for their nastier jokes.

After he saw her for himself he would decide what to say. With the grumbling discontent of age he continued to worry around the prospect of the coming confrontation.   He longed to dodge the encounter altogether, which, if he had accepted old Enrico's invitation to Tivoli last week he could have done. Ecch!

Forty years almost it must be. Dear God, why did it have to resurrect itself like a bad drama now, when most of the principal players were dead, as he himself would very likely be soon enough? One didn't make long range plans in the seventh decade. He walked from the kitchen into the drawing room and looked about him with appraising eyes, as he often did.

Small but fine, it had been one of old Catalbi's summer residences, the *dono* that Lorenzo had bestowed on him at the end. Not undeserved really even when he thought of Lorenzo's beautiful wanton daughter, Marinella, whom he hardly ever thought about in these last years - until now. But a gift well-deserved if he chose to recall just half of the services he had provided through the years to Lorenzo and the rest of that high-living clan.

The details of the room engaged his eyes. Most

of the furnishings were his own, pieces that had descended from his family or from Dora's, with a few acquisitions along the way. But there still remained some pieces from the original villa furnishings, the only reminders left of the Catalbis. Except his memories, of course.

Thank God that all the members of that ancient Roman line were now extinguished. They had never been an admirable family even in the remote past. Except for that one poor old scrap of humanity, Cosimo, a cousin only, who was nearing the end of his vacuous days in virtual senility at a clinic.

The line was quite dead. He was convinced of it. Well, perhaps not entirely in the strictest sense. He moved slowly out of the doorway to his study across the hall. Once there he looked at his books and research papers, the large piles of notes that he had accumulated and which focused on one period of Ostia's ancient past. He would try to fill the next few hours productively to stop the thoughts from bombarding him before his visitors arrived, although he doubted that his hobby would be able to divert him today.

❀

The sound of the car's engine could be heard before it entered the driveway. Luigi Bracci dropped the slat of the blind back into place. He stood there and waited. No he didn't want to see her, yet he had let it happen. When he had agreed to Cesare's request, despite a strong reluctance to revive anything of the past, it had been simple curiosity. Vanity, and he'd always had plenty of that in his youth, made him want to believe that his efforts so long ago had achieved some good purpose after all.

Wretched interfering fool of a son. What was Cesare doing anyway driving around with another man's wife? He should have settled down and married years ago, like his sister, and produced beautiful little grandchildren as she had done.

The low musical echo of the doorbell sounded and he left the room to go and open the oak door.

Maureen looked up into the stern face of the man who stood there and was swept with shyness. She had the wild impression he was a character from some ancient drama, or a statue come to life. His face had the severe outline one sees on old coins.

In the well of blackness surrounding him only his hair and complexion were differentiated. His open necked shirt and trousers were black too and his flashing black eyes were fixed only upon her until she felt isolated from the presence of Cesare beside her.

Speaking in English, it was Cesare who broke the tension of the moment for her. "We made good time, Father! I think the Via Mara is faster than the motorway these days. And it was a chance for Maureen to see a little of the *campagna* along the way.

"This is my father, Maureen, Dottore Luigi Bracci. Father . . . this is Mrs. Maureen Standish."

Cesare had stepped forward as he spoke, guiding Maureen along with him into the doorway with a hand at her arm. Luigi Bracci moved aside to let them pass and in slow but fluent English he finally spoke. But his gaze was still occupied by this amazing woman at his son's side.

"Welcome to my house, both of you. You are very kind to visit an old man out here . . . when the pleasures of the city are so many." There was an undertone of irony to the resonant basso voice.

"Well you know why we are here today, Father," Cesare responded evenly. "And I do come out to visit you very often."

They had moved along the hall into the drawing room and Cesare continued, "Clara sent something for you, of course." He put the small covered basket onto a table near the door. "Has your Maria arrived yet? We would appreciate some coffee after the journey."

"*Pazienza, pazienza* Cesare! She has already heard your car arrive I am sure." Then he turned to address Maureen directly for the first time. "Please be seated Signora. You must tell me what has brought you to Rome, and in September. Your own country as I recall, has a more preferable climate at this time of year."

Maureen was prevented from replying immediately when the comforting domestic image of Maria entered the room, bearing a large silver tray. With voluble enthusiasm she greeted Cesare, who kissed each of her round cheeks. Then she acknowledged Maureen with a smile before pouring and presenting her with the first offering of coffee from a floral patterned jug. This was followed by a plate of small pastries that smelled appetizingly of almonds.

Given the chance to delay her response a little longer, Maureen bit into a piece of pastry first and sipped her milky coffee. She was sitting on one of the two couches that faced each other and had noticed that Cesare had chosen to occupy the one across from her.

Luigi went to stand in front of the fireplace and

after sorting through the pipe rack on the lintel above, he selected one and began filling the bowl from a small leather canister. He finally turned to stare again at his guest before lighting the pipe.

In a hesitant voice, Maureen began to describe the medical conference that was taking place in the city. She could not know that Luigi Bracci had stopped listening to the content of her words shortly after she started.

The young woman seated before him was certainly not Marinella Catalbi, of course, and he was grateful to see that. Instead she was her re-creation, the living image of that lovely girl from the past, but as though nature had perfected and refined the original. All of the same physical attributes were present, tempered now with a divine feminine modesty, a sense of restraint and control that Marinella had lacked.

In his mind the years began to roll backwards like pages riffling through his fingers, returning him to that fateful summer of 1939, and the rural surgery in England - at Lingford Oaks.

Chapter 9

<u>August 1st, 1939</u>

"Luigi! Welcome - *Benvenuto!*"

When the carriage passed the platform ramp and the station sign appeared he had lowered the window to lean out. He heard Alan Forbes' shout before seeing him break into a run to accompany the slowing train.

"Alan, my friend, *come stai?* You fool of a man!"

The forty-minute train ride from Liverpool Street Station had borne him into ever greener countryside. From his seat by the window he watched the drab north-east London suburbs eventually recede. A flat landscape of fields and streams had gentle undulations between the small towns and villages. He looked forward to fresh air after the stifling heat in the city.

Seven years had gone by since those nine months spent at St.Thomas' Hospital, where he had met Alan Forbes. Their interest in medicine, history and politics had developed into a durable friendship. In 1932 the posturing and plans of Mussolini and Hitler were more often risible than contentious subjects. The laughter that had been echoed in pubs, bistros, tavernas and beer stubes had long died out.

England was now a visibly beleaguered island. General conscription was underway, gas masks had been distributed, and the city's schools were closed. Newspapers described plans for the imminent evacuation of children out of the capital.

He shared England's scorn for Italy's fatal Abyssinian venture in 1935, along with the seizing of Albania this Spring. But he realized his country's signed pact with Germany three months ago was regarded as more ominous by the English than by Italians.

He had wondered about his reception this time, but although an obvious Mediterraneo he still felt comfortable here. It was Germanic types that were unpopular. But then handsome men were always tolerated by at least half of anyone's population. His vanity, however, did not lean toward amorous diversion. Always somewhat purist about physical matters, he cherished the stability his life with Dora provided. As the train stopped he reached up to retrieve the bag from the luggage rack overhead.

"What a pal you are."

Alan rushed up to shake Luigi's free hand and slap his shoulder with the other.

"I needed a change, Alan. We are probably both crazy but so is the world right now."

After waiting to claim the heavier bag from the luggage van they walked out to where Alan's blue Austin was parked.

"Your rooms at the Pensione d'Este have been arranged," Luigi said. "The Rinaldi's have my car in their garage, and Alberto will deliver the keys to you when you arrive."

He hefted the bags into the space under the back hood, which he knew was called 'the boot,' after Alan lifted the lid.

"I really appreciate what you've done, Luigi. This may be my last chance to see Mother for a while. I'm glad that she's decided to stay in Italy." Alan latched the boot. "And I promised Susie we'd have a real honeymoon before the wedding."

"Here," he said. Moving around to the passenger side he tossed the keys across the roof to Luigi, who reacted in time to catch them.

"You might as well start learning the old girl's tricks before you drive us to the train tomorrow."

He opened the car door. "Everyone here knows war's inevitable now, but the general belief is we've got another six months."

Luigi got in and looked at the young man beside him. His junior by several years, Alan's air of staunch optimism was in marked contrast to his own cultural trait of cynical fatalism.

"Perhaps yes, perhaps no, Alan. Europe's tradition of war has been to wait until the harvest is gathered. This time . . . well, you make certain you return before the end of August!"

On the mile and a half drive through Lingford Oaks the hedgerows and gardens looked timeless under the blue sky. They talked of what was on every mind, aware that if the unthinkable came their profession would be conscripted too.

"Susie and I will take you to the 'King's Head' tonight. Introduce you to the local citizenry!"

Outside a two-story residence with a small garden in front, Alan helped Luigi retrieve the bags and looked up at the house-cum-surgery with pride.

"My bride's future home in three weeks' time. You'll like her, Luigi - and I'll soon be an old married man like you."

Luigi laughed. "She will make a real man of you, Alan."

"Let's dump the bags, have a cup of tea, and I'll show you the surgery. We'll run through patient records and you can meet my stalwart Nurse Hughes. She damn near runs the place."

August 6th, 1939

"It is I, Marinella."

Her voice was the last he had expected to hear when he picked up the telephone on Alan's desk. Two people waited for visiting hours to commence in the room outside.

A flood of emotions raced through him, none of them pleasant. So carefully had he disciplined himself to think, as well as speak, in English only, he was slow to respond in his native tongue.

"Where are you calling from?" he said.

"From London. I am with the Montagues in Chesham Place." Her voice acquired a teasing quality.

"But you don't sound happy to hear me, *mio caro dottore*. Are you not - a little bit excited?"

He bit back an angry retort. "I have patients who wait to see me."

"And that is why I am calling - I too am a patient. You are still the Catalbi family doctor, no?"

"Marinella . . . if you are in London, I can recommend several excellent - "

"No, Dottore, I want to see you. Now. Today."

"But I cannot get to London at this time."

He wondered how she had reached him here, then realized it had been easy. His whereabouts were known to mutual friends in Rome, even if she had not yet contacted her family.

"But I will come to this . . . Ling-what-is-it. They have trains, do they not?"

In his mind he pictured her incongruous presence in this village.

"If it is not urgent, as obviously it is not, I can come to London on Saturday. In two days."

"No, *today*. Tell me how I must go to get there."

Now thoroughly rattled by her imperious insistence he knew he must comply, if he didn't want her father to learn later he had ignored a Catalbi demand, much less that of Lorenzo's runaway daughter. The accounting could be savage.

"Very well. There is a train that leaves London at fourteen-ten. I will meet you at fifteen-hundred."

Before hanging up he gave her the directions. In no good mood he looked at his watch and went across the room to open the door. A young mother, leading a six-year-old child were the first patients of this morning's surgery.

As he looked down at the rosy-cheeked little boy and soberly extended his hand towards him, a smile stole across his features.

Just four passengers alighted at Lingford Oaks that afternoon. Luigi's first thoughts were not only that Marinella's slim beauty set her distinctly apart, but her clothes did too.

How on earth could she tolerate wearing that full-length mink coat, on such a glorious summer day? Her beige straw hat with its demi-veil was seasonal. He was attuned to becoming attire and fine decoration.

She stepped on to the platform. An alligator purse swung from the arm that held her coat closed. Brown suede and lizard skin court pumps completed her expensive outfit.

When Marinella caught sight of Luigi she smiled and began to walk over to where he stood beside the station's ticket barrier. Not about to move forward to greet her, his expression remained stern and impassive. Yet once again, and in this unlikely setting, he couldn't help but appreciate what an arresting and lovely woman she was. As she advanced he automatically, but not quite consciously, registered a difference about her. The memory of their last meeting, on a November night, was still one that he tried to forget.

It wasn't until they reached the car and he turned to open the door that the shock of what the difference about her was hit him with jarring recognition. Of all the reasons he had speculated for her visit, while waiting for the train, this one had not occurred to him. Marinella was a woman he never expected to be humbled in this way. Not now, and perhaps not ever.

Released from her arm, the coat had slid apart. She met his astonishment with a bold smirk, like a child found out after it had achieved a ridiculous goal, too late for remonstrance or punishment.

"Yes, my dear doctor. That is why I want to see only you at this time."

Luigi blanched. "Get in! We'll go at once to the house. But where is Tuornovici? He should have travelled with you. Is he still in London?" Marinella pouted her mouth. "Oh, Gabi went back to Italy months ago to play brave soldier for the cause. I wrote, but he has not replied."

❀

Her air of calm assurance and light banter had dropped. It was replaced by an uglier mood which Luigi had not seen her display before, but he could well believe it always existed. Her father and his brothers exhibited a similar streak of hysterical ruthlessness when thwarted or opposed, which happened on occasion, despite Catalbi position and influence.

"I won't keep this brat. It can be orphaned to the devil for all I care. And **you** will arrange it!"

Seated on Alan's sofa, in the lounge at the back of the house, she had kicked off her shoes. The beige silk gown flowed around her in sharp contrast to the worn chintz of the sofa. Narrow matte ribbons stitched vertically onto triple tiers were a designer's inspired deflection for the broadening effects of pregnancy.

Despite his protest she drank white wine, after refusing to have tea or a soft drink.

"You see, I didn't know, not until I was more than four months along."

He sat silent and she went on. "And I did try to get rid of it. But the doctors I saw in London said it was too late. They would not take the risk."

Luigi kept his features impassive as he watched her.

"I tried everything." She lifted her chin, her eyes had an excited light. "Those old wives' tales - gin, hot baths and quinine . . . and lots of sessions with a big strong man."

At last Luigi looked away from her.

"Stavropoulos was in town for the races. And that Alexos . . . he's built like one of his stallions."

She gave a laugh that was lewd. "I thought he would die from it. He called me an Italian bitch in heat."

Her expression changed again, her voice flat. "But he failed me too."

Marinella put the wineglass down and from her purse withdrew a gold cigarette case and lighter. She clicked open the case and looked at him. When she saw he would not rise to perform the courtesy with her lighter, she lit the cigarette.

Luigi sat with elbows on his knees and his large hands clasped together. He would allow her to express all that she wished. His thoughts twisted and turned as she continued.

"The Swiss doctors could have rid me of it. But for much money. And I could not call Papà."

Her movement was graceful as she extended a hand where the Orinici emerald sparkled. It had been presented by the family at her last birthday.

"I even tried to sell this, but there's a glut of old jewels on the market now. Too many German Jews selling cheap. Tiresome of them."

Luigi got up and in an unusual departure at this hour poured himself a glass of wine. She seemed to have wound down at last so he resumed his seat.

"Marinella . . . *I* will talk to your parents. They will welcome this child - they want you to return. And Gabriele will be accepted, eventually. I assure you, you are not the first Catalbi this has happened to!"

She looked at him and a malicious smile narrowed her full lips. "But have you not forgotten something doctor? Count the days. It may not be Gabi's child." She picked up her glass and drank.

"Would Papà really accept a Bracci bastard into the family?"

Luigi restrained the impulse to fling the contents of his glass over her. Instead he slammed it onto the table as he stood up.

"This is a wicked madness, Marinella. And you know what you say is not true."

He paced over to the window that overlooked a small garden, then strode back through the room. He stopped to stare down at one of the three zinc buckets filled with sand that were lined up against the wall. Alan had explained the required preparation for anticipated air raids.

For all her profligate ways and her long affair with Tuornovici, he was not entirely sure that her taunt was without possibility. One foolish act of revenge. It was unlikely but the doubt haunted him.

It had to be Tuornovici's child. Yet she could, and indeed would use the threat to achieve her purpose, of that he was quite certain. She was a Catalbi through and through.

Her eyes had followed him but she maintained the same pose as if relaxed and impervious.

"Cesare and Catarina would be amused to have a half-brother or sister at the *palazzo* - but not Papà."

In a sudden move Marinella raised her arm and hurled the wineglass. It shattered on the wall. The fragments rained into the bucket at Luigi's feet.

"And certainly not me!" she screamed. "Do you **hear**? Signore D-o-t-t-o-r-e Bracci."

❀

August 7th, 1939

The young woman Nurse Hughes led into the surgery looked as fresh and healthy as a ripe apple. Her pregnancy, that was nearing its term, had sat lightly upon her. Luigi noted the tanned face, contented demeanour, and a shine to her light brown hair.

"No need to undress, Mrs. Lyle. Nurse Hughes examined you last week. Just step up here onto the table and lift your robe, please."

Her cotton print dress was standard maternity wear. He had seen duplicates on excursions into Cheniston. After the baby came it could be belted until the next baby was started, or put away with the outgrown baby clothes. The years of depression, and now the threat of war, could damp the desire to conceive more children.

There were clinics in every major town of this Anglican country where the solution could be obtained, if the devices and instructions were not ignored. In Catholic Italy, this peasant woman's equal had little choice, especially after Mussolini promised reward to those who bore as many as possible.

"So. Tell me what you eat, and how you feel, Mrs. Lyle?"

He took the stethoscope from a pocket and hung it about his neck. If Alan's white smock were kept unbuttoned it just fitted him. Feeling her wrist he noted a normal pulse rate.

"My appetite's good, doctor. I eat just about everything." She gave a shy giggle. "Lots of tomatoes and strawberries these days."

"Do you sleep well? And do you walk each day?" With a gentle touch he placed the stethoscope over the crown of the abdomen.

Odd - the emphatic boom of an eight-and-a-half month fetal heartbeat, that should have assailed his ears, was absent. There was a lot of gurgling and pulsating from the gut, of course.

Grace Lyle was complacent and relaxed.

"I'm that full of energy these days, I've been helping out in the market garden."

His glance at her was sharp but he saw her country girl's acuity deduce his thoughts.

"Oh, just for a few hours each morning. 'Tisn't anything I have to bend down for."

His features became impassive as he kept sounding with the scope. Lower, and higher, then round the sides of the tautly swollen belly. Nurse Hughes was a midwife, and she told him all looked normal four days ago, except that she was not able to detect activity that was present the week before.

Not for the first time he acknowledged the ability of these women, trained by experience more often than professionally. He always listened to their observations.

"Well that will be all for the moment. You can get down, Mrs. Lyle." Attentively he helped her negotiate the footstool beside the examination table.

"Everything's all right, then? People do say Nurse Hughes is fussy. I reckon the little'un's getting plump and a bit lazy."

Her air of happy confidence had penetrated his professional mask.

"That is right. The baby is not so active the closer to term we come." It was untrue but he needed time to think.

He picked up the card from Alan Forbes' file that Gwyneth Hughes annotated each week. The voice of his mentor came back to him. 'Listen to your patients. They will guide you to your proper response.'

"I will just have Nurse Hughes take a little spot of blood from your finger - a precaution only. Then all will be ready for a few weeks from now."

He put the card back onto the desk. "Did you tell me how you were sleeping?"

"Like a top," Grace Lyle replied.

The expression baffled him but she had said it with such a positive smile.

"Much better than last month."

"Good, good. So do only what is comfortable now, and not too much." He walked ahead of her to open the office door with what he trusted was a confident smile.

"Dr. Forbes will return before you are due. And I am here if you need me before then."

"Thank you doctor."

Grace stole another shy look up at him before going out. He couldn't know she likened his dark-eyed looks and strange accent to romantic movie idols, occasionally seen at the Cheniston cinema.

He heard the nurse and the young woman talking outside and sat down to study her record again. Then he laid it back on the desk. No one else was waiting in the surgery outside.

It was a stillbirth. But his intuition, and the midwife's too, must be sublimated until every possibility had been checked. Could he have missed the heartbeat? If the foetus had turned, or doubled sideways in the uterus, it would be faint. Nurse Hughes had probed the vagina a week ago and felt the head. Normal presentation position. Any turning now could mean breech delivery.

Alan Forbes had indicated the Lyle girl was due at the end of the month and he would be back before then. When they had gone through his patient records he'd laughed. It was the only possibility Luigi might lose any sleep from while he was gone. The rest of his practice was run-of-the-mill rural accidents, or children with chicken-pox and measles, which had been epidemic this year. He never saw the exotic ailments of the city.

Luigi went to the bookshelf beside Alan's desk and took down Granger's 'Gynaecological Compendium'. He ran through the list of probable causes, quickly rejecting the extreme and unlikely, and over two he paused. Parental blood incompatibility would be tested by the blood sample taken. And measles - it was possible, yet how could he tell for sure?

But she looked so healthy! She was nineteen and if she had been exposed to rubeola she may have developed no symptoms herself. The deadly virus could have simply entered her system, crossed the placental barrier and killed the child. He would have Nurse Hughes check family and neighbours for exposure. What else?

As he sat and thought of how to handle this new complication, two ideas occurred in almost simultaneous order. He would try to reach Felix Mendell in London. He was one of the group of medical friends back in '32, and Luigi had learned that he now specialized in gyno-obstetrics. Felix could give him guidance.

The audacity of the second idea stunned him. But it had a perfect logical synergism to it. That it also warred with the foundation of his ethical beliefs and every tenet of his medical posture, he accepted. It was such a beguiling and simple solution, faced as he was with some hard physical facts of life.

Marinella and her unborn child, which in spite

of her crude attempts to kill it would no doubt arrive in perfect health. The answer was being handed to him like a gift from the gods. The idea that he would also be acting like a god made him shudder.

Agnostic in personal beliefs, yet decisive in his professional tasks, he savoured the practical mind of his cultural antecedents. A pantheon of apposite deities, who used mortals as hapless pawns in their outrageous games, made sense - a more rational premise than that eternally forgiving, omnipotent and kind, but otherwise utterly ineffective creator.

The gods were a bunch of bastards. Yet they had just presented him with his own . . . not salvation - for he didn't believe in that either - it was simple escape. Not just from Marinella's threat of blackmail, but from his own weakness, revenge, sinful lust perhaps, and certainly professional indiscretion. All could be tidily exorcised, banished from memory in a far-off place that was removed from his own world of endeavour. The conflict on the near horizon would further the distance and blur the act.

Not whether he would do it but how, was the exercise before him. And Marinella, selfish and deter- mined to be free, would applaud. Only she would relish the irony of the prince-to-pauper tableau he was about to stage manage.

But was it possible she would change her mind after the event occurred? When nature released, whatever it was, that created that vital biological bond between mother and child - the link that was strangely absent until the actual moment of birth.

It was unlikely. She had never been maternally inclined as a teenager after pubescence, as his own Caterina had been - the age when little girls became charmed by living versions of their cast-aside dolls.

Marinella had been too involved with her own adornment and the satisfying reaction it produced in every male who crossed her path.

Not so fast, Bracci, he reminded himself. There would be a price to pay for it sometime. The gods would also demand their retribution. But he couldn't worry about that right now; he only hoped it would happen when he was old and less caring of life.

There was just the stratagem of the problem to be solved. He had accepted the challenge. One didn't ignore a gift from the gods.

August 8th, 1939

The call to Felix Mendell confirmed his suspicion. The rubeola virus was strong enough to fatally damage the lungs and respiratory tract of the unborn infant Grace Lyle carried, and her exposure had been confirmed. The vulnerable eighth month maturation process had ceased and parturition might well occur at any time but probably at term.

The scheduled date was tentatively set for August 28th. Felix explained how he could induce the process but warned it was still a questioned procedure among practitioners. He advised Luigi to engage the service of a second doctor if he chose this method.

"Thank you, Felix. You have been of great assistance. Is there any chance I am wrong and the foetus is still viable?"

"I don't think that's at all likely from what you've described, Luigi. I'm confident of your ability in this. How you handle it is your choice."

"Of course."

"As *locum in situ*, you can avoid it, or do a favour for young Alan." Felix excused himself for a minute and Luigi could hear a voice in the background, before he continued.

"For the patient . . . well, one could look at it as a blessing with the coming war. She's certainly young enough to have more children."

As a final courtesy from his specialization Mendell instructed on the various procedures.

"When you tell her, before or after, depends on her psychological stamina and her personality. You're the best one to decide that."

Luigi sat with the Lyle patient card in front of him. The foetus could still-birth on the 28th, or spontaneously abort at any time before. Perhaps it could occur around August 19th. A better date to . . . to induce the process.

He picked up Alan's cardboard ring calculator and rechecked his other set of figures. When he had examined Marinella two days ago and questioned her, he had selected August 19th for that careless little beauty's probable due date.

Now he computed again: two-hundred-and-eighty days from the onset of her last menses. Nor did he forget to include November 7th as a possible conception date.

Staring at the figures he underlined August 19th with a pen and dropped it onto the desk beside the calculator. Leaning back into the chair he looked at the wall without seeing it, his mind racing through the necessary preparations and permutations to accomplish what he desired, and planned to do.

Before Marinella had left, he had agreed that he

would drive to London this coming Sunday and bring her back with him to Lingford Oaks. He had already reserved a room for her confinement at the nursing home near Cheniston, but he had not yet arranged for an orphanage. He'd planned to drive there tomorrow and talk to the staff.

Marinella had acquiesced to everything he had proposed, but not because of his scolding that her drinking, smoking, and general lack of responsibility could bring about the birth - and complications - at any time. Her body had become tedious and ugly to her, of course, but she was conscious of rejection by the Montagues.

Her idle playmates had initially been amused by this Italian aristocrat, with her outrageous lifestyle that so easily meshed with their own Bohemian habits. They had lost interest in her now. Cooing over cribs was not the sort of fun they indulged in and the outcome would be tiresome.

The quiet ticking of the clock over the desk was the only sound in the silence of the surgery. The improbable, fantastic, but logical plan began to take shape in Luigi's mind. He was wholly immersed in all the details.

As if unseen forces had prepared the scene to be played, the characters required to perform in it began to assume their positions on stage. The principal actors were about to slip into their roles and recite their lines.

Nurse Hughes tapped on the door and opened it a few inches.

"Doctor Bracci, may I come and speak with you for a moment?"

Luigi turned his head and slowly stood up.

"Of course, Nurse. Please come in."

He gestured to the chair beside the desk and resumed his seat. His hand reached down to place the patient card over his pencilled notes.

"I'm so sorry to tell you this, Doctor, but I've received some sad news. It's my sister - who lives in North Wales. I'll have to leave my post here with Dr. Forbes and return to take care of her."

Gwyneth Hughes explained this would have to be no later than Sunday, August 20th. She proceeded to describe how she would arrange for another district nurse to fill in before Alan returned on the 21st.

"Perhaps the new Mrs. Forbes could help out in the office - just until he hires a permanent nurse."

As though the same unseen forces had placed a script into his hands, Luigi Bracci stepped into his role to recite the prologue.

In eloquent and convincing words, he explained what he would like to accomplish - to wring a humane solution from the tragedy that awaited two unfortunate young ladies, and for one as yet unborn live infant.

With flawless timing he added just a hint of pathos to his reasonable and logical solution. The sorrow that awaited Grace Lyle, that could be averted. The shame and misery of a victim of love and an intolerant family, that could be avoided. Marinella had taken on sad enhancement in the telling.

When they parted that evening, Gwyneth Hughes went home to her rented cottage with a renewed admiration for this noble Italian doctor. Such wisdom and courage were rare; and his subtle inference of a small gratuity for her selfless devotion to her family, brought a glow to her heart. She would willingly cooperate with this gentleman of medicine.

Bracci, when he had retreated upstairs, allowed himself a nod of cautious triumph. He opened a bottle of the finer red wine, and poured a liberal amount into one of Alan's better glasses. He noted they were only two in number, so reminded himself that a wedding present was in order.

Now he was convinced he could pull it off, with Nurse Hughes' competent assistance. He drank from the glass and held it up to the light to admire the colour. Then he allowed himself another nod of achievement. An incidental, but important detail.

Marinella's child, the only true innocent in the proceedings, had been given an additional safeguard in life. Not only would it be placed in a secure household, but the one individual who might later be tempted to commit an indiscretion would disappear from the scene. And it was unlikely that Gwyneth Hughes would ever return to Lingford Oaks. So no village gossip or schoolyard jokes would haunt the child as it grew-up.

Chapter 10

The sun had shifted its angle of light through the villa windows and now reached across to the couches. Luigi had finished speaking and a stillness surrounded the three people in the graceful old room.

Cesare was first to break the quiet mood that prevailed. He uncrossed his legs, stood up, and looked at Maureen, who sat motionless as an artist's model.

His father still stood before the fireplace, the pipe long spent and cold in his hand. He too looked down at Maureen.

To the two observers she seemed lost within a solitary meditation, her thoughts hidden and unknown to them. She gazed at the windows where the cypress trees stood just as motionless in the sunlit gardens.

"What is it that you feel, Cara?" Cesare inquired gently, when another few moments had passed. "Your mother, the one in England I mean, she is really . . . "

Luigi brusquely waved a hand to silence him and spoke. "Signora. Nothing you have learned from me today can alter who you were before you came."

He received as little reaction from Maureen as Cesare had done but continued.

"For each of us, our lives are whatever we choose to make of them. Events may happen that are sad, unfortunate, or even tragic. But it can mean no more than we decide it shall mean."

When no response was elicited from the lovely but unnaturally silent young woman who sat immobile before him, his voice became stern and emphatic.

"Signora Standish, I do not excuse those actions I took so long ago. It was a difficult time . . . and a difficult decision was made. I was committed to preserving and protecting life."

He was irked that she still had not deigned to even acknowledge that he spoke to her.

"You appear to be a healthy young woman. One who has fashioned her life, and I was told it includes a fine husband, and children. You have been blessed. So . . . what you have just learned is unimportant now. Believe it when I say it is but a fragment of history. It cannot change your life."

Luigi's voice held a darker quality as he slowly intoned. "If my son, who stands there, had learned I was not his father, would it change his life? Of course not! So I warn you - *do not permit yourself to weave fantasies* or allow your imagination to stray."

"*Padre! Non penso . . .*"

"*Silenzio, Cesare! Non ti immischiare* - This does not concern you. Well now . . . Signora?"

Maureen at last dropped her eyes from the windows. She looked at each of the men in turn as though aware for the first time that their entire attention was concentrated upon her. Their dark eyes had an intense stare that seemed to demand her thoughts be made known to them.

A smile started to lift the corners of her mouth and then disappeared. The room had felt so comfortable while she had sat there. There had been the ambience of an accustomed environment about it. She looked up into Luigi Bracci's stern gaze. Her question was asked in a firm voice.

"What about the baby? You didn't describe what it was like."

Luigi frowned with a look of puzzlement.

"I mean the other baby - was it a little boy or a girl?"

A vexed look of distaste spread across his features and he pursed his lips as if an unpleasantness had been displayed before him. When he replied his voice was curt.

"If I recall correctly, it was a boy. Male infants generally have a higher mortality rate than females. Which may go far to explain a lot of our history."

He turned aside, his movement an unmistakable signal to them both that for him, the subject was over. When he had tapped the contents of the pipe into an ashtray and replaced it in the rack on the mantel, he moved a few paces from where he had stood.

Luigi was eager to bring the unwelcome recall of the past to a swift conclusion now. He felt tired. The continued presence before him of this uncanny stand-in for the long dead Marinella had begun to have a strange effect on him, one he had no wish to examine or explain. He wondered if he would ever look at that couch again without the image of this girl on it in his mind. There was a sadness about the thought.

Maria must surely have the midday meal ready. He would be eating later than he usually did. He hoped she had not overprepared for he had no intention of being gracious to these two young intruders by inviting them to join him. Ecch! And now Maria too would be put out. The traditional courtesy was something both of them would ordinarily have welcomed - a variation from the daily routine. But his patience along with his energy had been tried.

His presentation of the story had gone well, he thought. Condensed, finely edited, and glossed, of course, and only somewhat embellished. All of the characters had been generously ennobled in the telling, none more so than Marinella. She had been endowed with a poignant concern for the safety of the child she carried and for her parents' threatened status in the fascist regime of her native land.

Tuornovici, the penniless artist and unwitting father, had received the briefest of biographies. Sheer creation for the most part. Luigi had not known much about him, having seen him but once or twice, and then only in passing. When Clara had mentioned years ago that Gabriele had died in action he had felt little concern. The portrayal of the young man's irredeemable lower class had been subtle but compensated by the great talent Luigi had accorded him. A brave man with future promise, but unfortunate. That he was unlucky enough to get himself killed should intimate he was of no consequence for valid remembrance!

It all made for fine opera, Luigi thought, and with just about as much regard for substance and reality in its libretto. Created for acceptance only rather than close scrutiny - an inconsequential *divertimento* in the broad canvas of life.

He knew he could rely on his son in all this.

Although he would be aware that Marinella's image had been purified, he would not be able to challenge his father's record of past events.

Cesare was circumspect and mannered and would not readily admit flaws of character in his countrymen, or women. Though not a practising Catholic, his religious upbringing would tend to prevent him speaking ill about the dead. Luigi believed that any old scandal and gossip from those times must seem stale by comparison today. In modern terms they might even be quaint and tamely unshocking.

Yet he was well aware that Cesare would return to him later with his questions about many things he had learned today.

Maureen suddenly stood up. With a light feminine gesture she smoothed her skirt around her hips and reached down to retrieve her leather purse. Her stance, upright and graceful, she looked at neither of them but at the purse in her hands. When she spoke it was in a clear formal voice.

"I wish to thank both of you. And now I really must return to the city."

In amazed disbelief Luigi and Cesare looked at each other; a rapid appraisal on which of them had upset her to provoke this response. Whatever either might have expected, it was not a curt dismissal, with no further comments desired. The subject of the past hour was hardly one of trivial occurrence, a mere incident that dimmed before the next social engagement. Luigi felt concern for her true feelings, that she was so obviously able to repress. He would have preferred she had voiced them.

Cesare reacted with a quick movement towards where she stood.

"But of course, Maureen. We can go now if you wish. And we shall have lunch somewhere before I return to the Clinic."

Maureen led the way to the door and opened it before either of them could reach it. When they had moved down the hallway toward the big main door of the villa, Maureen moved aside to allow Luigi to step ahead of her.

As he opened the door and the sunlight spilled in around them, he reached out and laid his hand on her arm, and she was forced to pause before moving through the portal onto the steps outside.

"As you depart, Signora, please keep in mind one very important fact about your visit. Always know that you have made an old man happy." His eyes now held a warm glow in them and he at last smiled as he looked at her.

"You are . . . a very lovely woman. And the knowledge that you exist - the memory that you were here - will allow me to die contented."

Maureen looked up at him and an unexpected emotion swept over her. It registered with an impact that did not alarm her. The sense of otherness was very strong again and she felt she was going to step out of herself. The desire for it to happen was intense and pleasurable. She was . . . physically aware of him with an attraction that made her aware of herself. She wanted to move close and touch him. Then the feeling was gone.

"Goodbye, Dottore Bracci."

Into her voice, though still clearly her own while pronouncing the brief formality, there had crept a different undertone. There was a gentle warmth that was also playful.

Luigi stood and watched them depart. He gave a

deep sigh as Cesare and Maureen walked away from him down the drive toward the parked car. For him there had been no noticeable change in her manner as she left. She was a correct and formal Englishwoman in every way, of course. Yet he had experienced a momentary urge to bend his head to her and press his lips on that smooth cheek.

Then he had been assailed by a strong sense that it was Marinella who stood before him again, not her remarkable image. He could have even persuaded himself that he smelled once more that musky Jasmine fragrance she always wore. Dear God, how powerful are the memories that can still remain . . . and after all these years.

They made a handsome couple even viewed in retreat with their backs toward him as they walked down the drive. Something about the angle of carriage, their bodies close as they moved together, with Cesare's hand beneath her elbow. A sort of intimacy existed between them, which they might not be aware of themselves. Damned fool of a son!

Cesare swung the dark green sportscar into the fast-moving stream of cars on the motorway with an expert ease. Headed north towards the city, he executed a series of aggressive manoeuvres to position himself into the traffic pattern before he spoke.

"We shall have some lunch at somewhere very quiet and simple. And then we can talk, Maureen. I know a place near the Piazza Venezia that is perfect. We still have much time."

"Just take me straight to my hotel. Please." He looked across at her in surprise. "But . . . I can not do that yet. You must talk first. I must know what you are thinking now! It was a *trauma*, a shock, yes, what you learn from my father? So you must say, and tell me."

Maureen sat rigid, in as upright a position as possible with the low slung bucket seats of the Alfa Romeo. Her features were composed and her hands lay together in her lap. She decided that if she forced herself to look straight ahead she might avoid any nervous reflex.

Around them a flurry of lightning dashes were occurring. On each side cars cut into their path, and then cut out again, to be replaced by others. It seemed to be some kind of game that was mutually understood, she concluded from the enthusiasm displayed. She had not missed the expressions on the faces. They were challenges to Cesare that seemed outright invitations to mayhem.

It had been different on their way out to Ostia, along the Via Del Mare. But earlier this morning, a lifetime ago, she had been different.

Now she was changed. She had become a new person, with an entirely new background. And now she was someone else, someone she had to get used to. It was a little scary. Because . . . it had always been there, waiting to happen. The explanation to so many things in the past, so much that had happened to her recently. She wanted to be alone for a while. She had to come to terms with this new version of herself. There was so much to think about, which was why she controlled her body, her voice, and every remark she was forced to utter.

But did she really feel scared to discover she was someone new? Could it also be euphoria that had her in its grip? A heady joy and a sense of - yes, wild excitement. She wanted to laugh, to react to the astonishing information she had just learned. A part of her felt giddy and flamboyant. And it was lovely. And scary.

In a cool voice she answered him. "I don't want to talk about it. And not to you!"

"Why? What - "

"You *knew* it all the time, didn't you? Right now I want to return to - "

"You want to return to being English again, eh? Forget what you just learn! Hah - everything returns to the way it was?"

Cesare kept looking at her and she had to bite her lip to stop herself from screaming at him, 'Watch the road, for God's sake!' Which was what she certainly would have done, if John had been at the wheel.

John. Oh dear, how would . . . but she couldn't think about him right now. What had Cesare just said? 'Return to being English again.' She wasn't English anymore, of course, or was she? Not really. She was an *Italian*. Why did that give her the immediate urge to laugh out loud, with happiness?

But she must not let down her guard. She had a sense that if she did, then all her feelings would tumble out of her and around him. He was impossible. A nefarious, secretive, self-assured . . . she could hit him.

More than anything else in the world right now she knew she wanted something from him. She wanted the comfort of this impossible man's arms about her. What was worse, now she felt she wanted to cry. But she never cried, and if she started crying it would really make everything just too . . . Italian.

But she *was* Italian. It was all too much. She

had to get back to the hotel. She had to be alone.

"Just keep driving, Cesare."

It was said in the dispassionate voice she always used to discipline the children.

He expressed his exasperation with a click of his tongue, and swung the steering wheel over and roared ahead of the red Lamborghini which had threatened to cut in front of him. The bold move put an admiring grin on the face of the other driver.

The outline of the city came into view and within minutes they entered the wide Gregorio to circle the Forum onto the Via Fori Imperiali.

Cesare drove the little car out of the traffic stream and turned into an alley of a road. Halfway down it he braked, slid into a narrow space beside a building, and switched off the ignition. He sat back, turned his head to look at the straight profile of her face, and waited.

Maureen gave an imperceptible sigh and prepared herself to face his questions in a coherent way.

"All right. Yes - it was a shock. And maybe after I've had time to think about it - alone, I will talk about it."

She avoided the impulse to look at him and studied the narrow roadway ahead instead. She was conscious that his eyes were still on her.

He moved, and his arm came across the back of the seat and around her shoulders. She felt the light pressure of his fingers through her jacket.

"*Cara mia*, I didn't know before we went. Not for certain. It was . . . a possibility, sure! There was that special place - "

"Okay, if you say so. Fine! Now let's leave."

"But . . . what we just learn from my father. It is important. A reality. And now I feel . . ."

"You feel! What about me? You know what I feel? I feel that you're like some, some . . . Svengali!"

Maureen had turned to face him and the green eyes flashed in anger and frustration. She knew she had almost shouted at him but she didn't care. When she saw a humorous look creep into his eyes she was unaware that her outburst of emotion was a quite familiar and appropriate one to him. It was such an Italian reaction.

"No, no *cara*," he said in a mild tone. But he couldn't help the smile although he tried.

"You mean Machiavelli, *carissima*. Svengali was fiction. A Hungarian musician."

She gasped and her hand flashed out for his face. But he caught her wrist and held it as their eyes locked. Then he slowly pulled her towards him. As she leaned forward to be taken into his embrace, the pent-up tears began to flow down her cheeks.

The stifled emotion set free by her tears was of joy, not sadness. She felt another more profound sense of freedom course through her. Cesare held her close to him and let her tears tumble onto his hand and his jacket. His whispered words were in Italian as he moved his lips through her hair, over her brow to her eyelids.

When at last his mouth closed over her own, the kiss was long and deep. A brief pause and then they kissed again; and once more, as they let themselves spin out into the whirlpool of physical attraction and desire.

After a while Maureen pushed away from him a little so she could look into his eyes. In their glance the age-old knowledge was exchanged, accepted, confirmed. The invisible bridge had been crossed and the way back already forgotten. A new terrain awaited.

The wordless covenant had been made, and the quiet civil country left behind could never be regained.

With two fingers Cesare flipped the wave of her hair back off her forehead and reached into a pocket for his handkerchief. With careful strokes he blotted up all the wetness that remained on her face.

His voice was calm and matter-of-fact. "Now we go and eat."

He pressed the same two fingers over her lips as they parted to protest. "And you will learn that I know what is best.

"I want to have some wine and bread - you *need* some wine and bread. And then we talk. So . . . first things first."

They sat apart across a minuscule table, but were so close as they leaned forward, that their fingers brushed as the glasses of wine were lifted and replaced.

The little intimacy was discreet and Maureen felt confident the small dark restaurant was an unlikely one to attract tourists. A part of her mind was still cognizant of her status, the wife of a conference participant, but the rest of her was exultant and happy. She had no inclination to think ahead and beyond the immediate pleasure of the moment.

Both of them had been so intrigued by their new preoccupation, that the trip to Ostia had been late on the agenda for discussion. Now the assorted plates of food that constituted their light meal had been picked at and removed. The mellow red wine had relaxed some of the keen tension that gripped them.

"Your father was right, Cesare. I feel my whole life has changed because of this. But I know that some things will stay the same."

"You are wrong. Everything *has* changed now, *carissima.*"

His eyes and voice were soft and evocative. She could feel herself responding to him and his charged meaning.

"You know what I mean. Because my parents were Italian, doesn't - "

"I know what you mean."

There was a languid smile on his face as he looked at her. Maureen's wore a subtle feminine confidence. She was the goddess with two faces in life's eternal mating dance; the claimed and won, the claimer and winner.

She looked away from him for a moment. "It is so strange. To come to Rome like this and to . . . do you suppose there really is such a thing as destiny?"

"Oh yes."

She laughed, "You're just saying that. Because you want to believe it."

"Yes. I want to believe it."

"That's not a very scientific attitude for a medical man, is it?" Her words were soft now, the scold was gentle.

"But I do not feel scientific right now."

Their gazes locked and a field of charged energy sparked across the table.

"Right now, I feel . . . only like a man."

Maureen lifted her glass to drink and dropped her gaze.

"*Cara*, for me it is not important if your mother was . . . Cleopatra, and your father, Ghengis Khan. It is you who is important for me."

With his little finger he hooked hers that was around the glass, and smiled.

The sigh she made was slight but the contact of

his hand had physically aroused her. For the explicit promise that lay ahead she felt a hunger, but there was still the urge to delay.

"Cesare, please stop. For a moment."

"Why? I like this moment. I don't want to stop."

Maureen put down her glass and leaned back into her chair. "Don't rush me. I think I need more time."

"No rush," he murmured. "There is time. We have lots of time."

"I mean - "

He reached over the table, took both of her hands and folded them into his own.

"Maureen . . . I know what you mean."

He raised her hands to his mouth and while his eyes held hers she watched him gently impress his teeth onto the tip of her finger.

"But I want you. And I want you now," he whispered

What had been a constant low flame became a sharp blaze - a pain of longing that she was aware she had never before known. At the same time she realised that what she craved was familiar and right.

Why postpone what she knew she must have? He belonged to her and he would lead her to the heights of the mountain and down the other side, until she was quelled, and satisfied, and complete.

Whatever else she should have considered, it must wait. The consequences would remain to be faced. But later.

❀

The journey from the restaurant to his apartment was made in silent amity. Their own private world of suspended desire. Cesare drove through the portico into the old courtyard of the building and parked the car. With hands linked they walked back over the paved stones, past the small fountain, and rode up in the empty lift. The key to his front door turned with a smooth click and they walked along the hall to the door that led into his bedroom.

Cesare neither knew nor cared whether Clara was around, for her presence would not be seen until and unless he should call her. She was a servant from the old days and the old ways, and well versed in the master's occasional variations in routine.

He closed the bedroom door behind them, took off his jacket and tossed it onto the couch at the end of the bed. Maureen watched as he pulled his tie loose, threw it down, and unbuttoned his shirt before moving to her.

He put his hands around her waist and lifted the silk jacket up and off in one simple move, to drop it beside his on the couch.

For one long moment that tantalized he paused to look at her before taking her into his arms. Her body curved into his as he found her mouth and commenced the first slow overture of love. His hands moved over her and found the tiny loop around the button at the neckline. Her dress slid down her shoulders and fell at her feet.

They removed the rest of their clothing and stood for a second in quiet admiration of each other's body. Cesare slid an arm around her waist, the other beneath her knees and swung her up in his arms to carry her to his bed. The ancient proud gesture of a man who claims a woman, but in grateful intention to please as well as love; an act ignored when casual lust and the urge to move on exists.

Maureen knew she was two different women on the short journey to reach this point.

Mrs. Standish had noted the streets as they passed, remembered the apartment entry, and observed the unknown room. On a separate level that woman had even reviewed the potential for disaster that was here and devised the strategies to cope. But the other woman who existed inside her was dominant now.

She cared only for the sensations that had begun. Cesare's skin was warm and her arms wrapped around him with delight. Her hands slid over him and her fingers combed his hair, and then went down to stroke the hardness that was pressed between her thighs. The movement of his body upon her and the hard thrust of his entry brought an unbearable thrill.

This other woman had lost herself in a novel world of pleasure. When the throb of her release started an image flashed behind her eyes. She was a silken-clad, copper-haired girl, with pearls around her neck, and a confident smile on her face. She was the woman in the portrait.

The image faded and Maureen became conscious of herself. The memory of where she was returned, as did the man she held in her arms. She had never known a feeling of contentment like this before.

Chapter 11

Their love had been reignited, explored and fulfilled, and then joined once more in bemused wonder.

Sated at last of desire, Maureen's dual personas had merged.   Mrs. Standish was a changed woman. No tendrils of guilt had infiltrated yet to mar her content, as they lay together in spent happiness.

Cesare eventually lifted an arm to look at the watch on his wrist and met her glance of inquiry with a smile.

"It is early. We have more time."

"More time . . . for what?"

His confused expression was at once humorous to her. She delivered a light punch to his shoulder, and they both started to laugh like children.

He propped himself up on an arm and leaned over, brushing her hair back onto the pillow. She reached for his arm to look at the watch.

"It is only twenty-five before four. We will shower, and then I will drive you. His smile faded. "Back to the hotel . . . "

Maureen studied his face, then reached up to smooth his cheek.

"Thank you."

He laid his head down on her breast. "But I don't want you to leave, Maureen."

There was a moment of silence. "I have to go, you know that."

After a few seconds she slid away from him and sat up, but as she swung her legs over the side of the bed he reached out to take hold of her by her waist. She turned to look at him.

"But do you not want to stay? If you did not believe you had to return?"

She looked at the dark wavy hair and sun-coloured skin of his lean body. The urbane and attentive compatriot. The friend . . . who had just become her lover. That last thought should be upsetting to her, surely. Returned to feeling like her normal self more-or-less, after the turbulent emotions of the day, she only felt pride in it.

"What are you saying, Cesare?"

He leaned down to kiss the flesh of her hip. When he raised his eyes to gaze up at her they were serious.

"What I am saying is . . . *ti amo*. I love you."

Maureen sat up straighter. The thought that he had become her 'lover' did not involve the idea that he 'loved' her, or that she 'loved' him. That was a different concept and it governed how your life was arranged. But the act of 'making love' should mean you 'loved.' It was a word with multiple meanings and connotations. This was something else that she would have to think about now. She would have many adjustments to make after this day.

She moved away from his hands and stood up.

"Please, Cesare. We really should go."

❀

In the lift as they descended Cesare took her hand, bringing it up in his and tilted her chin to face him.

"I will see you tomorrow, yes?"

Maureen thought which day tomorrow was. "I don't know. It depends . . . John may not attend any sessions at the conference - he does plan to see some of the sights around Rome."

Avoiding his eyes, she studied the modern pattern of the carpet, feeling guilt that her response had been vague. But did he feel she was committed to see him because of one afternoon of passion? When she eventually looked up she saw the line of his mouth was severe.

"I am not a young man, Maureen. I do not anymore make love with a woman for . . . physical need or vanity. What we share together, it is not a casual thing."

"But - "

"You are a part of my life. You cannot leave and forget that it happened. There is now a change for both of us."

A tingle of fear skirted the edges of her exasperation and she was abrupt.

"Oh for heaven's sake! You know I'm married. I can't just change my life to - "

His move was sudden and caught her off guard. She was pressed against the lift wall as he held her tight and tried to kiss her. She struggled to evade his mouth on hers so he buried it into her neck. The quick panic turned to a dull sensual response as his tongue found her skin.

She gasped,"Cesare, stop!" But she let his mouth

take her own again.

Both of them were oblivious that the vehicle had come to a halt and the doors had slid open. At last she pushed him away and opened her eyes.

A portly man in his sixties with a briefcase in his hand stood outside. Imperturbable eyes behind thick spectacles watched them as he politely waited.

"*Buona sera,*" he said.

His head inclined toward them in deferential greeting as they disengaged and started to vacate the small space.

"*'Sera, Vecchi,*" Cesare said in a calm reply as he led Maureen out.

Clara sat in the immaculate kitchen and stared out at the rooftops. Her features were set in the same stern expression but her eyes had an anxious, sad cast to them.

As the faint hum of the lift faded, she sighed. One gnarled hand turned the folded magazine over on the table, and turned it again and again. In her simple regulated life these days it was an unusual measure of her distraction and concern.

Beloved son, my darling boy, she silently intoned, why is it your fate to meet your woman too late?   And such a one as this. The vision of the bronze-haired replica of Marinella, who had captured her Cesare's heart, came into her focus with painful clarity.

Clara's peasant superstition, never far from the surface, was uppermost this evening. "The past has come back to haunt us all," she muttered. "The Catalbis will never be dead. From the grave itself they reach out to touch us still."

And there was poor Maria Tuornovici, Gabriele's grief-stricken mother, herself dead these many years. She had never been able to clasp a grand-child to her heart.

✤

Maureen was relaxed again during the drive back to the hotel. Cesare had been strangely quiet but she was grateful for that. As they neared the inter-section she asked him to stop the car.

He pulled to a halt beside the curb just short of the corner that led to the Via Apollo, and then stared straight ahead with both hands on the wheel.

Although he had collected her in front of the hotel this morning she didn't want him to draw up there now to let her out. The return to her other life was best accomplished alone and without unnecessary complications.

"I have to buy some toothpaste first."

She had made a mental note of it this morning. There was something else she had to remember too, but at the moment it remained elusive.

"Ask for *dentifricio*," he said softly. "You will learn to speak Italian soon."

His statement had a proprietary ring to it and she turned to look at him. A part of her immediately felt amused, self-satisfied, that he was attached to her life. But she wanted to be rid of him now. When she snapped up the door handle and prepared to get out she saw him move.

"No, don't get out, I can manage." She knew what he wanted of her. "And tomorrow . . . I will call you, Cesare. As early as I can."

He touched her arm to delay her. Reaching

into his jacket pocket he extracted a slim gold pen and a wallet. On a business card he wrote some numerals.

"This is my home number. Call me at any hour. Clara will answer, speak slow - but she will know who you are. And my office will relay a message to my house if I am not there."

He looked at her as she took the card. A wide smile spread across his features and she could see that he was suddenly at ease and his normal self again.

"I am so happy, Maureen. And I am believing, hoping, that for you it is the same, with this happiness. Soon it will be all right, good for us. You will see."

As she watched his eager face and listened to his words a slow, lazy smile formed to tilt the corners of her mouth. Her eyes sparkled with excitement. At that moment she had never looked more like Marinella. Cesare had at once made the connection but was as much beguiled as amazed.

Her voice was low and it teased. "*Arrivederla*, Cesare. But . . . perhaps I am now allowed to say, *arrivederci, Dottore mio* ?"

"*Brava, brava, mia cara. Anche 'ciao,' mio amore. Ti amo.*" His eyes were liquid with love.

In spite of her need to leave him and return to that ordered and ordinary life, she was filled with delight. That landscape she had left behind this morning had changed as much as she had.

But if she was to survive and maintain her integrity she must observe a different kind of role-playing than before to protect all the people she loved, which now included one other. She was no more just a wife, a mother, a woman devoted to pleasing and assisting only three other people. Her life had become wider, more complex and more exciting to her. Deep within she sensed the new impulse that stirred, with its element of craving. It was like an addiction right now.

She stepped up to the concierge at the desk, the little package of toothpaste wrapped like a gift in pretty paper. She saw at the same instant as he that the key was gone from the hook above the pigeonhole. He smiled at her and she smiled back.

With a confident air she turned and stepped purposefully toward the staircase, ignoring the lift, her smile still in place. The concierge, with a discreet sideways glance, appreciated the way the peach coloured silk tightened around the hips of this oh, so attractive woman.

"Where the devil have you been?"

John slammed the telephone down as she came in. His vexed expression matched his voice.

"I've just tried to reach Laura. What were you doing out at this hour?"

Maureen held the little package up for him to see as she started to walk towards the bathroom.

"I forgot that I was out of toothpaste and - I must have wasted time exploring the shelves."

She gave a hasty glance at her reflection in the mirror over the bureau as she went by.

"Well thank God you've dressed, at least! You know the reception starts in half-an-hour."

She looked at her watch as she stowed the toothpaste over the sink and saw it was almost six o'clock. That was what she had not remembered, the conference dinner party tonight at the hotel where some of the meetings were held. John had reminded her at breakfast.

Damn. He thought she was ready so she couldn't change her clothes. The tailored silk dress and jacket would have to do.

"Can I just change my earrings first? And these shoes don't feel right now."

"Oh come on, Maureen! We should have left by now - how can you be so bloody careless? You know it's a conference do."

A stinging response sprang to mind, 'what the hell are holidays for anyway?' but she was careful not to voice it.

"I'll be ready in a second."

Quickly she washed her hands, applied lipstick, ran the brush through her hair and sprayed on some perfume. She considered telling him to leave ahead of her but decided it would provoke him again. Today, for the first time in her life it seemed, she had lived from moment to moment. For herself alone. Unusual as that was, it had felt good. Now that she was back in her proper life, the surge of rebellion she felt made her aware of a fundamental truth - which was that she had enjoyed being carefree. All at once it suited her nature. John was putting on his jacket and beginning to sort through his inside pocket as she emerged from the bathroom. She tugged off her earrings and reached for the small jewel case inside her travel bag. Then she opened the cupboard and retrieved high heeled pumps. Slipping them on she turned to face him.

"Okay, I'm ready. Let's go," she said with a bright smile.

Inside there was a little quake of uncertainty. His anger that she was holding up his plans had made her resentful, yet she knew she was at fault, for lapse of memory if nothing else. But the 'else' could not be considered, not now. So this is how guilt feels, she thought.

Outside, they walked through the streets and squares for the half-mile or so it took to reach the hotel. As they went Maureen parried John's questions about her day by first asking her own. She knew he would easily be deflected by queries about how the conference was proceeding and whether he found it worthwhile.

Their destination was in sight before she mentioned taking a trip to Ostia. Details about how she travelled there were neglected; she knew there had to be buses and trains. When he asked if it was an interesting place to visit, her response was indifferent, only so-so, quite dull really. As she said it, she realized it had been an honest appraisal. The suggestion of Tivoli for a weekend trip with the Grants was readily accepted.

It was several hours later, well after the dinner was over, that she moved through the press of people in the lounge bar, glanced across the mirrored semi-circle bar, and saw him.

He was looking directly at her, and at once she knew he had come to look for her. Their eyes locked and a strong magnetic bond isolated them in a private world. From a room outside the melody of an old Cole Porter song could be heard, and the reflection of dancers moved over the mirrors through an arched doorway beyond.

She had not expected he would put in an appearance at this event and he had not been at the dinner. She was certain, because she had looked. At the same moment that her heart leapt with joy, she fretted he would want to come near, but they could not, must not be seen together. He must know that. A surge of emotion that was new and out of character flooded through her, a sense of triumph he was here.

The music and the movement in the mirrors made her imagine. He would lead her out there and she would enter his arms and their bodies would move together as one on the dance floor. Their eyes held each other as though the same thoughts flowed between them and the clever, romantic, sophisticated lyrics to the refrain ran through her mind.

"Oh . . . my . . . God, what have you gone and done. Now you're in real trouble, Mo."

With a jolt she was brought out of her fantasy. Laura's voice had been quiet but intrusive.

Maureen dropped her gaze at Cesare and turned to the woman behind her. She had been oblivious they had walked together through the crowded bar.

"What . . . what do you mean?"

"Look, I wasn't criticizing, just reminding you where we are right now."

"But how did - ?"

"Hey, it can happen to the best of us. And the best of us hope it does - at least once before we die."

"Oh hell. Was it . . . that obvious?"

Laura took Maureen's arm and began to steer her towards a vacant bench well away from the bar, and they sat down. The music outside had stopped and only a muted roar of conversation surrounded them.

"From great depth and insight the answer is, yes. But I knew where you went today and who with. Remember how early you called this morning? But if you both keep looking at each other that way, others will soon catch the drift!"

Maureen felt a rush of gratitude that Laura was not only so understanding but alongside her now. A situation that she hadn't quite accepted herself had been calmly acknowledged by the other woman.

"Laura, believe me, something else happened first, and it wasn't - "

"Hold it right there - save the details for later. I'm not a voyeur. W-e-ll, just a teeny bit perhaps." She grinned and reached over to squeeze Maureen's hand.

"Here we had The Grand Mystery to uncover, and there you go, galloping into The Grand Romance! Slow down until I catch-up."

"You're probably thinking that I'm just - "

"Fast and loose? Not a bit of it. There but for the Grace of God, etcetera. It's just - I wouldn't like to see you mess-up a nice life. Which is too easy to do. There's England, and your children, and so on."

Maureen looked at Laura. "I do love John and the children. I know that."

"Exactly. Which doesn't mean you have to be a saint. A little itsy-bitsy one-time fall from grace never ruined anyone. Just don't go and risk everything on one throw of the dice - if you'll excuse the mixed something or other."

Laura looked at her watch. "Come on. We'll gather our legitimate cohorts and leave. What time tomorrow do you want to meet?"

Maureen slowly stood up and thought about tomorrow. They both started to walk away.

"I suppose we should meet early, because I promised - "

"Oh, I'm sure you did. So breakfast then would be wise, I think.   And did you remember we're supposed to look at the portrait at noon?"

"I forgot about that."

Laura stopped and looked at her. "Well I hadn't, and I'm curious. And I think it is important for you. Come on, Mo, put the lid back on the chocolate box!"

Chapter 12

Exhausted when she climbed into bed beside John, she was as terse as he when they said 'goodnight'.

The series of events since she left the room this morning had become a blur of tired concern - an amorphous shadow tinged with guilt, and with a dark core of excitement. Maureen had eyed the bed like a refuge on her return. All she wanted was to climb under the covers and forget everything.

John was more edgy and gruff than usual too, but she knew the reason was tension. Tomorrow he would deliver the paper he had written several months ago: The Importance for a Physician in General Practice to Determine and Evaluate a Patient's Education, Habits, and Environment before Treatment.

It carried a cumbersome title but the content was sound and included solid case histories. For months she had typed his notes and the finished paper last week. But he had added and amended right up to today. As she switched off the bedside lamp she felt grateful he wasn't in an amorous mood.

In the morning, before she woke, confused scenes of a dream had played in her mind. The recall was sketchy but it had included John and Laura in loud argument about something. Cesare had been there, in a long white smock, and he had examined her daughter Sara's tonsils. A spatter of blood had been on the pocket of the white cotton fabric.

With quiet efficiency she helped John look for his black socks and replaced the items in the drawer that he had strewn around in irritated haste. Then she sat on the bed, to give him all the space he needed in the bedroom. The day was an important one for him and she did want it to go well.

Laura called right after John left and suggested where they would meet before the visit to the palace gallery. Maureen decided to skip breakfast downstairs and wondered how early she could call Cesare.

For a second or two she debated whether she should skip seeing him altogether. But once his image had been called forth in her mind, an intense longing to be with him started. To watch again the easy elegant grace of his body as he moved, the expressive dark eyes.

She tried to imagine him swearing about losing some socks and failed, but knew that was un-charitable of her, and dangerous territory. After all, he wasn't on holiday and he could probably afford to buy dozens at a time.

Laura had reminded her today was Friday, and Michael and John would be free for the weekend. Maureen knew it had been a warning and silently blessed her good fortune in Laura's friendship and support. When she withdrew the diary from her purse to check the date and make notes, she had a sharp pang of disappointment to see they would fly back to England next Wednesday. So soon, in just four more days after today. She seemed to have lost track of time and if she didn't see Cesare today . . .

As she dressed she remembered that phone calls would appear on their hotel bill when they checked out. The awareness that she had now become devious didn't sit too well, but seemed a minor sin compared to others. Checking her purse for change she decided she could call from the kiosks around the corner, before meeting Laura.

After buttoning the dress she studied her reflection. The caramel coloured linen hugged her body to the hips then flared in godets. The effect looked stylish, even in the discoloured mirror of the wardrobe.

But contrast was needed, she thought, and twisted a burgundy patterned silk scarf around the waist in experiment. Too ingenue. Wrapping it bandanna-like around her forehead, the ends trailing on one side, she admired the gypsy effect, before pulling it off. Refolded and draped around the deep veeline neck, she tied a neat Windsor knot and was satisfied.

That it took longer than usual for her to dress this morning she could understand, on a simple feminine level, but the sudden desire for boldness was unusual. Indecision over the gold drop earrings that she only wore at night and the simple garnet studs went in favour of the studs. But her heeled taupe pumps won out over the flat tan walking shoes she would have chosen in London.

Maureen listened as the b-r-r's were repeated three times and a woman's voice answered, *"Pronto!"*

"*Dottore Cesare Bracci, per favore,*" she said, wondering if she would be asked to identify herself.

"*Un momento,* Signora."

After a pause his voice came on the line. She heard him say, "*Eccomi.*" There was a surge of relief, and some other feeling that brought warmth to her face.

"You wished me to call you today, Dottore Bracci."

His soft laugh was infused with such an obvious delight she could almost see his face at the other end of the line.

"So very, very much. I have been waiting!"

"Am I interrupting you?"

"No . . . and I want you always to interrupt me now. Even when I work - which I am not. How soon can we meet?"

Maureen had thought about that already. "Not until this afternoon - I have to be with Laura all morning."

"But we must have lunch together, *cara,*" he murmured. "Please."

"Well . . . about 1 o'clock?"

"That is good. Where you will be at that time?"

Because she wanted to wait to tell him about the visit to the *palazzo,* she tried to think of another location. The little piazza sprang into mind and was quickly rejected. Then she knew.

"The Piazza Navona would be nearby." She heard him laugh again. *"Perfetto!* I want us to celebrate. There is a special place near the Camera del Deputati. Be at the centre fountain - I will find you."

"All right. *Ciao.*"

Her smile of happiness was noticed by a man

walking his dog, and he smiled too at the vivacious woman in the kiosk.

"*Ti amo.   Ciao!*"

❀

Maureen was surprised when Laura placed their order at the outdoor cafe, in abbreviated but very passable Italian. This earned her a smile of admiration and a hearty *"Brava, Signora"* from the waiter.

"See? Don't think you're the only one who fits in around here, my girl."

Maureen laughed. "Is this in preparation for our trip tomorrow?"

"That too . . . but I've decided I'd like to come back here again, sometime. And you're looking very smart this morning, Mo. I like that outfit. No doubts about seeing the portrait again?"

Maureen shook her head. "No. Now I'm as curious as you."

"Good. Do you want to talk about yesterday - or leave it till later?"

Laura was conscious that Maureen looked different in another way this morning. There was a new self-assurance about her, a little assertive manner in the way she held her head. She looked entirely at ease and quite unlike the cautious woman she had met a few days ago.

"Well, you've already guessed part of what happened, Laura. And I'm still confused about that. I feel guilty as hell, and not very nice."

"A small price to pay, I should think." Laura grinned. "Where's the queue to buy 'Wickedness'? I can't wait to have the same sort of glow you've got."

Maureen ignored the salacious chuckle.

"Telling you about that can wait. What happened after we met his father is the important part."

"All right. I'm all ears."

The waiter brought the tray and Maureen used the interlude, while they stirred the milky contents of their cups and selected from the assorted breakfast rolls in the basket, to begin the recital of what took place in the villa at Ostia.

As Laura listened to the story that Luigi Bracci had related to Maureen, she was held in fascinated silence. That such a remarkable occurrence could take place, and in a humble English village, was unusual enough. But how would it be to discover new origins, she wondered, when you were as advanced in life as thirty-six.

An entirely new set of progenitors; not a situation where one had suddenly learned about just one, perhaps errant and unsuspected parent. That was almost a commonality. It was quite different from finding out you were adopted.

To discover that you were from a dissimilar culture to the one you had grown up in would also be an exotic surprise to assimilate. From a somewhat distinguished segment of it no less. Well, one half, at least. How would it change your current life, and your perceptions about yourself?

Maureen had finished the story and they sat in silence for several minutes before Laura asked her first question.

"Did he tell you who your true father was?"

"His name was Gabriele Tuornovici." As she pronounced it, she realized she had remembered the name without pausing to think. Yesterday it had been mentioned only once, perhaps twice at the most. The emphasis during Luigi's recital had been on Marinella, and the switch of infants.

"And he told me that he was 'a penniless artist.'"

"You mean there is another kind?   Anything else?"

"I don't remember . . . it was a lot to take in all at once. He just said he was killed in the war."

She wondered why she hadn't asked anything more about Gabriele Tuornovici.   After all, there might be descendants of his family who still lived. The older man had expected her to comment, to ask questions, she knew. But she had been so excited to learn that she had different parents, more exciting ones than those she grew-up with, and she had only asked about the other child. No wonder Luigi Bracci had looked a bit disgusted.

"So he was the one who painted the picture for the poster? While he was in England?"

Maureen's answer was swift. "Yes."

She sat back then and thought about what she had said. Laura had just made a random leap to that connection, but she suddenly knew, without a shadow of doubt, that he had. The picture she had retained in her memory for so many years had been painted by him she was sure.

Yet Luigi Bracci had not said a word about Tuornovici's art. He had mentioned nothing about whether he had painted while he was in England. Would Cesare know, or could he ask his father?   Did she need any confirmation for what she was convinced was so?

"I suppose it was awful of me, but I forgot to ask him when he died, or where."

"Well, never mind, Mo, you can find out later, but I think we should get going now.   We don't want to upset The Kind Lady Of the Wristwatch, do we?"

The gallery looked different in the morning light.

Their guide, Signorina Torcello, they had learned when they entered the building and exchanged names and effusive smiles, had switched on all of the lights. Before she departed and closed the door she reminded them again, in an apologetic voice, that thirty minutes were all that could be allowed.

Maureen walked down the left side of the room to where she knew the painting hung. It seemed that the more dark and sombre paintings that covered the walls looked even more forbidding today; and the brighter ones looked more alive.

When she looked up at Marinella's faint smile again she held her breath for a moment, and then let it out. It was a lovely portrait. Glints of light came off the textured ridges of oilpaint, and the dress, the pearls, the hair, the green eyes, and the ring all sparkled but the principal subject would have never needed any highlights or enhancement by the artist. She would have shone if painted nude and in a cave. Light was something she emitted like an inner fire.

Maureen experienced less shock this time, for the memory of her image had been with her for days. The initial impact, of alarm and dismay that first evening, had been replaced by a new shock - the thrill that she was now at one with her. How lovely Marinella was.

Then something else began to stir in her consciousness as she gazed up in charmed silence. An unwilling thought crept in, and a sharp edge of scrutiny suffused her admiration of the confident young woman from a privileged background. This woman was her real mother, who had abandoned a child - the love-child she had conceived with Gabriele Tuornovici. Maureen searched the expression now for a hint of the strong practical will that the act required. She had no idea if the portrait had been executed before or after that event, and decided it must have been painted earlier. She couldn't have looked so assured and contented with herself. Could Marinella have been so scared of her parents, and the thought of war, which had not yet arrived for Italy? Did she really love the young artist? Had she ever wondered about the baby daughter she had left in England? Would she have tried to find her later, if she had not died?

Marinella gazed back at her; the air in the gallery had become chill. Words began to form in Maureen's mind, unbidden, vagrant words that emerged out of nowhere, surely not from her own imagining. They were carried on the current that seemed to flow from the portrait to where she stood. 'Well . . . and so there you are. But are you not alive, *figlia mia?* So go now - and live, *live* , while you can!' Maureen felt the hairs along her bare arms lift in the rush of cold air.

Caught up in the strange thoughts, it was a few seconds before she responded to the voice behind her and the question it asked.

"When was it that he said she'd died, Mo?"

Laura had been truly startled at the likeness. She had stood in silence and marvelled at how two people could look so much alike, however closely related they were. If Mo were dressed in a similar gown they would have appeared identical: the variation in their ages was not apparent.

There was no doubt in her mind that Maureen

was the daughter of this proud young beauty. It was a genetic fluke so rare she had never witnessed it before in any family she had known. Laura thought about her own sister, who most resembled their mother, but could never have acted as 'stand-in'.

Yet, a subtle difference existed. She wondered if in personality they were in any way similar. Laura was astute in her observations about people. She had the Celtic trait, to discern character from appearance. Marinella looked as though she could have been a totally selfish bitch most of the time. Maureen was reticent, not bold, too vulnerable to the needs of others. She would never seek the attention that Marinella would demand as her right. Whatever determined or shaped personality, it was not genetic inheritance alone, direct or indirect; and the condition of being born into a family with money and prestige did not confer confidence. The times you were born in, and where, could hardly be factors. In the nature-or-nurture debate, Laura was sure some things would always remain obscure.

"I think he said . . . 1943, but I might have got it wrong."

Maureen turned and walked back to where Laura stood.

"No - wait. Go stand beneath it for a second, Mo, and face me. I want to see something. You don't mind, do you?"

"Of course not, if you tell me what it is you see."

Maureen moved back to stand beneath the portrait. She was interested to read Laura's expression, but it was her words that caused the smile to subside.

"You look quite different now from when I first met you. It is since you arrived in Rome - and especially after yesterday."

"Different? In what way different?" Her tone was defensive. What happened yesterday included a minefield of sensitivity for her.

"Don't take that the wrong way, silly! My God, now you look like the old Maureen again." Laura made a face at her.

"I meant, since you learned who you are. Last night at the hotel, and this morning in the cafe, you looked different. It has changed you."

Laura tilted her head as she studied her and her tone was gentle.

"It's as though you've finally uncovered your real self . . . you've become stronger, and you now display more depth than anyone suspected."

Maureen thought about the frank comment and wondered if it could be considered a flattering one.

"Don't you feel different now that you have discovered you're really a thoroughbred Italian?" Laura chuckled. "Not a dull old English matron anymore."

The smile gradually returned and put a glow in her eyes, but Maureen was quite unaware that as she stood below the painting, she had precisely duplicated the smile on the woman above her.

Laura gazed in awe and immediately knew she had skated to the brink of very thin psychological ice. She decided to restrain herself from any more spontaneous comments about the other woman's newly discovered past for the moment, but Maureen didn't hesitate.

"Yes, I do feel different. But not because of that. At least, not yet. It's too soon, I think." She paused.

"It's something else. About being here, in this city. More than the sun and the light, it's the people. They make me feel . . . I can really be myself. Does that sound odd?"

"No, it doesn't. If I could live without macs, cardigans, and umbrellas, all summer long, I'd become so pleasant the Pope would beatify me."

The sound of the door opening caught them by surprise. Signorina Torcello leaned an anxious spectacled face around it. Like guilty schoolgirls they turned and began to walk towards her. Maureen slowed her pace to let Laura go ahead. She cast one more quick glance at Marinella.

From this new angle the expression had altered. The smile had acquired a mocking quality and the lustrous green eyes, played fully on Maureen, moved with her to the door, as the eyes of gallery portraits often do. It was probably a trick of the light, Maureen later thought, but into the glance had appeared a hard, fierce spark that bore into her. It projected envy.

When they reached the Navona it was as busy as always, and they were forced to walk at a slower gait. Maureen was suddenly reluctant to say that she planned to be in a certain place, at a certain time, and started to invent a lie about her plans for the afternoon.

Conscious that the option she had always avoided was now her first choice, it surprised her how easy it had become. Rather like a game really. Easy to learn, and with an agreeable sense of triumph when successful; but she failed this time and incurred Laura's wrath.

"Oh come off it woman. You told me last night who you're meeting. Sort of."

"I'm sorry, Laura - and I feel awful that we were going to do things together."

"Shed no tears for little me. I'm having my final fitting with Bruno today, who is as adoring of me as he is of my money. No competition from you, please."

"But I was supposed to come with you, wasn't I?"

"Well I'm glad you're not. Just be sure you're at the hotel early - no later than five. I want everyone present and in a happy frame of mind, before we go out."

Laura gave her a quick hug and strode off to disappear soon among the crowds. Maureen watched her depart with a pang of regret. Everything could have been so uncomplicated if . . . but then she gave a light shrug of her shoulders. Laura was independent. They would have other times together.

With a lift in spirits she made her way towards the central fountain and glanced at her wristwatch to see she was ahead of time.

He had come up behind her shoulder.

"*Mia Bella Signora.*"

Maureen spun around, her breath caught on a suspended intake. His voice had been pitched low in the voluble racket around the area, but penetrated her concentration at once.

After she had slowly circuited twice she had stood with her back to the fountain, and had become absorbed with watching the artists. At least seven easels were spread along the verge of the paved island.

Maureen sighed. "Hello, *buon giorno, dottore,*" she said softly.

His eyes were direct and intimate in their

admiration of her. The thought skittered across her mind that no one who saw them together, like this, could mistake their intentions.

In conflict with the mental picture of him she retained, he was dressed in a pale grey suit. She had only ever seen him in darker shades. The blue shirt flattered his Mediterranean colouring. A handsome man . . . how much is that a part of what we love or where we love, she thought. Am I 'in love' . . . or just attracted to that which is beautiful?

Maureen's emotions wavered and there was a shyness now. He was here and the rendezvous had been kept, but the tacit agreement it entailed for them brought on that new emotion for her, the possession-submission factor, with its appealing new power that began to blossom and grow. With a casual motion of his head he indicated the direction they would take.

"The restaurant is behind that corner building, not far."

She noticed that he made no attempt to take her arm or guide her by the elbow as they began to walk across the square - the small contact, that was a routine gesture, a mannered protection of women in public places. It would have been an acute intimacy between them now, and no longer innocent.

The restaurant gained, they were ushered to the table with some ceremony. She was seated on a plush banquette and faced into the room, with Cesare seated opposite across a wide expanse of crisp white damask. It was an impressive establishment, fine crystal and china tableware and restrained decoration.

Cesare exchanged comments about the dishes with the waiter as she surveyed the room. Fish in all its variety and culinary fashioning seemed to be the speciality, but a few meat dishes were offered.

Maureen noticed few women present at the crowded tables of diners, but without exception they were expensively turned-out and jewelled, and of whatever age they were attractive. She was glad she wore her antique garnet earrings, and for the most part was at ease with her appearance.

They had attracted brief regard when entering. Several of the men had looked up as she passed. If the table included a woman, she too would look, to see who had lured away her companion's eyes. All of the Roman ladies had favoured Cesare with their approving glance.

No one greeted him, Maureen had noted, or turned to a companion in excited comment. She knew so little about his life, or his friends, and how Isabella fitted into it. She made a mental note to explore that subject, when the opportunity came about, sometime later perhaps.

Between them there now existed an unvoiced but mutual accord, to refrain from any personal comment. There was no hint of how the rest of the afternoon would be spent. Maureen was aware they had now indulged in a game, assumed new roles. For a brief interlude, among a cast of urbane strangers, they would play parts, unlike those they would otherwise perform elsewhere, or if alone.

The game carried a curious tantalus. Maureen was conscious of it and knew Cesare was. The power of their physical attraction suppressed, its high voltage concealed behind a facade of casual conversation, the pressure built. Their proximity to each other was at flashpoint.

That knowledge gave Maureen such an urgent longing of anticipation, it was almost an ache. Her toes tingled as she flexed them inside the pumps beneath the table.

Cesare was talking about the politics, and the politicians who made up most of the complement of the restaurant's patrons. He gave some humorous comments and told stories. Maureen concentrated on appropriate replies and asked some informed questions about the present government under La Malfa. Interested and abreast of topical world events, she knew Barzini's writings, and asked about his current attitude, as parliamentarian with the Christian Democrats. She saw the quick flash of surprise in her partner's eyes turn to an admiring consideration.

On Cesare's part, like all men who fall into love with sudden passion without prior consideration or prolonged reflection, he experienced instant relief that the object of his love possessed a brain. The beauty of her body had a matching counterpart. She not only would engage his physical desire but his mind as well.

And in the future, sometime soon he hoped, when they were together all of the time, he would delight to see her move within his larger world. In those hours that remained, when he had indulged all his desires of moving within her.

But for right now . . .

Before the lift came to rest at the third floor his urge to possess her again almost overcame him. He held himself in constraint from any attempt at even slight physical contact.

During the ascent, only his eyes that stayed locked upon her, focused in passion, betrayed him. Maureen sensed the force that drew her. The response was compelling. She held herself apart from him in the narrow enclosure.

In slow and measured paces they reached the door to the apartment, walked into the hallway and along it, and gained the door of the bedroom. Before it could swing closed they had turned and joined.

Without pause or separation mouths crushed and probed, tongues penetrated. His grasp lifted and carried her forward, and their bodies sank down onto the bed.

The sound of ripping fabric reached her as the dress, pulled apart by Cesare's hands, sent a button flying. Released from the lace cage, her breasts were grasped by eager hands, and one rigid nipple at once covered by his mouth.

As he indulged himself to her exquisite delight, her legs began to separate beneath his body and his response to her want was immediate.

Alternately straddled then leaned on, she felt the constriction of clothing being pulled and tugged away. His pants, her pantyhose were thrust aside and at last he pushed hard into the warm silky moistness that awaited him.

Their coupling was wild and intense, and executed to swift completion. The past hour's game that had led to the final arena of struggle, had awarded the claim-all trophy, and the winners now lay in panting satisfaction. He still lay upon her as their breathing slowed.

"Maureen . . . *tessoro mio* . . . I am sorry," he said against her ear. "I was too rough, I could not stop. Please tell me if - did I hurt you?"

Carefully he eased himself away and looked down at her with an anxious expression, smoothing the shiny strands of hair back from her cheeks and forehead. She looked up at him in a green-eyed gaze, the mass of bronze hair spread over the white bedspread beneath her head. A smile started that lifted the corners of her lips, still moist from the bruising force of his mouth.

"It would hurt . . . if you had waited one more second." With a lazy hand she reached up to lift damp hair back from his brow.

"Does food always make you like this?" she said. "They should put a warning notice in restaurants."

He grinned in contented relief and got up, bending forward to pull her gently upright. "May I help you to remove your dress, *cara* ?"

"I still have one?   No, but it was my favourite."

"I will buy you a new one - lots and lots of new dresses."

From the bathroom he brought a dampened facecloth and some towels. Avidly he watched as she removed the rest of her clothing. He unbuttoned his shirt and tossed it aside. Then he picked the garments off the floor to place them on the couch below the bed.

He threw back the covers on the bed, and reached for her, pulling her down beside him onto the cool sheets.

Running his hand gently down her smooth stomach and around her hips he drew her close and put his mouth onto her lips in a long, gentle kiss.

When he stopped, Maureen pulled her head back a fraction to look into his eyes.

"Cesare . . . ?"

"Hmm?" His hand slowly stroked her skin, and then moved between her thighs with gentle pressure, as his tongue explored her neck.

"It's not possible . . . so soon. You can't - "

"No?" His hand stopped the coaxing. He took her hand in his and pulled it down so that she could feel the hard proof of his intention. "You think not?"

As he drew her beneath him to cover her body with his own again he spoke softly against her ear.

"But this time I want for us to be slow . . . to wait. Ah, Maureen! My beautiful, passionate one . . . "

Long after, in the time ahead that had not yet arrived for them, Maureen's memory of that aftenoon was hazed with a dreamlike quality, the details blurred. Their bodies, whether still or in motion, stayed one.

Curled into each others arms, in a separate world of their own sensation, their pleasure had no clear divisions. Roused again to join and share his want, to accept his possession and respond with her own blissful demand, she at last drowsily pushed Cesare away, only to look at him in joyful wonder as she held him.

She accused him of being a greedy boy. He tiredly claimed he had never known such hunger and desire when he was a boy. But when at last Maureen began to end the idyll, and prepare to return to that other world, she found Cesare was resistant to releasing her.

In the huge marble bath which they both now occupied, he held her against him, his chin over her shoulder in the soapy water.

"You must promise it, Maureen. Say the words to me - now."

"But how . . . I can't promise it."

"You must!"

"But Cesare, there are the children to think about and - "

"The children will be with you and here in Rome - all of you with me, that is understood."

He moved her around in the water to face him, tilting her chin up so that she met his eyes.

"There is room here, or we will buy another house, with a garden. I love you. I want to marry you, Maureen. So, say you will apply for the divorce."

She looked at him and a new cloud of worry hovered and formed. "It will take time, I have to wait. When I return next week, I can't just - "

"I know that. But not too long. In November I come to London, as I told you. Before I leave for New York. So we must plan for our future."

Maureen stared at him in mute dismay, unwilling to think about the disruption ahead. She was locked in a dilemma. Her love for this man who held her and the established love that waited for her return.

"Maureen, say that you will." His hands gripped her shoulders and gave her a gentle shake.

"You have said you love me, have showed me, and I love you. We must now be together. You see this, do you not? There is no other way. Say you will divorce!"

"I do love you . . . I think I do. But, please Cesare -"

He bent his head and covered her lips and his hands slipped around her breasts. In the steamy water their bodies slid together. But she wanted to resist him, tired of the pleasure that now threatened her. It was all madness, her madness, and now it would shatter and change her world. She wanted more than anything now to bring to an end this golden, reckless afternoon, and to escape his demand that she alter her life.

Lifting her arms she slipped them around his neck and in the long kiss she acceded once more. It could be the last time, she thought. Hiding her ambivalent intent she allowed him all the time he desired.

Before he let her leave, she said, "I will get a divorce but . . . I must have time, Cesare."

Chapter 13

The tension that had escalated between the two men who now faced each other across the broad kitchen table, created a palpable field of energy. Orso's dense dark pelt stood upright in the statically charged atmosphere and he uttered a low feline growl of displeasure before fleeing to another of the villa's rooms. The darkness outside the windows concentrated the lights in the kitchen into a tableau, encircled by shadows. Two pairs of dark eyes glinted and flashed as they glared at each other.

Cesare had driven to Ostia late that Saturday afternoon. A telephone call in the morning had confirmed that his father would be there, and alone, free tonight from the occasional visit of a chess-playing archeologist crony who lived nearby. It was now nine o'clock and they had both moved out of the dining room to the kitchen, where Luigi prepared and served coffee. The dishes were rinsed and ready for Maria's attention when she returned in the morning.

During the simple but ample meal Maria had prepared for them, Cesare had begun the questioning of his father, curious to explore in greater detail the circumstances that Luigi had circuitously touched upon during the visit of Maureen on Thursday.

Luigi had fully answered each of the questions his son posed, but without any elaboration, more in the manner he would have adopted with a medical colleague rather than a family intimate, carefully skirting personal opinions and without emotion. But the preceding hour of questions and answers, probes and responses, parries and ripostes had suddenly become very intimate and personal. Father and son now faced each other in an atmosphere of hostile confrontation; one wherein an objective onlooker might be forgiven for identifying the bedrock similarities to a Greek tragedy.

This new mood of acrimony was initially provoked by Luigi, in an unguarded moment, when he finally became the interrogator, questioning Cesare's involvement with Maureen in disparaging admonition. By rapid stages it had segued into the classic spectacle of an angry father voicing shocked dismay at his son's surprising, and defiantly emphatic admission: he not only had made love to Maureen repeatedly during the past days but was declaring he was now in love with this woman, as with no other in his life before.

Allowing his anger to betray him, Luigi had hurled that last guarded secret at his son like a weapon, with the vain but absolute certainty that he would be undermining as well as deterring what he still believed was only a manifestation of Cesare's foolish excess, a middle-aged madness. An achievable lust, perhaps even excusable, but nothing more. So using the spectre of genetic probability, invoking mankind's taboo of incest, he shouted out the revelation of his own brief sexual act with Marinella.

Even as he voiced the damning words his mind wrestled with whether it was really parental stricture, medical prudence, or some other reason that caused his violent outburst.

With a glass of grappa he had earlier poured for himself now clenched in his hand, Luigi faced down the shaken countenance across from him as Cesare hit back in censorious disbelief. With a concentrated fury and a voice that was steely with barely controlled passion, Luigi baited the recipient of his own disgusted admission.

"How? You are asking me how such a thing could happen! What are you? A man of this world - or some sterile ascetic, removed from reality, living on a monastic hilltop?"

"But you were the family doctor! She was the daughter - a little flirt, yes, and also a tease if you like. Marinella was a spoiled playgirl and a hedonist - but she was only a young girl!"

"Marinella was a woman before she was sixteen!" Luigi roared back. "She seduced her own cousin for the simple joy of it! Before he knew what his apparatus had been designed for, for God's sake!"

Cesare glared at him. "But my mother was still alive then!" His voice had risen to an anguished wail at this last shouted imprecation.

Luigi's hand crashed down onto the table and the fluid in his glass sloshed over the rim to form brown puddles on its scrubbed surface as he shouted back. "D-o-n'-t y-o-u dare mention your sainted mother's name to me in the same context, you sanctimonious pup! What the hell do you know about our life then? And what the hell did you ever know about any of the Catalbis? Nothing !"

In the stunned pause Luigi finally reacted to the

late, slowly-dawning recognition of the heart-broken
young boy that had called out; that still existed beneath
the polished but superficial veneer of the mature male
animal standing across from him. He made a great
effort at self-control. Straightening himself into a
more erect stance he held up his arm, palm turned
outward as he studied his son's belligerent face before
speaking in a slower and lower tone of voice. Luigi
wondered how he had failed to see the effect of Dora's
death as a wider consequence in Cesare's life. He had
believed that certainly Caterina, and he himself, had
been the ones uniquely cheated, but they had each
accepted their own loss more philosophically and
moved beyond it in their lives.

"Stop it, Cesare. That is enough of this stupidity
between us. I owe you an apology . . . as a father . . .
and as a man. I am going to tell you how it happened.
And why I think it happened, my young innocent! But
do not sully my wife's memory by mentioning her
name in the same context as that sorry episode." He
sighed, an exhalation that only an old man can invest
with the same morass of memory. "I loved your
mother. Since before the day I married her, when I
was still eighteen. She was the only woman for me.
Then, now, ever!"

Slowly turning away he walked across to the
kitchen doors before reversing to face Cesare again.
"Come. Let us sit down together like reasonable men.
It is a long story - and I want you to understand. Perhaps in the telling I too will understand at last." He
waited to gauge his adversary's reaction. "Pour yourself a drink and bring the bottle with you."

Maintaining his rigid posture and hostile
countenance throughout, Cesare inclined his
shoulders slightly and made as if to consider whether

he would move or remain. Without any hint at concession but more as one according habitual civility to the older man, he eventually advanced a few paces. After a prolonged pause he walked to where his father stood waiting, collecting the bottle from the table as he went.

Reaching the lounge they moved towards two armchairs placed together at an angle. The cat, hastily moving again, now vacated the comfortable cushioning as Luigi approached and prepared to sit down. Amber eyes alert and unblinking, Orso leapt lithely across the carpet and on to the windowseat to watch these two human antagonists from a distance, assuming the classic feline crouch of repose that affords a springing departure if events should suddenly warrant. The silence around them hung in suspenseful wait that was marked by the faint ticking of a clock across the room, as Luigi took a slow sip from his glass before placing it onto a table beside his chair. He stared off into some far recess of his own memory.

"You will remember that a large summerhouse once stood on these grounds. It was partially destroyed by bombing during the war; but the foundation is still there, buried somewhere beneath the undergrowth. I have let it remain so all this time . . . I think now perhaps as a penance. Unseen but always there - the evidence that must also be tallied, along with every other act in my life."

❀

Wednesday, November 2nd, 1938

The final days of 1938 were drawing toward the close of the year with a spell of unseasonably hot weather as November began. The Fascist government of Benito Mussolini was gaining increasing attention and a renewal of support among the majority of the citizens of Rome, as well as in the rest of Italy. For the city's established classes and among the intelligentsia a growing concern was being evidenced however, but with ever more muted criticism these days.

For Lorenzo Catalbi and his brothers, Il Duce had changed from a subject of scorn and offhanded humour to one of foreboding and discreet curses. Today Lorenzo had quite enough on his mind already without having to learn that his younger brother Carlo - of all the idiocies - had made yet another girl pregnant, this one a farm girl from the largest village of their family's landholding in the country around Cerveteri. Not that it was without precedent among any of them over the years, but these inflamed times made it altogether different. They could not afford either monetarily or visibly to pay off the girl's family in support and acknowledgement as they once would. To draw attention to themselves in the fascist-sympathizing countryside could be fatal now. Had it been a servant within the social milieu of the city's families it would have been a different matter; an understanding between equals could be reached and accommodation quietly made.

Trying to find a discreet physician, one beholden in some way, to eviscerate quickly the growing seed of a casual Catalbi pastime, would be impossible now. Such a simple, harmless and often unnoticed process to effect - so it always appeared to Lorenzo, who shied away from any intensive medical description if he could avoid it, as it didn't contribute anything important to man's necessary knowledge of his own body. It was a process especially easy with a dull-witted girl, even if she was quite happy to bear a Catalbi bastard for the added substance to her meagre existence; and one which probably gained her a measure of prestige among her own people, he thought. He had sometimes recognized a few of his family features around the villages, evocative merely of his grandfather's, father's and uncles' more uncomplicated lives in happier times.

He was going to have to lean hard on Bracci this time. There must be some way to reach behind that faultless air of propriety the man always wore like a mask. Surely there was some acceptable bribe that would work now, although not money of course for there was less and less of that available. His face set into hard lines as he thought of having to endure Bracci's subtle if silent manner of aloof disdain whenever he was presented with the fleshly ailments of any normal man's reasonable lifestyle that had to be dealt with. Damn! But there was little other acceptable recourse available. One other minor but troubling fact was that he truly respected the man without ever analyzing or quite understanding why he felt as he did.

He would also have to demand that Bracci drive out to the villa at Ostia this evening to meet him there, which put him at an added psychological disadvantage, asking an additional favour of him before broaching his appeal - but it was unavoidable for two good reasons. First because Lorenzo himself had to go there later this afternoon, to take that idiot of a local mayor to task for permitting the Fascist rally last night to get so out of hand. There had been damage done to a few of the family-owned properties around the area. The stupid cretin should be soundly thrashed! Who did he think he owed his petty functionary office to, from which he could be tossed out tomorrow if he, Lorenzo, so chose?

The second reason was the privacy he required. Bracci should meet him in Ostia because the coercion and hard-leaning he planned for him could be freely voiced in the seclusion of the summerhouse there; it was prudent to do it well away from where any servants or family members could interrupt or eavesdrop. The doctor was a respected friend of his family and well liked by all of Catalbi's household, administering to them readily when asked and often without expecting to be paid.

It was with these thoughts, aggravated and compounded by the second telephone call of the morning he had received, that sent Lorenzo storming out of his office on the ground floor of the Palazzo d'Orinici. Striding down the marbled hallway he wasn't in any mood for the sight of Marinella slipping out of the library doors ahead of him.

"Nelli!", he shouted at her. "What were you doing in there? Come back here at once, miss, I have something to say to you!"

Marinella spun slowly around to face her father with a little tremour of foreboding at the anger in his voice but careful to present a winsome smile on her face.

"Papà! I was just finishing a letter before going upstairs to see Mamma now."

Lorenzo surprised her as he came up, grabbing her shoulder in a fierce grip and pushing her firmly towards the door. "Get back in there!"

She knew immediately that someone must have already telephoned and told him where she had been seen that morning. Mentally running through an assortment of likely reasons she could offer that might diffuse his obvious and unusually severe temper, she quickly selected one that could serve her.

Inside the huge book-lined room with its heavy leather chairs and dark wooden tables, Lorenzo confronted his daughter, standing with his back to the doors that he had slammed behind him, consciously blocking her means of escaping from him.

"What do you think you were up to even appearing down at the Palazzo Venezia, you stupid fool?" he yelled at her.

"But Papà, Francesca Petrone asked me - "

"Don't lie to me, you silly little bitch! That filthy peasant will destroy us all without you prostituting yourself, along with the name of your family!"

Marinella flushed with anger, as much from the severity of his attack as at the unaccustomed scorn and crude choice of Lorenzo's words. "How dare you speak to me this way, Papà, I was just - "

"You were flaunting yourself in front of that lascivious poltroon! Isn't it enough for us to endure that you consort with riff-raff boys of the Trastevere - that you must now also prance in front of that bald-headed pig of a Dictator!"

Marinella let out a small breath to steady herself, believing she had witnessed the worst. Lorenzo's anger had surely all been vented now, a sudden violence like a volcano's occasional outburst of rocks and sulphur gas, leaving a dissipating cloud but without any further massive eruption to follow.

She attempted a faint appeasing smile. "Gabriele Tuornovici happens to be a very fine artist. And . . . everyone praises our great Mussolini, Papà - these are new and exciting times we live in."

His hand flashed out slapping her hard across

the face with a suddenness and force that surprised them both. The sound alone was a shock. Especially so to him, for he had never hit her before, not ever. She had always been his favourite among the children. God knows she was more lovely than her mother had been at the same age, and with a leaner body and a livelier wit. He sometimes thought she was also smarter than either of her two brothers.

As much from astonishment as from the force of his blow, she dropped to her knees in front of him, catching her breath again, momentarily stunned. As the red marks appeared and spread across her cheek she steadily held his eyes with her own in a fixed stare, an exchange of wills silently engaged. A new boldness slowly crept into her eyes, taking the place of astonishment. There was a subtle mocking in her quiet response that followed the silence as they looked at each other. A little smile once again began to form around her mouth.

"But Papà, haven't you always told me that I am just like you? That I am a Catalbi . . . and we like the variety that life has to offer? Francesca mentioned to me your . . . interest in her last week at the dinner party. Was that before or after you had more fully explored her maid upstairs? The poor child was in tears, Francesca said."

Lorenzo stared at her a long while before sighing deeply to himself. Indeed she was a Catalbi. He wished at that moment that the often diffident and restrained behaviour of the Orinici side had predominated, in just this one area of her personality. Young as she was, she revelled in her seductive ability, discovering as many unique opportunities as a man might have done to gratify her sensual appetite. The same way that he had always done. He doubted his sons ever indulged or availed themselves as much. The immediate problem had now become how he could marry her off quickly and well, so that some curbs and discretion could be achieved. After that it would be her husband's problem if she exploited every gardener's cock in the afternoons.

"Get off your knees, Nelli! It doesn't become you. From now on you will watch your behaviour. A woman becomes easily soiled in men's eyes, especially an unmarried one. I think you should be sent away from Rome for a while." Lorenzo turned away from her, his anger fully spent for the present. She stayed watching him as he opened the door and walked out of the room.

Still smarting from the surprise and indignity of being slapped by her father, Marinella got up. How dare he strike her like that? She knew how much he loved and admired her, just as she loved him too, but she held no illusions or respect for him, of course, not as a man. She had never respected any man. Once she had made them capitulate to her wants and her will they either became quickly tiresome or merely useful to her. They were like silly schoolboys, always pestering for more sweets, until she became bored with them. The married ones the greediest. Gabriele was different, of course, for he was entirely her own; he would always belong to her no matter what she did.

Her father must obviously have problems she wasn't aware of yet, besides money. She knew that she would have to be more careful and not provoke him again. Leaving Rome certainly didn't appeal to her at the moment, even though Gabi kept talking about Switzerland. Yet there was a dangerous petulance starting to seethe behind her sense of relief that the ugly scene was over, and a desire for revenge was starting to form in her mind. That, too, was a well-known Catalbi characteristic over the years.

The summerhouse was completely enveloped in darkness now. As Luigi stood in the middle of the large hexagonal-shaped room he ignored the hot, humid atmosphere left behind from the sun playing on the windows all day. He was as angry as he had ever been in his life by the recent exchanges between him and Lorenzo Catalbi. His adamant and repeated refusal even to consider performing a curettage to rescue Carlo from the consequences of his actions, had led to a coarse shouting match. It was one of the few specific acts that he as well as any skilled physician was capable of, that he would not accede to. Not because he was ethically or clinically opposed to the procedure - he had often debated the merits among his own medical associates - his refusal was a primitive self-protection. A quite simple and stubborn avoidance of throwing his own medical standing into jeopardy. Although Lorenzo's demand was clear, he had refused to change his mind despite threats or bribery - the latter especially insulting to him. Some old rancours and private errors had been bandied about between them.

Over the years that the two men had known each other a curious sort of friendship and superficial liking had developed between them. The fascination of opposites perhaps, because Luigi was as direct, open, and morally abstemious by nature as Lorenzo was devious and libertine. It could have been that each regarded the other as an anomaly, producing a curiosity that attracted, by wondering how each could function and be content in his own lifestyle.

Aside from that aspect of their relationship, which Luigi regarded as a learned and copied trait as much as an inherited character-failing, he had always respected Lorenzo's hard-headed practicality. The man had an undisputed generosity and without question he possessed diplomacy and a charming grace when dealing with people or in philosophical argument. Only when faced with blunt opposition did the ruthlessness and malicious force surface. As a family, the entire Catalbi clan could be objectively regarded as a degenerate species in some lights, but they were not altogether without charm and purpose on occasion.

Alone at last after Lorenzo had finally stalked out, Luigi tried to dissipate the lingering rage that the meeting had created in him. Not one charitable thought for the other man permeated his mood at this moment. He had been called away - demanded to come in fact - from his clinic in the city where he had been intensely busy today. The drive out had been slow and even hazardous because of the amount of people, the Fascist supporters, still congregating along the way after the recent marches and demonstrations in the locality, and now he would be late getting back this evening, leaving Dora alone yet again. She would have already retired to bed before he could reach home, as she seemed to be doing so much earlier each night.

He loosened the knot of his tie further, tossing it onto the chair where his jacket already lay, unbuttoning and spreading his shirt collar wide, when his attention became focused on the image, through the glass doors and windows, of a burly shadow approaching down the darkened lawns leading to the summerhouse. The shape bore something carefully poised midway in front of it. As it reached the doors he recognized one of the elderly house staff carrying a tray with a jug balanced upon it. He stepped forward to open the doors before Bruno had to position the tray on one arm to perform the same act.

"It is so hot, dottore, Maria thought you would appreciate some lemonade."

As Bruno entered and placed the tray upon the glass table near him, Luigi's throat constricted as he saw the means of quenching his suddenly acknowledged thirst. He looked at the beads of moisture condensing outside the crystal pitcher and automatically swallowed. Chips of ice floated alongside thin slices of lemon on the surface of the cloudy liquid. Beside the jug was a crystal glass and a silver domed plate.

"And there is a little ham and bread before your journey back to town, dottore."

"Thank you, Bruno. Please tell Maria how very much I appreciate this. It was kind of you both to bother."

"Not at all, it is nothing, dottore. Is there something else that I can do for you - anything?"

"Nothing more at all," Luigi assured the servant. "No, no - don't bother putting on a lamp. I shall be leaving immediately after I drink. I am very grateful, Bruno."

As Bruno turned to go Luigi added, "Is your master still up at the house?"

"Il Conte has already left for the city, dottore. There is no one of the family at the villa now." He paused in case there was a further request of him. The good young doctor was respected by all of the Catalbi staff. He never hesitated to inquire about their health even before they needed to approach him and readily provided the nostrums for their assorted ailments.

"Good! That is all then, my friend. Good night to you!"

❀

Still caught up in the mood of smouldering irritation he stared out into the barely discernible patterns of shadows made by the trees on the villa grounds against the evening skyline. During festive events the grounds could be brightly and colourfully illuminated, but tonight there were just the perimeter lights of the entrance gates and walls lit.

It took a full thirty seconds for the sound of a door behind him, softly clicking open, to register. As he hastily returned the glass to the tray before he spun around, he was quite unprepared for the dimly silhouetted feminine outline framed in the doorway. The curving shape of her hair to her shoulders was only made visible by the faint backlighting coming from the lower grounds through the windows of the room behind her.

"Did I startle you, dottore? Forgive me, please."

Luigi swallowed hard and tried to moderate his annoyance at this new Catalbi intrusion before he replied. "Marinella! What the devil are you doing here? How long have you been in there?"

She slowly advanced towards him into the larger room leaving the door open behind her. "I just arrived and I was curious to see where Bruno was going with a tray at this hour. So I came in by the back way." She bent down with agile grace and slowly ran her index finger up the side of the sweating pitcher, bringing the wetness on it up to the tip of her tongue.

"I thought that the villa would be free of any of

my family tonight. I saw Papà's car leaving as he passed me on the road leading here."

Angered by this unexpected interruption Luigi retrieved his glass from the tray and finished the contents in one quick draft. Then he plucked his jacket and tie off the nearby chair.

"I am just leaving to drive home. So the house is all yours now!" His voice was curt and harsh as he spoke, even to his own ears.

"Please, don't rush off yet. I want to know what it is that is wrong with Papà today. You won't believe it but he - he actually struck me this morning, for the first time ever."

Luigi looked down at her standing in front of him. The heat and the humidity inside the summer-house were now emphasizing for him all of the odours present in the room. The sharp tang of lemon slices in the pitcher, the dry reek of upholstered furniture, the fetid aroma of decaying flowers in a vase somewhere, and the jasmine scented exotic muskiness of Marinella's perfumed skin. His mind unconsciously and unbidden had appreciatively detected the inimitable sensuous appeal and aroma of young vibrant skin. For a doctor especially it was always in acute contrast to the stale odour of ageing flesh that filled a clinic each day.

"Would you please look at the bruise he made on me?" She laid the palm of her hand against the damp shirt on his chest as she stepped close to him. "Tell me please, what it is that is bothering him. He really hurt me."

Luigi had barely begun to say, "Marinella, I haven't - " before the unbelievable shock of reaction surged through him. She had pressed her flat warm stomach and hips against his lower body and was now slipping her arms around his waist as she laid her head against his chest. He could feel the nipples of her bare breasts under the thin silk of her dress, pressing into his chest hairs. The scent of her hair filled his nostrils, and his body started to defy every instinct and control of his mind by the instantaneous arousal that was occurring.

He put both of his hands firmly on her shoulders preparing to push her away but she spoke to him quickly. "Please don't leave me yet, dottore. Help me - I need comforting. And . . . I need a man tonight to give me relief."

"Good God, Marinella, you have half the young men of the city in your hands - " Her body moved slightly as she pressed closer.

"But young men are not good, they are too quick to please themselves." Her voice dropped lower in register. "I've never known what it is like with an older man, an experienced man who could show me properly." As she tilted her face upwards she found his mouth and delicately impressed her own.

The tip of her tongue was a soft warm presence between the fullness of her lips, wetly probing in little stabs, and one of her hands slid down from around his waist. The warm pressure of her palm, held flat against his penis, brought on the imminent and threatened hardening. It began straining against the fabric of his pants as her hand curved to accommodate the bulging of his willing eager member. He stood there in stunned silence, as her fingers caressed him in tantalizing movements. Then her lips moved softly on his as she breathily murmured.

"Oh yes, please, take me."

Whether it was his confusion and embarrassment, coupled with an unwillingness to resist the strains and discipline and negations of this tiring day, or simply the inverted means to revenge himself upon Lorenzo, he could never later explain to himself. As she took his hand and pulled him forward he blindly followed her.

Slowly moving backwards she led him into the other room, and he abdicated all thought and resistance anymore to her mesmerizing and seductively scented spell. Mutely he watched, as she raised her arms in the shadowy darkness unhooking the dress at the back of her neck; his breathing rapidly increased as it fell to the floor. Avidly he inhaled the odour of her desire coming from the moist labyrinth under the silky bronze patch of hair between her wonderful legs, as she again came forward to push against his body in all her naked lovely softness. There were a few seconds only while he savagely groped and flung off his clothes before his large hands came up to clutch her to him. Zealously he started to explore these sudden riches in this hot, dark treasure cave of the summerhouse.

On the padded couch in the humid shadows he took her with a forthright and studious satisfaction. Successively he strove to incorporate and relentlessly execute every act of sexual repertoire with a thoroughness which had her gasping for breath. Her pliant accommodation and eager response to every demand he made of her supple body only fanned the fires of his madness. He was a large man with a sturdy muscular physique, and for this interlude, at least, beyond any restraining consideration. The previous silence of the room was now punctuated by the incessant creaking stress of the couch under his weight and movement, and his grunts of exertion as she received the force of his plunges with small groans.   It seemed as if by primitive physical force alone he could expunge all his troubles of that day, punishing Marinella as well as her arrogant father, even though aware that by doing so he was breaking the ancient respected code by which men lived and could be called civilized.

The aftermath was brief. As he rapidly got to his feet and struggled into his clothes, Marinella, who still lay prone on the couch in front of him, in exhausted and supreme satiation, murmured dreamily. "Thank you, dottore. I knew that it would be different. This will be our little secret now - our little personal revenge." He could hear the happy smile in her voice behind the words.

As he hurried out through the door he spoke as much to himself as to her resting body when he said, "This was an aberration, a horrible dream. It never really happened."

Chapter 14

A quiet stillness permeated the room, the tale and its telling absorbed by the night. Prior antipathies had been diluted, exorcized, and left to depart into the shadows.

Then a subtle stirring occurred that marked the closure to what had passed. The subject would not be referred to again. The cat yawned, stretched a hind leg behind him and resumed his pose. As if on cue, Cesare exhaled a light breath and uncrossed, then recrossed his legs. Luigi still stared ahead but emitted a soft, "Ecch, an old story, an old shame."

Cesare studied his father's face and the indelible lines of age that furrowed his brow and scored his mouth at each side. The emergent sense of compassion he felt had been reluctant but total. Yet his understanding was now tempered by a dark cloud of doubt, one that he was not quite ready to confront for a while.

"How was it resolved - or was it? I mean with Carlo Catalbi."

"Quite well. And with some unexpected benefit." For the first time that evening Luigi smiled, with a genuine if sardonic humour.

"Once more I meddled with people's lives. But to good effect this time, I believe."

He settled back into the chair.

"When next you are in Fiumicino, look for a large red fishing ketch and the man who owns it. His grandfather was a patient of mine, a sad old man who was raddled with arthritis. His wife had died, his eldest son had been lost at sea, another was killed fighting in Ethiopia, and except for the third boy he had no other living relatives.

"In November, 1938, that last son had received his conscription notice. I went to see the old man and we talked for a long time. In December, before the boy left for military training, he met a girl from a village further north and they were quickly married. She moved into the little fisherman's house in Fiumicino. The old man now had a healthy young woman to clean, cook, and care for him."

Luigi smiled again as he recounted. "Next summer his first grandchild arrived, to great rejoicing. A sturdy boy who would carry on the family name, and in time be taught to handle the family fishing boat for a livelihood. This did much to rekindle the old man's interest in life.

"You see, the Catalbi lawyers had presented him with deed of ownership for the fishing boat and for the house. That generous act occurred after his son had married, in December.

"I'm told his grandson is known by the nickname his school friends used, 'Il Barone'. He was always a born leader. Now he is head of the local fishermen's union. Intelligent, well-liked, and good looking too; but a devoted family man I hear."

Cesare smiled along with his father when the story was finished. He reflected on the contrast between his father's generation and his own. Those times had required an entirely different set of hurdles to be surmounted, within an inflexible societal framework. A doctor then would often administer more than medicine to the community.

"A sort of justice then, Father. And it all stayed in the family too."

"Yes. Which in essence was how the lawyers phrased it, when they handed the pen to Carlo."

The two men looked at each other in compliant accord, Cesare conscious they had talked as equals, not older and younger man, or father and son. Two men who mused on the vagaries of life and its challenges.

The moment passed and another element engaged them. Their relationship to each other was in focus once more. The knowing look in Luigi's eyes, that was really a question, was precursor to the weightier issue between them, one that still must be addressed. The older man was offering him the initiative, before he assumed the offensive - a play of power between father and son and one that touched an archaic core in the affairs of men, with biblical overtones.

But the younger man was now ready and would take command in this arena. He was, in fact, the ultimate logical executor, by a quirk of fate or some strange destiny.

"Surely you cannot have lived all these years since then Father, and truly doubted that Marinella's child was any other than Tuornovici's?"

Luigi's face reflected an habitual impassive stoicism.

"Long ago I resolved not to think about it."

"It is the only logical assumption."

"Another possibility exists."

"But it has to -"

"Why? We are talking about a mere fourteen days variation." Luigi's voice became impatient. "No one computed with more precision than I. And no one can be certain."

The idea that had formed itself in Cesare's mind during the past hour was the only solution, of course. Just as he was the only responsible processor. Any other course was unthinkable. Whatever the outcome he had to know, for his own peace of mind. He had to live with the knowledge so he must uncover the truth.

But there also lay within his means the ability to offer a release to the older man. Possibly. A last final solace before he died. There had been enough prejudice and hostility between them tonight, and the years of doubt that the other had lived in were sufficient expiation for a youthful folly.

Cesare knew that until resolution was obtained the dark cloud that had descended around him would affect everything in his life.

"You know that today, Father, we can eliminate your doubts quite easily. Some research with medical records, of course, but - that is part of my work."

Luigi looked at him. "I thought those blood tests were never conclusive."

Cesare returned the look with a confidence he would now have to assume. "Newer antigen research is being developed all the time, and the tests have become fairly indicative. But we can still prove whether someone is not the father - even though we cannot entirely prove someone is."

"Would it not be better to just bury the memory . . . and move on?"

Cesare's chin came up. "That is what you have done all these years, Father, yet it didn't stay buried!"

"And are you sure you are prepared to face the other possibility?" Luigi asked, staring hard at his son.

Luigi got up slowly out of his chair and stood looking at Cesare. "For me, it is no longer relevant. But for you . . . it is that important?"

"Yes, it is." Cesare stood up. "It seems that there is such a thing as fate, or destiny, after all."

The two men regarded each other for a moment. Then Luigi moved to come forward and embrace him.

"What you say saddens me Cesare. But - perhaps it is so. Certainly my own life would not argue otherwise. The gods are all bastards, my son!"

Cesare returned his father's hug with equal warmth. "True, but if we are forced to perform in their games, we must devise the means to beat them, because we are men and have to live in this world."

Orso rose up off the windowseat and arched his back in a tall stretch. He directed a baleful glare at the infrequent intruder. Cesare caught sight of the movement and made an effort to lighten the sombre mood between them.

"That cat of yours is so incredibly ugly."

"He is, I know." Luigi smiled. "But women continue to seek him out - and cause him so many problems."

They began to walk towards the door under the scrutiny of their unlovely companion.

"It is late. Will you stay here tonight, my son?"

"No, no. It is an easy drive at this hour, and I have an appointment tomorrow."

Each of them was aware the subject of the evening would not again be referred to. Not until some development occurred. Luigi watched Cesare drive away into the night and closed the door. After he prepared the house and himself for the night, and retired to the bedroom, the prospect of sleep seemed a welcome balm.

He lay back on the pillows but his eyes stayed open. It was impossible after this night of recalling the painful past again, for him to prevent his memory returning once more to those final days during his time in Lingford Oaks in 1939, and the acts performed then that had now returned to haunt him.

Chapter 15

Saturday, August 19, 1939

Dawn arrived over South East England with a clear golden light and then swiftly developed to brilliant sunshine in an azure sky. Saturday would be another perfect summer day. The exaggerated heat and a first quarter moon that night, had weather-wise country folk predicting an imminent storm.

The morning radio news broadcasts still talked of Danzig and Britain's pact of alliance with Poland. Stepped-up military preparations heralded the greater storm that was already on the horizon. Most people would go about their ordinary affairs today in the usual way, content not to dwell on it, or to know that in only a matter of days their lives would be changed forever.

Much earlier, in the hours before the dawn, Luigi had neatly, painlessly, ruptured the embryonic sac to release the rush of amniotic fluid that would cause Marinella's labour to commence. While gently reassuring her, he was surprised and heartened at her attitude of calm cooperation. He instructed her to alert both the nurse and himself as soon as more powerful contraction pains began. She smiled at him.

"Don't worry, Dottore. I will be a good patient, you will see. Just tell me what to do and I will do it - I promise."

"Good girl! All will go well, *cara*."

By ten o'clock she lay in the narrow bed on sterile cotton sheets, and drifted in and out of shallow slumber.

Gwyneth Hughes looked in on the surgery's only patient every half-hour, each time admiring the rich sheen of copper hair that escaped onto the pillow from the cotton cap. Marinella restlessly tossed as the hours advanced and the pains grew stronger and more frequent.

If all proceeded as it should, in another four or five hours the full course of labour would be transited - and an infant safely delivered. For both Luigi and Gwyneth Hughes the hours of this day and evening would be critically busy ones. There was a measure of anxiety, of course, professionally suppressed, but they were well prepared, and all was in readiness for the arrival of their second patient. Around four o'clock, Nurse Hughes should be able to escort Grace Lyle into the second room that was prepared.

So far as that young woman knew, she would merely be keeping an appointment for a routine precautionary check-up as she neared her term. But Nurse Hughes would lead her back to where Luigi would administer sedative drugs and initiate labour, and eventually deliver her child.

They had discussed and rehearsed in detail how they would effect the happy result that was anticipated for Grace Lyle, before her family would be summoned to take the mother and child home.

❀

The day wore on in cloudless summer glory, and by two o'clock the temperature had climbed to 80 degrees. Marinella's pains were now harder and came in swift successive waves. A sheen of perspiration on her face reflected the strain. Each wrenching contraction took its toll and Gwyneth Hughes gently wiped the lovely features with a cool, damp cloth.

"You're doing so well, my dear. Try to relax between each one - and take a deep breath before the next. It won't be much longer."

Marinella gasped, and her hands were gripped around the metal bars at the head of the bed. She lay on her left side with both knees tucked high.

"I am trying, but . . . ahhh!"

Nurse Hughes grasped her shoulders and attempted to move her onto her back in order to check the dilation again.

"No! Let me stay here. Please! It's better like this."

"There, there. I know it is, my dear. All right. Now you can roll back again. But just for a short while."

In her experience she had often observed that women in childbirth, if left to their own instincts, would prefer to squat in a deep crouch, on the floor if they could. It was doctors and midwives who found it easier for themselves to deliver babies from women flat on their back in bed. So medical convention decreed that was how it should be accomplished. Gwyneth Hughes remembered hearing the old tales of the way it once was, in her native Wales - with the birthing stools that had a hole in the seat - and the baby grasped as it descended, with all the female relatives supporting the mother.

To all intents and purposes it had worked well, she had heard. She often wondered if less suffering was involved than with the modern way.

But then, it didn't seem quite proper for an elegant young woman of class to have to squat like a rude peasant, although childbirth was the same experience for every woman, no matter her pedigree.

Luigi walked into the room and went across to the bed. He gently put his hand on Marinella's forehead. At his touch she opened her eyes and released a hand from its grip on the bed rail. She reached out to grasp his and he firmly clasped it.

His eyes silently questioned the nurse, who calmly shook her head to convey that it wasn't quite time yet. On a side-table was the nitrous oxide cylinder and mask, covered by a towel. It was there in case Marinella's strong resolve deserted her at the last. He would not let her suffer unduly, but would prefer not to risk damage to the infant, nor delay labour any longer than was necessary.

Nurse Hughes held up her hands to signal another half-hour to forty-five minutes. Luigi acknowledged with a nod of his head and looked at his wristwatch, then again at the nurse, before turning his gaze back to Marinella.

Completely absorbed with the task he was about there was scant regard for the personal in Luigi's professional manner. Only on the fringe of his consciousness did he allow himself to be aware that the woman on the bed before him was in some way special. As eager as she for the event to be concluded, his attention was partially directed toward what was ahead, with the other young mother who would soon arrive - and the other-than-normal birth that must be effected.

"Not long now. You have been wonderful, Marinella - keep it up. Not much longer."

In their own language he had murmured the words to her in semi-distraction.

"Ahhhh. I hope not. Ahhh *God!* Please make it be over soon."

"It will be. Very soon, I promise. Be brave."

With a gentle squeeze he released her hand and she at once grasped the rail with whitened knuckles. He watched as another pain gripped her body and subsided to leave her panting in relief. Fresh beads of sweat dewed her face.

It was the first time in his career he had witnessed the full progression of labour. Normally he would be summoned for only the last sequence before birth. Even during his residence at a training hospital he was never obliged to monitor the transition at close hand. This day he would actively attend the entire duration for two women.

With Gwyneth Hughes, his co-conspirator, he would also be involved in a far stranger series of events today, and for everyone's sake - not just his own - it must be performed with a successful outcome. To this end, Dottore Luigi Bracci had studied, prepared, re-checked, primed, and steeled himself to practise at the highest level of his ability. As though he faced the most stringent board of medical examiners, all his faculties were alert and engaged. Every exigency and deviation had been tallied and alternatives prepared. Paramount was his own sense of confidence.

The distant rumbles of the storm that began minutes ago approached quickly and grew to loud crescendos. Darts of jagged fork lightning illuminated the windows with flashes of piercing blue. The rain drummed onto the roof tiles and increased the volume of sound everywhere.

One mighty crash of thunder exploded overhead and coincided with Marinella's last scream. The fuzzy damp head of the baby emerged at exactly one minute past three.

Luigi and Gwyneth Hughes, now a synchronized team of efficiency, each experienced a surge of elation. That breath-taking moment when new life appeared was always a wondrous marvel, however often it was witnessed.

The baby's eyes were quickly bathed with boric lotion, and the little body slipped out; then the umbilical cord was tied and cut. Perfectly formed in every way she was crying lustily. Nurse Hughes lifted her away and proceeded to clean and swab, rub with a towel and swaddle the infant in a blanket.

Luigi eased out the placental afterbirth and examined it. He was delighted that for a primipara, Marinella had delivered well and with ease. Her co-operation to their every request had contributed to the process. Because they were careful she experienced no tearing or complication.

The exhausted mother now lay there in serene respite at the cessation of the ordeal of the past hours, with her eyes closed.

"Do you wish to see your daughter, Marinella?" His voice was quiet.

Slowly Marinella opened her eyes and looked up at him, ignoring the activity beyond his shoulder which could well have been viewed if she chose.

"No . . . just tell me that she is all right."

"She is perfect! And beautiful too."

For all his calm demeanour he was unable to suppress from his response the sense of elation he was feeling.

"That is good."

She closed her eyes again with an expression of peaceful contentment on her features.

Gwyneth Hughes cuddled-up the crying infant against her bosom, gathered up some linen, and prepared to leave. She looked across at the young mother and was impressed at how she could be so calm at this exciting moment. Such restraint and determination, she thought, as she left the room with the precious little bundle.

In the succeeding hours and on into the evening the rain had abated then returned in force, as the storm rolled around the countryside. Now overhead, then echoing at a distance, it moved in a circular pattern. When actively in the area, lightning of blinding ferocity lit the dark outside the windows.

In drowsy repose Grace Lyle lay back with just the lingering after-effects from the drugs. When Gwyneth Hughes entered the room and approached her she opened her eyes and smiled. Seeing what the nurse was holding she raised her arms to receive the blanketed bundle.

"Oh, my little darling. Isn't she sweet?"

"She is that, Grace. She's the loveliest little thing I have ever seen." Placing the baby in the crook of Grace's arm, she said, "What are you going to call her? Have you a name picked-out?"

"No, not for a girl, we haven't. Jack was so sure we would have a boy. His family hasn't had any girls for generations!"

"Well . . . what about Maureen then? It's a lovely name - and a good Celtic one."

Gwyneth had been quietly calling the baby Maureen for hours. In the little room down the hall she had kept a loving watch over her, and whispered the name as she suppressed the sound of her brief crying sessions, half aware when she did so, that Maureen had been prompted by Dr. Bracci's use of Marinella, when he spoke to the baby's mother.

"Maureen . . . Maureen. Oh look, she opened her eyes. I think she likes the name! My little Maureen." Enchanted, Grace Lyle gazed at the pink dimpled face that nestled in her arms.

The baby's mouth moved with sucking motions and Gwyneth leaned across.

"Let me help you put her to the breast, Grace. Your milk will start in a few days."

The amazing efficient factory that was the human body, ensured lactation would commence normally with stimulation of the baby's mouth, even after parturition of a pre-natal mortality.

The storm had moved off again. Luigi glanced once more at the little form on the table before him as he completed his medical records. The body of the infant, slightly macerated, presented no readily identifiable abnormality on its surface. Two small patches of indentation were faintly evident on each side of the cranium. He had always avoided using forceps, but in this case he knew no further damage could be done to the dead infant and during the sluggish birth presentation it had been more saving of the mother to use them.

Into the section of the record marked 'Probable Cause,' he wrote 'Rubeola'. The placenta had been secured in a glass container for histological evaluation by pathology, and now - all was ready.

The private ambulance would soon arrive to take Marinella off to the nursing home in Cheniston for her nine-day confinement. The result of her pregnancy would be wrapped and sealed, and would travel with her. He knew that it would be sent on to a London hospital for analysis.

When he had checked on Marinella a little while ago and confirmed her normal progression, they had talked. She had promised him she would return to Italy on August 28th, as planned. He had himself verified that her reservations for the ship and the train were in order. This time he emphasized that she must not remain in England any longer. Her luggage had been sent ahead to the shipping agency, and just two small bags were to accompany her now.

Earlier, Grace Lyle's husband and her mother had excitedly arrived after being summoned. In their market garden van they had driven off home with her and her baby, where everything had been ready for months to receive the new addition to the family. A wry smile lit Luigi's face as he recalled their profuse thanks.

Nurse Gwyneth Hughes had said she would visit the Lyle household tomorrow morning, before she herself departed on the train for Wales. The temporary District Nurse she had recruited would make the family her first responsibility on her Monday morning arrival.

When he had presented Gwyneth with the envelope, a shared glance of visual triumph had passed between them before their effusive farewells to each other.

The soiled linen in the surgery had been attended to and replaced, the instruments had been sterilized, and Luigi now had only the other records left to complete for Alan's files.

When the ambulance arrived he went to escort Marinella, as she was wheeled out on the trolley bed, in the capable care of the two attendants.

"So, Dottore, I thank you . . . once again, you did not fail me."

Luigi bent to kiss the hand that she raised to him.

"You be good from now on, Marinella. God speed."

Alone at last he stretched and walked back into the house to retrieve his pipe. He could allow himself some relaxation now before finishing up.

Dawn was breaking and streaks of gold in the eastern sky were interspersed with silver grey strands. They cradled a crescent moon that still rode high on the horizon. The day would be a little cooler perhaps but promised continuation of the fine summer.

The storm had washed the air to crystal clarity and the shrubbery and grass around the house sparkled and dripped from last night's rain.

Luigi had fallen asleep on the couch in Alan's living room, still dressed in yesterday's clothing. He roused with a feeling of exhaustion - but a profound sense of cautious content. This last fine day would be entirely his own before he began the welcome journey back to his Dora and the children.

Walking out of the door he stood in the small garden and gratefully inhaled the cool air. As he looked at the sky he rubbed his shadowed jowl that was heavily whiskered.

He stretched and lifted his arms above his head. A sudden rustle of leaves startled him and a bird flew out of the nearby hedge. The rising sun caught the white image in its silent flight.

Jubilantly, it seemed, it flew high and away into the morning sky. As Luigi watched his spirits lifted as though carried along with it in its flight.

He didn't know what sort of bird it was, but as he watched it depart, devoid as ever of all spiritual bent, he suddenly received a strange sense of benediction.

Chapter 16

Cesare had risen early on Sunday morning after a restless night. Already showered and dressed, he saw the clock above the kitchen stove showed five-thirty as he prepared coffee in the *espresso* machine on the counter. He watched the relentless electronic spasm of the slim black bar proceed upwards.

"Time . . . too late, too soon, too fast, too slow. Always at odds to our purpose."

During the drive back from Ostia last night his thoughts had twisted and churned around the latest revelation by his father and his own obsession for Maureen. The sudden desire to take the fundamental and novel step of permanent attachment, to tie her to his life forever, he was still trying to accept and absorb. His concern for how to achieve that aim was fraught with doubt and uncertainty. The claim to her he had imposed was tenuous at best with no control over the outcome.

This new impediment was a greater obstacle, a shadow, that had forced him to re-examine his feelings, and with the microscopic scrutiny that affairs of the heart had never merited before. Little wonder his sleep had been fitful, fragmented by troubling dreams.

His temperament was one that demanded immediate action when faced with a problem and his training had emphasised that facet of his personality. Unable to rest when problems begged solution, he drove himself until resolution was obtained, in his work or in his life. The two were usually linked. Colleagues and family were familiar with his disregard for sleep - and even food - when immersed in the pursuit for answers.

This problem was unique, involving deep personal emotions, but the habitual modus operandi was engaged automatically. The original subject had to be examined, the veracity of the components scrutinised, and the strategies enumerated to prove validity. But the chances for swift resolution to this inquiry, with the need to eliminate the dark shadow of doubt, demanded a patience he was ill-prepared to accept.

Not one second of his time would be wasted, however, to prove he had not fallen catastrophically in love with his own half-sister.

"You go to the office today?"

Clara stared at him from the doorway. Instead of the casual tailored sportswear he should have worn he was in a business suit - and up and about far too early for a Sunday.

Lost in speculation as he stood there, he looked up with a distracted tender smile as her comment finally penetrated.

"Yes, *madrina mia*. Might as well . . . and I have to be on the Isola this afternoon."

A conference obligation would involve a few hours of his time, when he would host a tour and panel discussion for a group of dermatologists at The Fatebenefratelli Hospital on Tiber Island. Also called

St. John of God, it was the site scheduled for closing festivities Tuesday evening.

"Your sleep was not good, *figlio mio?*" She studied his face for a while. "You did not have words with your father!"

"Now Clara, you know I am too old to argue with father - stop fussing!"

He poured some coffee into a cup and thought how the heated exchange of Saturday evening would have shaken her to the core.

"Here - I made enough coffee for you."

Clara shuffled forward and collected milk from the refrigerator and a saucepan from the cupboard for her *caffe latte.* There was silence between them while she heated the milk and took her cup to the table to join him.

"In November you go to America, Cesare. Will be good for you . . . is good for a young man to travel, have changes."

He managed to smile at that. It had been a comfort always to have a Clara around - the mother substitute, who would always think him young, even when he was now past his forties.

To allay her obvious concerns about him he made an effort to respond to that subject.

"And you have already made a list of what you want me to buy when I go?"

A derisive burst of air escaped her lips and she jabbed her hand down in a dismissive gesture. Yet he knew that when the time came for him to leave she would hand him a little pile of clippings from American magazines that she had carefully hoarded, with voluble descriptions of the advertisements. She would also be offhanded and equivocate, 'perhaps if you come across, but not important if you don't.'

Right now her intuition was working overtime.
Whatever *Il Dottore* and his son had discussed last
night it had left this one with a strangely troubled
countenance this morning.

She felt in her bones it all had to do with the
beautiful girl. That young image of Marinella. The
English woman . . . who could not be English. Who
had the not-so-right English husband, and probably the
English children too, who knows? The one who was
so right for her Cesare finally to give his heart to. The
fates were being more than usually unkind.

In the past there had been enough tragedy and
loss, but the feeling in her bones told her there could be
more to come. She wished it was tomorrow, he could
leave for America, get him away for a while.

Clara's mention of the New York trip prompted
Cesare to remember something - to have his airline
tickets include a stop-over in London. Perhaps he
would also arrange a courtesy visit to the London
Hematology Society while there.

Try as he might to resist it, an insidious thought
flickered across these musings. If the results of his
research were incomplete, or went the wrong way,
perhaps he would not be flying to London. Idiot - of
course he would go. Whoever Maureen's father
proved to be, of one thing he was sure, he had to see
her again. Whether for the last time or . . . he clung to
the fantasy . . . to make plans for their future together,
he knew he would go there.

Silence surrounded Cesare at the Clinic where
he spent most of the time at his desk. He knew that in
the laboratories above and below there would be some

technicians at work, but in the office suites he was alone.

He had first unlocked the Records Library after arriving and searched the files, then left a handwritten memo on the Senior Librarian's desk. It requested an immediate trace on any medical data for two specific names: Gabriel Tuornovici, to include military records; and Marinella Fiorenza d'Orinici Catalbi, including all hospitals in Rome.

Neither of the names, nor the request, would generate any special interest with the librarian or her staff. Time and ingenuity would be needed to hunt down the old records that could well turn out to have been lost or destroyed over thirty years ago, and this might vex the librarian, given the rush demand. Still, she would work hard to comply; Cesare was a favourite of hers among the clinical staff.

Back in his office he started his own file and careful effort went into a graph. He knew the blood type of his father and mother as well as his own, of course. The memory of his first experiments with testing as a student returned as he worked.

The class had taken samples of each other's blood and the young professor, full of modern innovation, had then speculated on the probabilities of what their parents' classification could be. And, even more intriguing to them all, what it could not be.

Cesare's had been A, the second most common group. The fellow student he had drawn blood from had been the rarer AB, which less than three percent of the population possessed. Later, they had all rushed home to collect the evidence and determine their parents' blood type. Customary juvenile humour had abounded with risqué allusion and infinite variation to, 'it is a wise man who knows his own father.'

Cesare's father had been AB, so he could indeed have fathered his classmate, along with his sister Catarina's B classification, and his own A. But his mother's A type blood, combined with his father's AB, precluded them from being parents of an O type child.

In retrospect it still surprised him that only one of their class had become sullen and withdrawn from the general hilarity afterwards. Like Cesare, he too had the common A type blood. Sadly, his acknowledged parents had each possessed O type.

Their chagrined professor - after emphatic reminders of the vast propensity for error in the unknown void of medicine they must conquer - had hurried them all on to the loftier subjects of antigens and alleles.

Though he could chart it from memory, Cesare reached for his copy of the A-B-O Mating Table to scan again the permutations he knew so well. His fervent hope was that Marinella and Gabriele would not prove to have been an A and a B respectively, the singular combination of blood types that could produce offspring from all four groups, O, A, B, and AB. That result would mean a hung jury, even with protracted and finite antigen tests on Maureen's blood.

Since Luigi's AB blood type prevented him from siring an O type child, then O could be a desirable blood group for Maureen to have. But the O gene is also an amorph, able to be carried in the parents' genes undetected. And there was no possible way he could ever obtain four sets of grandparents' blood types to verify.

The problem he faced was twofold: to acquire a sample of Maureen's blood immediately; and to learn both Marinella's and Gabriele's typing. Gabriele's was the possible key. The odds of proving non-paternity were tilted to the highest percentile of probability. Even though it was a meagre sixty-two percent, he would be grateful to accept it. He refused to consider the odds for coincidence, a wild card possibility that Maureen was AB, Marinella an A, and Gabriele a B. Determined to suppress all emotion from the task at hand, Cesare placed the graph in the file and locked it away in his desk drawer. But as he made his way out of the building his thoughts strayed to Maureen again, wondering where she was right now, and the self-imposed restraint of scientific discipline slipped away.

He had been strangely attracted to someone. For the first time in his life he was truly in love. An emotional and physical bond had been forged that he had never known with a woman before. Beyond the exciting sexual gratification and pleasure, Maureen fascinated him, had touched and laid claim to his soul.

Was it possible . . . had he been drawn and snared by that ancient lure, the mystical kinship of blood? With a shudder he rejected the horror of the thought that pervaded his otherwise practical mind.

Oblivious to the city's charms that day, the infective happiness of Sunday strollers in the sunshine, he drove towards the Ponte Fabriccio to cross to the island, the Isola Tiberina, and forced himself to the practical problem of how he would obtain a sample of Maureen's blood. Tomorrow was best; there was so little time before she flew back to England.

Cesare hoped she knew her blood group and could tell him, even if some verbal ingenuity was demanded to learn it. He could not casually ask when he inquired about her weekend travels, after he kissed her and before he made love to her.

The more probable situation was she did not know; few people did. So he had to devise a way to take a sample himself, without alerting her to the reason. Bad enough that he had to live for a while with the torment; to reveal it was unthinkable. Not only would it destroy everything good and wonderful between them, he would never impart his Father's shameful secret.

❀

Later that afternoon, sun-bronzed, dusty and sated with sight-seeing, an otherwise happy foursome returned to the city. The rented car was returned to the agency and the Grants and Standishes parted to make for their hotels. A dinner at the Excelsior Hotel's renowned restaurant would be the indulgent finale of their weekend.

"Let's blow the bankroll, John, and live it up tonight."

"Good idea, Michael. After all that exercise I think we owe ourselves the finest."

John was easily persuaded. To dine well was an occasional luxury that made a worthwhile memory. In a London winter he was often too busy to eat proper meals at regular times. The ability to drop a famous restaurant name sometimes, among better-heeled associates, was an added *cachet* for him.

"Make it a late hour, fellows. I'll be a long time in the bath after all those catacombs we explored," Laura said.

Maureen had enjoyed the sojourn away from Rome and away from Cesare. In the hilly countryside of Tivoli she had recaptured, for short time spans, a semblance of her former self - the complacent housewife, with no outside complications in her life, on holiday with her husband and with friends.

While still unmistakably Italian, the area held no sinister lure and attraction for her as Rome did. No strangely attractive, all-consuming lover, to confront and uncover her own hidden desires.

Both Michael and Laura were merry companions and the four of them remained in agreeable harmony throughout the weekend. Two full days of exploring together had left little time for her and Laura to be alone and talk, which was a relief too. The secret they shared did not have to be raised.

Only once was she made to reflect on the past. The two of them had collapsed on a grassy bank, late on Saturday afternoon, after the two most famous villas, Hadrian and d'Este, had been toured. John and Michael wanted to see yet another site and Laura demanded they not return until they were ready to go back to the *pensione* and stay there.

"Michael always has to see everything - he was that way as a child."

Laura flopped back onto the grass and kicked off her shoes. She saw Maureen's curious glance.

"We're cousins, you know. So I've known him since childhood."

"Cousins? But I thought - "

"Well, cousins once removed, so it doesn't constitute a problem genetically. Keep in mind that grandparents had large families in those days, dear girl."

"And did you always know you would grow up and get married?"

"No. But we met up again in our twenties. Both of us were recovering from failed love affairs . . . and mutually consoled each other. Then after a few months we realised we had something special - a loving and comfortable relationship with a lot of respect. It's worked out well. How did you and John meet?"

Maureen thought a moment, surprised to recall the memory. "On a Sunday morning, at three a.m., at St. Bartholomew's Hospital."

Laura laughed. "Not a very romantic location. Were you sick?"

"No, my flat-mate was. Avril, a Belgium girl, became very ill after a party. The art students were always having wild get-togethers in those days. Not much money and bootleg liquor. John was the intern on night duty."

There was a pause while Maureen looked up at the blue sky above and thought back to those times.

"Well, did she recover?"

"Yes, after her stomach was pumped."

"And . . . "

"And John made a house call to check-up on her progress two days later. He . . . seemed so caring and responsible and dedicated - so different from the men around the art school."

Laura rolled over onto her elbows, looked at Maureen and let the silence grow for a while.

"So . . . it wasn't a 'love at first sight' sort of thing, either."

"Not really. Avril went back to Belgium, I found a job and began working, and John and I casually dated for a year - concerts, movies, walks. Then his residency ended. In the excitement of him starting in practice, we decided to get married."

While they talked Maureen had also become aware that in the short space of time she had known her, Laura had filled yet another void in her life, the role a sister might have played, trusted confidant and keeper of her innermost thoughts. The amity developed over the weekend between all of them, petty rivalry, camaraderie, gentle humour that also provoked, was shaded by the sort of relationship siblings would display.

With a small shift of focus that jarred she wondered if John now seemed more like a brother to her. Had she ever been passionately in love with him, or he with her? Certainly she had never . . . done with him the things she had with Cesare, nor felt inclined to. She could never be stirred in that way by any other man she was sure. So which was love? Or were they both love but of a different type? The thought made her sad, especially for the one whom she loyally, affectionately called her husband.

That her life had been turned inside out and upside down was a private agony, held in the dark corner of her mind that was her own little torture chamber. Even with Laura she had skirted her deeper involvement with Cesare, along with the formidable permanent attachment proposed. But she longed to confess that this was more than a brief flirtation. Last Friday in Rome, over coffee, Maureen remembered Laura airily dismissed her vague and circuitous allusion.

"It's a passing fancy, Mo. You've fallen in lust, not in love."

She clung to the hope it was true. Because then the agony and chaos would pass. Guilt she could endure so long as life could return to the way it was.

Then had come the insistent urge from the depth of her being. Did she really want to return to the way it was? Once known, could this new sort of love be ignored for ever, and forgotten?

❃

After the pleasant and restorative weekend, Monday morning arrived with a domesday quality to it for Maureen. Just two days were left until she must leave Rome.

When John left the hotel for his penultimate conference day she felt as edgy as she had during their breakfast together downstairs. Curious to know whether Cesare would call her this morning, she worried about whether she should call him. When he drove her back to the hotel last Friday they had not made plans. Or if they had, the emotion that surrounded their parting had scattered them from her memory.

Part of her wanted to retain the distance and peace that Tivoli had provided. Yet the return to the city yesterday caused her to step back into that excited mood of tension and a deep sensual yearning for him.

At the elegant restaurant last night she had been intent to study the occupants of the other tables and knew she looked for him. When she had dressed and made-up with precision, noting that her skin had a golden glow from the sun, it was for his appraisal. But he had not been there, and she ignored the discreet and admiring glances directed her way.

She could of course call him. Perhaps he expected it, but she resisted, even though today would be their last time together. Tomorrow she would shop with Laura for the take-home gifts, then pack and dress for the reception that closed the proceedings. That thought inspired a sudden urge, to buy a new dress. A vain and illogical thought, for she had enough things to wear, and was never excessive about clothes. Anyway, she couldn't afford to, so that was that.

But if she could, then something in white, and with a simple elegant line, in a soft shiny fabric, that caught the light. When the telephone rang, Maureen jumped. With a breathless leap of her heart she crossed the room to pick-up the receiver to hear the concierge inform her that a visitor waited in the lobby.

After a hasty check in the mirror, she collected her handbag and hurried from the room, pausing at the top of the stairs to force herself to walk slowly down. In the compact area of the lobby she looked around, puzzled not to see him at once.

The concierge smiled as he addressed her from behind the desk.

"Ah, *Signora*.. the young lady there."

Maureen turned to see a young Italian woman get up from one of the armchairs.

"*La Signora* Standish? *Buon giorno*! I am asked to deliver this to you."

Maureen thanked her as she took the envelope and prepared to turn away, but the girl spoke again.

"Please - you are to read and let me know. I am sorry, my English not so good, eh? *Dottore Bracci* say I now bring you to the Clinic, if okay with you."

Bewildered, Maureen slipped a thumb under the envelope and extracted the short slip of notepaper.

Please forgive the way of this request,
Maureen. A busy morning for me. Could you
come to the Clinic? Then I shall be free.
C. Bracci

Maureen looked at the girl who waited with a cheerful smile, as if it were a normal event in her daily round.

"Well, yes. I suppose so, but - "

"Good. We take taxi. No problem *Signora*. My name is Valentina Corraci."

When they were seated together in the back of the cab, Valentina said,

"I want to take you on my Vespa - but I think Dr. Bracci is right. You prefer taxi, no?"

Maureen had to laugh at the young woman's infectious smile and air of enthusiasm.

"I would have enjoyed a ride on your Vespa, Valentina. I've always wanted to try one."

"See - I knew. They are g-o-o-d! I take my mother to her favourite market on Saturdays. In Rome is the best way to go."

"How long have you been riding a Vespa, Valentina?"

Amused by her happy companion, Maureen kept up a conversation to avoid thinking about Cesare's strange summons to go to the Clinic, and why he had not simply called her.

"This one for six months, is new - and red, my favourite colour. Fabrizio, my boyfriend, he help me to buy. Next year we are to marry. My old one was, how you say, some other have it first - ah *si* - 'second-hand.' That one was small, this one big."

Within a short time, the taxi pulled up outside a modern building and Maureen saw the name Clinica Ematologica. She reached into her handbag for money to pay the taxi but Valentina touched her hand.

"No, is not necessary, *Dottore Bracci* give me the money."

Pushing open the glass doors, Valentina escorted her into the building and towards the lift. When it arrived at the third floor they stepped out into a carpeted hallway and walked down it. At a doorway she stopped and indicated that Maureen should enter alone.

"*Arrivederla, Signora. Si - Prego!*"

Maureen stood there for a moment and then hesitantly opened the door. A large office contained several desks at which three women and one man were busy. Beyond them, through a partially glassed wall, she saw Cesare, who also sat at a desk.

As one of the women looked up to smile at her, Cesare looked up at the same instant and sprang to his feet. He came out into the main room to greet her.

"Signora Standish - Maureen, I am so glad you are here. Please come inside."

He had spoken with graceful deference and a modest smile. Maureen looked at his eyes expecting to see a sparkle of suppressed humour at the mock formality, but they were merely warm. Missing was that intense and appreciative look she had grown used to and she was left a little off-guard as she went forward to join him.

Cesare closed the door and his voice returned to a more normal tone.

"I am sorry, *cara,* but I . . . I wanted to be sure you did not make other plans, and . . . something came up here . . . so I could not call you first."

He moved away to the other side of the desk and gathered-up some papers into a tidy pile. These he placed into a tray while Maureen stood and watched, and tried to sort and tidy his remarks into a coherent sequence.

"Look, if you are busy right now . . . I too have other things - "

"No." He looked directly at her then. "We must talk again. But away from here. Please, for a few hours only."

Maureen realized he had a pleading look that begged her understanding. She wondered if his changed manner had to do with the office environment. Was it possible, that the weekend had afforded time for reflection and a change of heart?

Confusion and doubt infected her thoughts and she felt a keen pang of disappointment. But her curiosity was piqued now so she said nothing.

He watched her and sensed her doubt.

"But I did want you to see where I work. When you return to London . . . you will know where I spend my time."

"Yes. Thank you."

Her response, after a pause, had been short. She wondered if after today she would end up feeling angry, relieved or simply foolish. Perhaps all those things at once, but she willed herself to wait and find out.

Cesare, aware that things had not begun on an auspicious note, hastily put the last paper aside.

"Well - now that you have seen my office, I must show you the laboratory before we leave, yes? This is one of the most modern research clinics in all Italy."

He came around the desk and guided her to the door and into the outer office. After a quick exchange with one of the ladies there he led her out to the hall.

They entered another door and Maureen gazed around a large white room where apparatus and machinery were banked around the walls and on a long table running the length of the room. Several white-coated technicians were busily engaged over screens and equipment.

"This is the small laboratory where I sometimes work. The main research is done elsewhere."

He began to lead her down one side of the room.

"It is one of your own countrymen we must thank for the major leap forward in blood research - William Harvey, in 1616!"

Maureen looked up and stared at him. He was reciting other names, talking about autoanalyzers, and haematocrit readings, and she wondered if this was a full-fledged lecture. Was he serious? He had said 'your own countryman'. Only days ago he had refused to let her think of herself as English, had been emphatic that she was really Italian.

She tried hard to believe he truly wished to share his work with her, but if he was busy why were they here, and why today? Now they had paused before one of the technicians who adjusted dials on a screen before he turned to smile at them.

"Do you know your own blood-group, Maureen?" Cesare's voice had a loud hearty quality.

"My blood-group? . . . No, I don't."

The question surprised her and she felt odd that she didn't know. How silly she had never inquired, for certainly enough blood samples had been taken from her over the years for one thing or another.

"Ah! Then Domenico can tell you it very fast."

Cesare lifted her hand, took hold of the index finger, swabbed it, and picked up a surgical pin. She quickly pulled her finger away.

"No - I don't want to. I mean . . . not now. It doesn't matter."

Both men stared at her and Cesare's mouth stayed open in surprise at her sudden reaction.

"But . . . it is important to know your blood-type, Maureen. Every person should, and it does not hurt. Just one small drop is required."

"I know that. But I don't want to bother right now." She folded her hands together as if to close the subject.

Domenico shifted his rapt gaze from Maureen to Cesare. What the hell is it with Bracci, he wondered, liking a prick before a poke now, some kinky Dracula fetish? Christ, who cares if she has Mongolian B-7, just feed her chocolates and wine and get on with it. Maybe it was his age. Wait till I tell Enrico.

"That's all, Domenico." Cesare glared at the technician as he took Maureen's arm and moved away. "My apologies, but you really should know what type you are. Of course, the work we do here is more complex, and for different applications."

Numbly Maureen nodded her head, relieved to see they had moved close to the door again, and hoped they could leave. She supposed it was always good to know your blood type but . . . a thought hovered at the edge of her mind, but she was unable to grasp it.

Cesare opened the door with a small sigh and a dismissive shrug of his shoulders. What had seemed a simple and direct solution had failed and with some embarrassment. Now what? There was another way he could learn it, of course, but it would be time-consuming and involve circuitous inquiry.

When they reached the lift Cesare turned to her, and Maureen saw that his eyes now held the familiar, intimate regard she desired.

"For these past two days I have thought of you so much, Maureen. And you . . . did you think about me at all?"

She watched him and revelled in his attention, aware of a shaky feeling inside and how much she had longed to return and be bathed by this look.

"Yes . . . part of the time."

Remembrance for the feel of his body warmed her and she relaxed. She smiled at him with a joy that was tinged with triumph, and completely forgot about all that odd nonsense back there in the laboratory.

When the lift arrived it contained an occupant, who greeted Cesare and inclined his head to Maureen as they rode down to the lobby in silence. Outside, in the sunshine, they proceeded along the pavement to a doorway which led to an interior garage. Within seconds they were in the car and out onto the street to join the traffic.

"Where are we going?"

"We are going to somewhere very nice that is across the river and above the Trastevere, where I think you have not visited before - The Monte Gianicolo ."

Maureen recalled the evening with the Mendells, just after her arrival, and the sinister grey area around the restaurant. In the bustle of traffic that sunny morning, with Cesare beside her, she felt too carefree and indolent to think about it.

"Where did you go, *carissima*, and did you enjoy what you saw?"

They had reached one of the bridges across the Tiber now and she was fascinated by the views of the river from both sides.

"On Saturday we went to Tivoli, which was lovely. We stayed overnight. And on Sunday we drove back along the Via Appia and visited one of the Catacombs."

"Tivoli is beautiful," Cesare agreed. "Every Roman swears he will have a villa there someday. Not so grand as the ones you visited, of course!"

He threaded the car through the squares and alleys of the old quarter and Maureen received a different impression in the morning sun. Still grey and shabby-looking, compared to the city across the river, it had the robust air of a true community with lots of residents going about their business in the small shops they passed.

Cesare seemed impervious to the surroundings as they sped along the narrow roads which soon gave way to broader avenues and more traffic. Maureen saw there were occasional fine buildings among the indifferent ones. They began to climb along a road that led to masses of umbrella pines with grassy expanses between.

Within minutes he had swung the car off the road and brought it to an abrupt smooth halt onto a paved area. They were on a high ridge that had a large statue of a man on horseback, pedestalled against some ancient stonework.

Maureen was surprised at how fast they had climbed over the city. Even from the low seat of the sports car she could glimpse through the trees, roofs and domes across the river.

"Who is the statue of, Cesare?"

"Over there are the city walls built by Marcus Aurelius, and that is Giuseppe Garibaldi, the Father of the Italian Republic. But I don't believe he really rode a horse into Rome."

They looked at each other and laughed. Then he opened the door, stepped out, and quickly walked around to open the door on Maureen's side. He gave her his hand and pulled her up towards him.

"But I did not bring you here to see Garibaldi."

He bent and put a light kiss on the tip of her nose, and with linked hands they walked along the balustrade for a little way. Then he stopped and turned her around to face the view down the hill with both hands on her shoulders, and drew her close against him.

Before her lay the expanse of Rome in all its architectural splendour. Framed by the trees of the gardens below them, the multiple hues and shapes and textures of the city sparkled in the light. Maureen wondered why none of the tours had included this unique and lovely view.

Beside her ear Cesare murmured. "I wanted you to see this view and remember . . . when you have left and gone back to London."

Silent and still against him, Maureen thought about what he had said, and what he would say next.

"Perhaps sometime soon I hope, you can return to live here - with me."

Through her mind raced the dizzy parade of new experiences during the past week: Ostia, the Palazzo d'Orinici, the little square, the Borghese Gardens. He had shown her another life. The warmth of his body against her now was having the effect of potent red wine.

He had offered her this view of Rome like a jewel on a velvet pillow. And he had offered her his love. Of course she wanted it, all of it, and right now. Under the golden sunlight it seemed so easy to accept. But it would entail a most wrenching and painful adjustment for others beside herself.

"It's a wonderful dream, Cesare, and I want it. But dreams have their price, and others would have to pay too."

"Yes, because everyone is touched by another's dream. But if it is also our destiny, are we not willing to pay the price?"

He began to turn her around to face him and she prepared to respond with passion to his expected kiss, but there was a serious expression on his face.

"Maureen, I am truly sorry for what happened between us last time."

Colour came into her cheeks and she started to respond, but he laid a finger over her lips and smiled.

"No, not for our love - that was honest passion. A sea of love that swept us away." He brushed the wave of her hair back from her brow.

"I am sorry for the impossible demands I made of you. You know that I love you, will always love you. But . . . you must have more time. To think and to decide."

Maureen paused, unsure how she felt now that the demanding lover she had fought to restrain had become so quiet and reasonable.

"You must decide with your heart and not in haste what is best for you, your life. And I will be here, when you have chosen."

She listened and examined the tone and the nuance of his words, then thought about his manner earlier while they were in his laboratory.

"Today you seem so different, Cesare. I thought, there is something that worries you. Or - that since last week, you have thought and . . . "

Maureen pulled away from his hands and walked a few steps away to look down the hill. She felt confused yet composed all at once, and when she turned back to face him her voice was precise.

"Don't apologize for what happened. I was a willing partner - so I can't have regrets, can I?"

She looked at him with eyes that flashed.

"You don't have to promise to marry me if it was just an affair. We're both grown-ups, and perhaps it was just that, an affair. I can accept it - especially as I may have to anyway!"

Cesare's expression changed and softened. He came towards where she stood and looked down at her haughty and remote gaze. A grin started that he bit his lip to try to suppress and a devilish glint lit his eyes.

"What a woman - I have to learn how to manage that fine temper you have."

He reached for her and kissed her with a hard intensity as she struggled to resist, then succumbed and joined his ardour as his hands moved over her.

Only conscious of the joy that coursed through her, Maureen was oblivious that they stood in an open place, in each other's arms, like a pair of itinerant teenage lovers. When they separated he looked at her.

"It was not just an affair . . . I love you."

"But then why, back in your laboratory - ?"

Inspiration hit him, like a bolt from the blue, as though the gods had handed him the gift of devious reasoning.

"You are so perceptive, my love, and I confess there are other things on my mind. But not what you thought. Here, let us walk."

They wandered off on the grass to pause beneath a tree, while he mentally rehearsed what he would say.

"I wanted to surprise you, later. Try to obtain some records about your father; you had said you wished to learn more. And . . . there is an idea for research perhaps. He was an artist and you are artistic too. There is the current notion that genetic inheritance for music or other talents are linked by DNA, which involves blood analysis, so - "

Maureen turned and burst out laughing with a look of happiness on her face. Of course, that was why he had seemed so awkward and reserved, so unlike the urbane man she admired.

"Oh Cesare, that would be marvellous if you could find out about my father. When I'm back in England I will try to find my blood type and send it to you."

She flung her arms around his neck and he sighed with profound relief. Their kiss this time was tender and long. As he held her he thought about the rest of the day. She smiled at him.

"Why do we keep having important discussions in a park among the trees and grass?"

He looked down at her with delight and tried to make his voice serious.

"Because we are classical lovers, just as in those old paintings." His arm around her tightened. "I did say we would only talk for a few hours - but do you think . . . ?"

He read the look in her eyes before she slowly nodded her head. The lazy sensuous smile on her lips made him catch his breath.

Above the rickety antique shop in a dark Trastevere street, they lay together in a narrow bed. He had explained it as a place used by the Clinic, for the students brought to Rome when being considered for interns.

Maureen looked about her with a sense of peace. The small room was clean but with an old shabby intimacy that was pleasant. Here their lovemaking had been different too, still urgent but not as wild as their previous couplings. Their passion was tender with a new and gentle commitment and a newer element that contained sadness.

Wrapped in each other's arms her thoughts were bittersweet. This was the last time they could be together like this. For a while, for a long time, or perhaps forever. This moment was one she would always remember, wanted to remember, and she pressed closer to him.

Feeling her movement, Cesare held her tighter, and gratefully lost himself again, drunk with the scent of her hair and her skin. He had blindly pushed aside the concern that had oppressed him earlier. The knowledge it might be for the last time had made his passion, and his satisfaction, more absolute, but also gentle.

In dreamy pleasure his hands caressed the silky curves of her body again, and he let the mood of sadness slip away. Once more, just one more time, my love. He wondered why they could not stay here forever in this simple shabby room, never to leave the bliss and surety of the moment.

Chapter 17

Two bridges moor the city's boat-shaped island to the shore. And when the conjurer of evening arrives to turn its stones into a deck, the romantic *Romani* come to promenade, and abandon the day's realities for night's illusions.

A light-hearted gaiety infused the finale to the 1975 International Medical Conference. Papers that had occupied and tested some of the participants had been read, the proceedings and panels were concluded, and among many a comfortable familiarity existed. The restrained formality ten nights ago, at the Palazzo d'Orinici, was now a distant memory.

At the noble old Fatebenefratelli Hospital, high conviviality reigned, with just a hint of abandon. The Do-Good-Brothers of its name accorded a liberal interpretation. John in particular, Maureen saw, was in a rare and boyish good humour. With some of the senior men he would eventually see again in London, he was informally jovial and relaxed, content within his own coterie. The reception occupied a large hall and flowed outside into a courtyard.

The women tonight were grouped with their own chosen associates. Gone was the earlier need, observed by tradition only but with scrupulous adherence, to remain beside their husbands. Theirs after all had been a separate conference, of different experiences, during the tours and excursions.

Maureen and Laura stood on a stone terrace that overlooked the river, amused by the general hilarity that reached them from the "men's club," and occasional shrieks of laughter from groups of women.

"Well, Mo, you won't be surprised tonight if a handsome Italian should accost you."

Maureen turned and smiled at Laura's innocent jest.

"That won't happen. We've already said our *arrivederci's* to each other.

Her voice was studiously laconic but a knot of emotion caught at her throat.

"No regrets, I hope. Because there shouldn't be."

Laura gave Maureen's arm a light squeeze when no response was apparent.

"He not only added some spice to your life - he gave you what has always been everyone's secret dream."

"What? You mean a cheap holiday romance? It wasn't like that, Laura - ."

"Hey, hey, don't leap off the deep end! I mean, he finally made The Foundling Fable come true. You know, when we were kids, didn't all of us say at some time, 'Those aren't my real parents, I must have been a foundling'?"

Maureen let her frown disappear and they both began to laugh.

"Oh, Laura, if you hadn't been here with me I couldn't have coped."

"Yes, you would. But don't forget we still have some family details to complete. That artist father of yours must have been a very nice person. Look how well you turned out."

"I don't know . . ."

"Well I do. Even if he wasn't as lah-de-dah as your mother."

They sipped their wine and watched the parade of couples who ambled along the paved walks beside the river. From the corner of Laura's eye she caught a movement in the shadows. Farther along the terrace where steps led down to the pavement, a solitary figure stood and looked in their direction.

"Don't look now, dear girl, but I do believe that someone wants to bid you one last *arrivederci.*"

Maureen followed the direction of her glance then quickly turned back to Laura.

"But I can't - "

"Go on! I'll go inside for ten minutes then come back here. Just see you return, and remember - others have eyes!"

Maureen looked again to where Cesare stood. A brief tilt of his head beckoned her and the chance to see him alone made her heart leap. She knew he would be here tonight but believed only a stilted and formal acknowledgement would be possible.

Slowly she walked along the terrace to join him in the shadows.

The tiny room was a sort of office located off a hallway connecting the main reception hall. In the distance figures could be seen. Cesare had led her there from outside when they walked off the terrace, around the building, and in by a separate entrance.

He touched a wall switch that lit a dim reading lamp on a desk, and closed the door behind them.

"For just a few minutes, Maureen. There is something I must give you before you leave."

They faced each other and he withdrew a circlet of gold from the pocket of his evening jacket. Holding it out to her she saw that it was a slim bracelet, chased in the Florentine style with a domed cabochon of perfect sea-green jade at its broad centre.

"Cesare, you shouldn't . . . I -"

"It is another sort of ring, yes? Until . . . some day perhaps."

He quickly undid the clasp and held it up, then turned it around to display the smooth golden back that encased the stone.

He smiled. "Can you see what I have had engraved there?"

She moved closer and touched it to examine the inscription. There was a small capital M in flowing script, and around it was carved a large plain C.

"That is for Maureen, always surrounded by Cesare's love."

Maureen swallowed hard and her eyes were shiny with tears. With the same soft smile he looked at her, his eyes reflecting a similar well of emotion.

"I would like to think you will wear it - sometimes. But tonight, for me . . . if you would."

He lifted her right hand, slipped the bracelet around her wrist, and fastened the safety clasp.

"And should someone ask - then there is another meaning. The C can also be for that other name. The one you have learned is now properly your own."

Maureen moved into his arms and closed her eyes, and he pressed his lips into the hollow of her neck.

❀

The plane lifted off the runway, flew south as it gained altitude, then banked and turned to the north.

Maureen sat by a window on the right side and experienced a flurry of emotions. Laura had hugged her before waving goodbye at the Leonardo da Vinci Terminal in Fiumicino.

"I'll call you next week, Mo! We can have lunch - and we'll see whether we can find that old railway poster."

Both John and Michael were oblivious to the exchange, involved in their own remarks.

The Grants had driven them out in the rented car they would use to visit Pisa and Florence, before they flew home on Sunday. John had demurred at first but Michael insisted it was a chance for them to see Ostia and the Lido before they headed off.

Maureen looked down as the plane completed its turn and the whole of Rome swept into view. A not so very large mass seen from above, all mono-chromatic terracotta-coloured. Several patches of green held acute memories for her. The perfect ellipse of the Colosseum clearly visible, along with the soaring dome of St. Peter's.

The River Tiber was a sinuous curve of dull aqua-green as it etched its way to the coast, to where the Grants would have already arrived. Ostia, where at the villa of Luigi Bracci, her past had been changed and rewritten. Could it only be one short week ago that had happened? The place from where she had fled with excitement, into Cesare's arms, to alter forever the concept of who she was. She continued to watch as the panorama grew small and then disappeared.

Maureen felt disconnected, the pang of departure tempered by curiosity about what her reactions would be when the plane landed. In just a few hours she would be home, in London. Back to her former life, and everything that was stable, and English. There was a sudden impatience to see Mark and Sara. They would now be noting the time to when they would learn what gifts had been brought, and how soon they could impart every detail of what had happened in their life while she was away.

The thought of seeing her mother again had a poignant aspect, and an awareness that she could acknowledge her in a different light. Separated from all biological bonds, Grace Lyle acquired a new status, that of an unsuspecting, but exemplary, woman who had raised her as her own.

When the stewardess bent over them to offer drinks and the lunch trays, Maureen relaxed and leaned back in the seat. The flight was a welcome interim, an ideal period of suspended void from the need to plan or decide. A temporary isolation chamber from all constraint and obligation that waited for her.

She was going home, but would not be returning the same woman who had set out ten days ago, for a holiday in Rome. Her life would be measured by new mental yardsticks. If there would be regret, for what was and could never be again, it was too soon to know. It was enough now to be distanced for a brief spell.

"Looking forward to seeing them?"

John had been looking out of the window too, an unopened newspaper on his lap.

She turned towards him with a warm, sad smile of affection.

"Yes, I am. You too?"

"Yup! I'm thinking how Mark's going to love that watch."

"M-m-m, he will. And Sara will just adore her necklace."

"Bet it's raining when we land at Heathrow."

"Probably!"

"And we'll lose all of our suntan within a week."

Maureen busied herself with the tray. In her mind a silent voice responded, 'I wonder how long it will take for our memories to fade'.

In linked proximity they sat in separate states, as each reviewed the events of their immediate past that receded with each mile, and anticipated a future that could not yet be defined. A bond of subtle harmony, seemed to share what was unsharable, the private domain of their own heart's desire.

❀

John had driven Mark and Sara to school when he left for the surgery next morning. A special treat to offset their protests for not being allowed to wear or tote any of their new acquisitions.

Grace had gone upstairs to complete her packing and Maureen tidied up the breakfast dishes.

Through the window she could see some of the chores that would need doing later in the small garden. When the sun's rays found the lilac tree, the first tug at her heart occurred and his image swam into her view. Trees and parks and sunshine would some day fail to conjure up a vision of Cesare. These were early days. With determination she turned away.

Her faithful old Mini, retrieved from the rented garage two streets away, gave a few hesitant coughs that indicated it might stay alive. She drove it around to the curb in front of the house and went inside to collect her mother's suitcase, a tapestry knitting bag, and an assortment of packages to stow on the backseat.

After Grace Lyle eased herself into the seat and the safety belts were fastened, Maureen set off for Essex. London traffic demanded her total attention as she manoeuvred the Austin, scuffed but reliable, towards the north east and the road for Cheniston.

She always enjoyed the sense of liberty gained behind the wheel of a car. This morning her spirits were lifted too by the necessity to leave the city, which was a curious anomaly.

The little terraced house in Chelsea was her haven. She always thought of it as part of her personality, a reflection of who she was. After being away she should have felt a strong desire to remain, or be eager to return soon. But today the diversion was welcome.

Against John's gloomy prediction the weather was fine and sunny, a comfortable seventy degrees. She wore a short sleeved dress but noted her mother still wore the camelhair jacket in which she arrived.

In Rome she had bought a hand-knitted mohair jacket in a lovely shade of amethyst that complemented Grace's silver hair and light complexion, but it was obviously packed away. Maureen mused whether it would always remain wrapped in tissue paper, and 'saved', rather than worn and enjoyed.

Grace's lifelong habit to conserve and hoard had always puzzled her - the 'best' china used only for special and infrequent occasions; the 'good' table linens that were still pristine from lack of use; all the cosseted things packed away in cupboards and drawers that the older woman should enjoy right now.   The material objects that in time would be all that remained; a collection of markers to indicate her passage through life.

But Maureen's interior criticism was now overlaid with revised compassion and she accepted the simple background that had fostered thrift. Into her mind came the thought of that other 'gift' Grace Lyle had preserved, when Luigi Bracci had made the human presentation to her thirty-six years ago, for safe-keeping.

This produced the urge to discover how much the other woman remembered. Once the outer ring of London had been left, and Grace allowed longer intervals between her nervous 'tutting' about the traffic, Maureen introduced the subject.

"You said how tall Sara is getting, Mother. Even I think she has grown a bit more while we've been away."

"Oh, she has, Maureen, she has. That girl will be as tall as you are by the time she's fourteen. You wait and see."

Maureen laughed. "Now that she's eleven it's hard to remember her as a baby. How the years fly. Can you still remember so far back - to when I was born?"

"Of course! Every woman remembers that. Since Jack and I didn't have any more children it was quite the event."

"I seem to recall you told me there was a thunderstorm too, when it happened."

In fact her mother had often recounted that detail while she was growing up. It had evidently been one of those violent summer storms that sometimes occurred after prolonged hot weather. But Luigi Bracci had made no mention of it.

"Oh, it carried on all day and through part of the night. Thunder and lightning. And rain so heavy it would have hurt to be caught out in it."

"I can remember storms like that too when I was young. And how good the grass smelled afterwards."

"Your Dad always reckoned it was the storm that made you such a wilful and difficult child!"

Maureen let the familiar criticism pass with a faint smile.

"That was the last good summer we had, seems to me. The same year the war started," Grace continued.

There was a pause as Maureen coaxed the car through the intersection, circled the roundabout, and exited on the road that led to Cheniston.

"So it was all happening while you were in labour. Must have taken your mind off it a bit. I don't remember you saying much about that - was it a long or a difficult labour?"

Grace Lyle sniffed. "Well it all happened so fast I don't remember suffering at all, if that's what you mean. Doctor was that foreign chap, who stood in for Dr. Forbes. Handsome man, and ever so kind, he was."

Into Maureen's focus came the memory of Luigi's stern features. The intense black eyes and thick mane of grey hair. How he had looked at her as she stood at the villa door before they said goodbye. He must have been a very handsome man in those days. He still was.

"I remember he gave me something beforehand. Said it would make me feel more comfortable. Next thing I knew, there you were."

Grace bent down to rummage in her bag for something.

"It was all a bit like a dream really, Maureen.

Can't think why some women go on about it so." She
blew her nose. "But then again, maybe I was one of the
lucky ones."

Maureen was silent with her thoughts. It was
clear Grace had not endured too much discomfort, and
had probably been asleep most of the time. The doctor
had indeed been kind, and efficient too. Was she lucky
not to have known about the baby that was stillborn,
the little boy that had been spirited away?

How kind and solicitous had been the act that
Luigi had performed, the gift he had given. A cuckoo
had been dropped into the Lyles' nest. They were forever denied a reality in their lives, the son they had
created. Although it had been dead when born it had
still been their own, to be looked at, cherished, grieved
for, then buried in the churchyard. To be remembered
down the years, perhaps, with time-honoured ritual as
a solace.

Luigi had arbitrarily given them another child to
raise instead, with a different origin and genetic make-
up. Perhaps if the Lyles had known that, then all the
puzzle and turmoil of the years might have been eased.
Adoptive parents and their charges seemed to manage
well from knowing. Instead, they had all been seared
by the conflict of differing personalities and emotions.

Maureen then realised what she skirted in this
peripheral musing - the thought that she herself might
well have fared better - or perhaps worse - if she had
been raised as an orphan. But that was something far
too late, and impossible, to ever know.

When they reached Lingford Oaks Maureen
parked so that Grace could buy fresh bread and milk
and some basic supplies from the village shops.

She looked along the familiar High Street with a detached and impersonal interest. It had stayed much the same as she remembered. There were a few changes in shopkeepers, different inhabitants in some of the cottages, but since it lay beyond a fast commute to London, minimal development had happened, unlike other villages down the line.

At the cottage she helped her mother stack the few provisions and watched her settle happily into the snug surroundings. While Grace prepared a cup of tea, she took the bag upstairs.

Along the hall she went to look in at the room again. On the shelves under the windowseat there were still a few of her old books, left for Sara and Mark to explore on visits. This room too was unchanged from her memories.

The hand-crocheted white bedspread that Grace had made with patience and love; the chosen flowered wallpaper her father had hung; just one framed print on the wall, of a chateau in France. Simple, neat, and untouched by time.

How eager she had been to leave it for a new life in London, along with Lingford Oaks and all it stood for, and Grace and Jack, with the incessant arguments and criticism. Out in the wider world she disdained ever going back. It held no identity for her. Sad to think that it was even further removed now.

Grace urged her to leave early and return before the children left school. Maureen knew she would make one more stop.

At the railway station she parked and walked through the ticket hall onto the platform. She paused first and looked around. Luigi had arrived here in 1939; and the lovely Marinella Catalbi had stepped from a train onto this platform. Would the poster have hung then in the waiting room, or was it placed there later? Would those two elegant, sophisticated travellers have seen it?

Maureen experienced an unbidden stab of doubt that was close to scorn. Would either of them have cared? Not that haughty beauty, who came here to abandon her child, with Luigi's assistance. Her family had not lacked financially then, yet she had not braved the shame and returned to Italy, and Gabriele. Could she really have loved the man who had fathered her child?

A few people came onto the platform for the next train to London as Maureen stood there. How strange that all those long-ago incidents happened here. Stranger still was the aura they had left, an aura that had waited to reach out to her.

Maureen walked toward the waiting room, her purpose all along, and entered. The room was empty and the painted walls had other posters displayed, bright modern prints that extolled Glorious Britain instead of foreign places.

With a measured pace she walked to where the print of an impossibly sunny Devon now hung. Closing her eyes she imagined again the scene that had drawn her into its mystical world: the piazza in Rome, the blue and white awning of 'Federico's', the facade of the Church, the life and colour that swirled around the square.

There was no stillness now in the echo of her memory. Perhaps it was finally exorcised, as Laura claimed, now that its message had been fulfilled. Then, as she concentrated, a gentle stir of air wafted over her. A few faint notes of the sad music from her dream appeared, and then vanished.

She would try to find the poster by the artist

Gabriele Tuornovici. Maybe more of his work existed somewhere. Just as hand-written letters reveal much about the writer, so artists too express who they are through their paintings.

It was Gabriele who had summoned her down the years. Marinella had only endowed the legacy of her appearance but her father had bestowed a more special gift, the singular talent she possessed.

A multitude of tasks kept Maureen occupied. The school dentist advised her one of Sara's teeth needed attention; Mark's feet had again outgrown his shoes; the gynaecologist's office reminded her of her annual check-up; and the plumber was called for the persistent leak in one of the bathrooms.

Prevented from idleness or reflection she had been busy. An anniversary gift was selected and sent to John's parents; a chatty letter written to his brother and sister-in-law in Salisbury; and his other sister was promised lunch next week, to arrange a family dinner in December.

John came home at his usual varied times and was called out twice - for a rash that confirmed chicken-pox in a six-year old, and a fever that meant influenza for one of his senior patients.

When Saturday arrived, cool but still sunny, John stayed seated at the breakfast table after Mark and Sara left to pursue weekend activities, and Maureen learned the reason for John's happy air during the past two weeks since they returned from Italy.

"Remember I wanted to find out about a switch from private practice into some kind of teaching, Maureen?"

She wiped her hands and left stacking the plates, picked up the coffee pot and came back to sit at the table.

"But I thought you decided not to after Brian joined the practice. It's going well now, isn't it?"

"Very well, splendidly in fact. Brian has really added to the patient list. Now he's found someone else who might want to join."

"So why would - ?"

"So, if I'm ever going to do it, now would be a good time."

Maureen looked at him. They had talked about it at length two years ago, when he first proposed interest. The different life-style that could include more travel opportunities, the not unlikely chance for personal recognition, longer holidays with the family.

"I don't understand. Why now?"

"Because now an opportunity has come along!"

"But you were worried about the time you'd have to spend on a teaching degree. And the cost. I thought you decided against doing it."

"Turns out that it might just mean a year, after all. That fellow I met in Rome, at the conference, Bill Simmonds, who's at the University of Birmingham, he told me of an opportunity that might occur up there. He called me yesterday, and said their department is going to expand. It's come along sooner - and there's even talk of a grant that might be available."

"But . . . Birmingham?" Dismay was evident as she pronounced each syllable in a slow cadence.

"It's a good university, an older red-brick, but their reputation has really grown."

"But what about London . . . our house, and the children's schools?"

"Oh don't be silly, Maureen!"

He jumped up from the chair and began to pace the small kitchen with a charged vitality of enthusiasm.

"Schools are just as good there. And we'd be able to afford a bigger house - a lot cheaper than London. We'd probably realise a tidy profit from this one the way prices have risen. We could pay off the mortgage along with Dad's loan."

Maureen sat and looked at him with a premonition that all the secure anchors in her world had just been pulled up.

"It's not as though we'd have to pack up and leave next month. I could go up there in January, possibly, to start in on the courses, and we could arrange the transfer on successive weekends. Then by March, say, the switch could be made. The children would adapt to new schools before the summer break."

She grasped for a straw in the wind, wanting to halt the scary changes that had assailed her.

"But you said you always wanted to do that at London University."

"And so I would! But it isn't possible, and this is. Anyway, who knows, a few years down the road, maybe I'll be able to transfer there."

She sat there and tried to think about what such a radical move entailed, and failed.

"John, I can't imagine leaving London now . . . not to live in Birmingham."

Her voice had been quiet and firm but he wore a satisfied grin of achievement as he continued to stride around the kitchen.

"Oh rubbish, Maureen! We're not in the Industrial Age - Birmingham is every bit as cultured as London. And the countryside around it is lovely."

Maureen got up and went to stand and look out of the window.

"So it's all been arranged, has it?"

"No, of course not. All the prelims have to be worked out. But Simmonds thinks it's a good bet, or he wouldn't have called. In a few weeks he's sending me details."

John turned away to leave the kitchen, and over his shoulder said, "And it's all come about from going to that conference in Rome - isn't it marvellous!"

Chapter 18

In the first floor committee room of the Clinic the meeting ended. Cesare made a notation in his calendar, glanced at the current date again, and got up to return to his office. Two weeks had elapsed and another was half over since the International Conference closed.

His life had returned to its normal routines and habits. Some of the memories were receding from his consciousness during the day. Each night he resisted too many tantalizing thoughts about her.

One of the papers that he planned to present in New York had been expanded and he could lose himself in the work with a studied purpose. He had a keen desire to be invited back to America next year, to see more of that fascinating country, with its well-funded laboratories and up-to-date equipment.

Varied pursuits held their same qualities. A new Fellini movie was seen, the small da Vasca painting he had been considering was purchased. He had driven to Pisa to see Caterina and Paolo, laden down like a good uncle with books and toys and chocolates for his niece and two nephews. He had taken Clara there too for her diversion and joy.

The ordinary pleasures were still there but changed in a subtle way. He found that when he was not involved with work or with friends, a little void existed, an empty space he was unable to fill.

Isabella had joined him twice and he still enjoyed the familiar and easy-going relationship they shared. They had returned to her bed after the first occasion, and indeed on the second one too, after a fine dinner in a new restaurant they had visited with friends. His arousal and fulfilment were as satisfying as before. Isabella was a warm partner in lovemaking, with a lovely body, responsive to his attention.

Absent was the deep joy when he had possessed and been possessed by Maureen. He wondered if that perfect unity of two souls could be realised with any other woman. A new appreciation of loneliness entered his life. Perhaps that was why his father had never remarried or chosen to live with a woman again. He had tarried with one or two.

It was not until Cesare walked into his office that afternoon and saw the record librarian's folder with its red tag, that the image of Maureen flooded his mind with an intense and sudden longing.

He lifted the folder to see the name it carried and was surprised it was Marinella's. Tuornovici's army records should have been the first and easiest to retrieve.

The folder was thin and he flicked it open to find it contained just three small pages, photo duplicates of hospital records. He sat down before scanning the first page for the vital symbol. His heart skipped a beat when he saw it, but a closer scrutiny revealed a single letter. Her blood type was A. The letter B that followed was part of the printed form, where data was graded by alphabet rather than numerals. The typed and printed letters were equal sized and close together.

Cesare unlocked the drawer and withdrew his file. As he copied the letter onto his graph he calculated that the odds were still the same, reduced a little perhaps. Until the other two types were determined it would remain inconclusive.

But the chances for Gabi coming up a B were low, if for no other reason than that less than ten percent of the population carried that blood-type. The B combined with an A could, of course, produce children from each of the four groups.

If he were a B, then absolute proof was impossible. His father could have impregnated Marinella, which would put all of his own recent acts with Maureen into a perpetual past. No further contact would be possible. By his own choice. That discouraging speculation had to be shelved until he knew.

Cesare picked up the folder again to look at the other contents and turned to the first sheet once more, where some wording had caught his eye.

Surprise froze him to the chair as he read. The blood typing was taken on September 8, 1943, at two-thirty in the morning - a hurried preliminary to the emergency operation performed at one of the city's old and respected hospitals.

A bullet had been removed from the patient's abdomen. Another had penetrated the stomach, moved diagonally up to the right lung and had lodged against the spine from where it was later extracted.

As Cesare read he automatically envisaged the procedures, as if he had stood beside the two surgeons. After the first extraction, with blood transfusion in place, the patient would have to be turned, a risky manoeuvre, and the delicate spinal probe made.

A deep sigh escaped him as he turned the paper over and continued to read in fascinated dismay. The stomach was sutured, abdominal bleeding staunched, and two pints of blood transfused. The outer lung membranes had sealed normally at points of entry and departure of the bullet. The patient had regained consciousness and been kept closely monitored for residual internal bleeding.

She died five hours later, at seven-thirty that morning. The surgeons' summary was that nerve and tissue trauma to the spine had been too extensive to sustain life.

Cesare sat back for a few minutes, then picked up the next paper in the folder. His astonishment grew as he read the contents of the admitting sheet.

Marinella had been brought to the Gemelli Hospital along with another shooting victim, Herr Oberst Klaus Richter, S.S., in a German Army Staff car, driven by Gruppenkaptan Heinrich Strasse. Richter was pronounced dead on arrival.

The last page in the folder was the official police document, prepared by an Italian officer, procedurally summoned to the hospital to report circumstances surrounding death of a native inhabitant of the city. Cesare was gripped by a range of emotions as he read the last document from beginning to end. It was the most moving of all for him.

At last he neatly replaced the sheets, re-sealed the folder, and laid it on the desk. Swinging his chair around to face the window he gazed out.

Until now he had believed Marinella died during a three-day period of heavy bombing around Ostia. That was what he had been told, or led to assume. Like others, her family had fled the besieged city for the countryside. Allied Forces were attempting to land at Fiumicino and Lanza. Survival seemed better closer to the new invaders. But the German Army that still occupied the city was reinforced with another full division, and they mounted a fierce resistance.

Cesare did not need much imagination to know how she came to be in Rome at that time, nor why she died as she did. Foolish, impetuous, amoral . . . and ever vital Marinella. She had taken a German Officer as her lover for the sheer novelty and pleasure, not for any material gain she or her family might derive.

There was no doubt he had been the seduced. Herr Oberst Klaus Richter must have thought himself 'King of Rome' while it happened, with such a beautiful and aristocratic mistress. He might have fostered the hope it would endure, have even fancied she would become his wife one day. That proud German officer would not suspect he was a mere diversion, her whim of the moment.

If Marinella had not died she would later have indulged herself with some American or British new-comer, to fulfil her sensual needs.

The idea that associating with a hated occupier of her country might be considered treason would be quite irrelevant to her. So in a city that was desperate and humiliated, an Italian resistance fighter, some un-known hero with his hidden weapon, had passed final judgement.

Or else it was unintended . . . for who would waste bullets on a pretty butterfly? Of one thing Cesare was sure, that Marinella would not have judged him harshly, but with a laugh.

When Cesare read the police report he felt he had seen into the mind of that Roman policeman, sitting by Marinella's bed with his questions, while the life she had lived to the full ebbed away from her.

Along with distaste for what he must have suspected was fact, there was that aura about the remarkable girl before him. Into the terse officialese had crept unusual words for typical police reports. 'Disposition quite unverified at time . . . ameliorating circumstances could apply . . . perhaps a tragic error . . . patient brave when admitting . . . not apparent that . . .' And most telling of all . . . 'Subject smiled when . . . '

Marinella, who lay dying, had smiled at him, and in the pre-dawn hours of a city under seige, that exhausted and undoubtedly overworked cop, had also fallen under her spell.

Cesare was puzzled how the circumstance of her death had been suppressed, then and later. How the bureaucratic blanket to obscure the event had been secured. Even so late the Catalbi's had influence, aided by the massive confusion before the Allies arrived and the Germans were driven out.

He had visited her grave much later, in the d'Orinici Catalbi family plot, and remembered the simple phrase carved below the customary lettering on the headstone: "A Beloved Daughter Resides With Us Still in Beauty."

Unable rationally to define the impulse, Cesare wanted to visit the grave again, reaching back across the years in his memory for the girl he had known, to an earlier time, when they had played and laughed. Children who grew-up together, in a world that held so much promise.

The cultural legacy of his Roman lineage included millennia of mystical beliefs, but he was of his time, endowed with scientific persuasion and reason. Yet in a flash, he was moved to invoke the spirit of Marinella.

So a few hours later on that day, in the early evening light, he stood under the cypresses and pines in the older part of the cemetery, and willed his thoughts beyond the noise of the traffic. Into the ether his silent assurance went out. Only the finest about her endured, and he cherished her infinity.

When Luigi's telephone rang he had just returned to the villa after driving back from Rome, and the call from Cesare surprised him.

His trip had proved tedious, made at the request of the Catalbi lawyers, the same office that administered a now vastly reduced estate. Their quarters, off the Via Apollo, had recently been modernised inside, and the building next door had become a small hotel, but Luigi had detected little else that was changed in that area since the old days.

Happily he had allowed enough time to take tea and empathy with Lucia Theresa, the distant cousin whose feminine company and fund of gossip varied the routine of his days, and her own he suspected.

His son's descriptions - and questions - now did not disturb him. Cesare was bound to uncover the old details during his research. It was just the coincidence of the timing that surprised.

Try as he would, and always had, adamantly to refute superstitious notions, especially all that modern 'paranormal' claptrap, he could still be caught off-guard sometimes.

"Yes . . . yes . . . I am well aware how she died, Cesare."

With the phone to his ear in the study he loosened his tie.

"Quite simple - another certificate of death was obtained. Yes, of course, he was. Lorenzo and Rinaldo . . . and myself. That same morning . . . we moved her to another hospital."

Luigi unbuttoned the neck of his shirt wondering how long Cesare intended to continue, careful to avoid sounding too dismissive.

"No, it wasn't difficult. Yes, very dangerous . . . but channels were by-passed . . . because of the disruption. No! Of course they did!"

He massaged his neck and refused to let his thoughts stray, to allow one image from that time and the event.

". . . and the formal funeral was held much later, yes."

But he was unable to suppress a loud snort of derision when he heard where Cesare had been.

Not for the first time he wondered if his only son had become unhinged, a temporary psychosis brought on by his involvement with Marinella's daughter. The sooner this madness passed the better, for his sake as well!

"No, no, Cesare. And there I agree. She was braver in pain, or adversity, than any man."

He closed his eyes and with finger and thumb pinched the bridge of his nose. Cesare's late eulogy to Marinella had begun to provoke him. With stubborn will he blocked out another image that floated on the periphery of his vision.

"You must remember - she was a Catalbi, inheriting virtues as well as vices."

When he at last put the phone down, he swore, immediately going off to pour a larger glass of red wine than usual. In the general direction of the kitchen door he called out as he went, "Leave the dinner, Maria, and go home! I shall eat later - or not at all tonight."

Without bothering to remove his city clothes first he walked toward a chair in the smaller salon, where he and Cesare had revealed all their past and present secrets a few weeks ago.

Orso's head received a scratch before a firm push that sent the large body over the edge of the cushion.

"Get off, Orso. Now I am home I will have my chair again, thank you."

All of the packets cleared from the deed box he had placed on his desk in the study. The few insignificant items that remained - some old and now worthless deeds - were of historical interest only. Just one small patch of farmland still generated a little money.

It had endowed old Cosimo's decline at the private clinic all these years, and would provide a suitable funeral next week. It had also supported the lawyers - so little profit would accrue this year. Hardly a princely sum to worry about in any case.

There had been family records, documents, a meagre collection of jewelery, without real value, old coins, medals, and some silver this-and-thats. Long since sold off had been the fine jewels and the valuable properties that once constituted the estates.

All the more remarkable then, that Lorenzo could not bring himself to relinquish it, that one last valuable piece - especially since it was an Orinici, not a Catalbi, heirloom.

Luigi drank a large swallow of wine and reached into his pocket. For some odd reason he had put it there, before he replaced everything else in the velvet pouches and packets.

In his fingers he turned the large marquis cut

emerald until it caught the reflected light. The diamonds around it flashed and it glowed with a dark green fire. An exquisitely wrought old gem.

He remembered the last time he saw it, when Lorenzo had been handed an envelope by the matron at the hospital. Luigi could still see the tears that unashamedly coursed down Lorenzo's cheeks. In truth, his own had not been dry. The ring had been taken from Marinella's finger, and the diamond pendant at her throat, before the operation to remove the bullets.

She was dead before they were able to reach the hospital. When they had kissed the pale cheeks only a faint blood warmth remained. How strange that Cesare should have stumbled onto that old memory this very day. He had no use, no desire, to be the recipient of this sorrowful legacy from the past.

Old Ugo Diecelli, the very same lawyer who had been privy to most of the Catalbi affairs, had questioned him today, about his knowledge of "any .. umm . . . ah, semi-related or possibly deserving . . . er, heirs . . . priorly unmentioned or overlooked." The dry and circuitous legalese that inquired whether any Catalbi bastards might remain.

As the family doctor, Luigi Bracci was the likeliest one to know, of course. He had taken a long time before giving a negative shake of his head, but the recent appearance of Marinella's daughter had made him pause. Then he had finally accepted the burden of the residue from the estate.

Luigi slipped the ring back into his pocket as Maria came to bid him good night. He drained the glass of wine and thought of what he would do about all this. Nothing yet. It could afford to wait. There was no hurry now, not after all these years. Catarina and

Cesare could worry about it when he was dead. Yet, perhaps . . . and the image of the lovely young woman, called Maureen, crept into his vision again. It was too brief a time she had been here at the villa. Now he wished he could have seen her once more, when the reason that had brought her here had been assimilated. Such a pity . . . that she lived so far away . . . and was married . . . because Cesare . . . .

Fesso! Luigi stood up so abruptly he startled the cat, which leapt onto all four feet. That damned son of his would make him as foolish and sentimental as he was if he did not watch out!

Chapter 19

The gloomy economic reports out of Westminster matched the weather. Cold rain off the North Sea had blanketed the South-Eastern counties for days under a pall of grey clouds.

Maureen knew it was time to retire the summer clothes to the back of the closets and resurrect the winter woollens. The telephone rang as she considered this. "Mo! *Buon giorno, come stai?*"

The cheerful voice was a welcome intrusion into her bleak mood.

"Laura! *Bene, bene, amica mia.* Well, not so bene really - only so-so."

"Hah! *Cos`i e cos`i,* eh?" Her smug triumph made them both laugh.

"I'm so glad you called."

"Well I said I would. What say we go look at some paintings next week?"

"You mean . . . you actually found out where we can?" She felt a pang of guilt not to have done that yet.

"The exhibition is over, but would you believe, I managed to cajole a nice young man at the London Transport Museum to let us browse around next week.

A-n-d, since they haven't stored the canvases yet - we can even see the exhibition ones."

"That's wonderful. My God, you're so efficient, Laura."

"Of course I am! But I have to call back with the date. He said after l p.m. is best. 'By special appointment only' was his charming phrase."

Maureen forgot her lethargy and grey mood at the prospect.

"Any day is good with me - Monday would take some juggling - but you decide what's best for you."

Laura didn't need to think about it.

"Wednesday it is then. Let's meet for lunch first, eleven-thirty outside Holborn Underground - there's bound to be a decent pub around."

"That's perfect. Thanks, Laura - I really mean it."

"The pleasure's all mine, dear girl. I can't wait to see this awesome picture from your past. For me it's like Madame Tussaud's, the basement exhibit." A throaty laugh sang down the line. "But I want to see *you* again, picture or no picture. We have lots to talk about."

The gallery and its contents were larger than they had expected. Printed catalogues of the recent exhibition, and one of the collection, were handed to them to study.

Laura's 'nice young man' had introduced himself as Tim Fenway, and they agreed that his oversized gold-rimmed spectacles were an endearing accessory to his shock of blonde hair and serious features.

Maureen described the details of what she sought but was unable to provide the year of execution which could have indicated the museum's acquisition date. Mr. Fenway wrote everything down and speculated.

"It could take a while for me to run through the archive register. The foreign section isn't large, but does include a lot of other stuff - continental trains and boats, steamship posters, and the like."

"We don't mind waiting."

She looked at Laura who shook her head in agreement.

"I really appreciate your taking the time with this."

A faint blush appeared. It wasn't often Tim Fenway had a chance to play curator, and to attractive older women.

The rooms at the top of the Transport Building that contained the art and the library records were high-ceilinged but not well lit. A not unpleasant musty odour of old papers permeated the air.

Laura grabbed Maureen's arm with excitement.

"Look, Mo - they have some by Graham Sutherland. Even little old me knows that name. He did that gaunt portrait of Winston Churchill. To think he started with a vase of flowers at a window."

Maureen gave her a tolerant smile. She had recognized many of the icons from her early studies: Edward Bawden, Anna Zinkeisen, Robert Gibbings, Clive Gardiner.

"He did one of the Queen, too. But advertising illustrations are done by real artists, Laura. And famous names can be commissioned. Or they already work in graphics for agencies. It's all art."

"Okay, feel free to lecture, you're the expert here.

Should I appreciate riding Underground escalators more?"

"Yes you should - never mind the subject, it was somebody's original and creative concept."

Tim Fenway came back to stand behind the broad counter. He wore a look of quiet satisfaction.

"Well, we do seem to have them, ladies. Sorry it took a bit of time to locate them, but I think I've found the canvases."

Maureen stared at him. "Them . . . you mean there is more than one?"

Earlier, when she had wondered if more of Gabriele Tuornovici's work could be found she had not thought of other railway posters. Her concentration on that solitary print had not allowed her to imagine others.

"Well, only two, actually." Fenway gave a modest cough. "Six were presented evidently, from the records, but just two selected. They're both of Rome but not part of our, er, more valuable holdings. By that I mean - ."

"No - that's all right, I understand. But the artist was quite young. And he died soon after."

"Oh. I wasn't aware of that. The provenance is a bit slim." He looked at her. "You, ah, couldn't have known him, could you?"

"I didn't know him. But he happens to be my father."

Both Laura and Tim Fenway looked at her in a respectful silence. The note of pride in her voice would have done justice to an heir of Canaletto or Picasso.

"But you do have the 'Piazza Santa Emiliana'? That one is rather special - I want to see the other too, of course."

"Well, it really might be better if I took you round into the stacks, if you won't mind the cramped space."

They followed him through a door into an area hung with racks and shelves. Most of the stacked canvases were in cardboard sleeves and on swing-out bars. Through a second and then a third room, floor to ceiling shelves were filled. Each shelf carried printed lists of the contents.

When he led them to the last room he walked to a central aisle and swung out the rack, pulling two framed canvases down. He eased them out of the sleeves and brought them out, propping them up in the narrow passageway.

Maureen experienced an immediate thrill as she gazed at the painting of the piazza. Disregarding the other, it was the focus of her attention.

But something was wrong . . . surely. The large rectangular canvas showed much more sky than she remembered and the church roof had other details.

Then quickly she realized, the poster print of her memory had carried large black lettering across the top.

As she looked at it she was overwhelmed by nostalgia, but not for the childhood scene of her memory. This was the place where she had paused, and where her life had taken flight into another dimension.

That was the table at 'Federico's' where she had sat, across from Cesare. Like a surge of airborne water, the memory of that afternoon rose inside her and brought another image, of the fountains in the Navona and his . . .

The present moment returned. With a mental shake she moved closer to study the brushstrokes. She thought that Gabriele's technique had been a fast application of his colours, the tones built up in swift succession, skilled execution and economy, so that the surface, when seen close up, did not have any distortion of line.

The canvas would have been brighter once and it could have used a cleaning. However well protected, oils attract grime that is always in the air.

Laura watched as Maureen stood in silent admiration. She concluded that no alarming reaction would happen now, so gave her attention to the painting.

The general effect was pleasant, she thought, but not remarkably special. It certainly had no ominous element, at least for her. At last she decided to risk an observation.

"It's quite lovely, Maureen."

Young Tim Fenway, discreet beyond his years, chose not to comment. It was a good work, of course, but not what he would personally favour, not when he thought of all the others that the collection contained. Always advisable to tip-toe, however, especially if ancestor worship was involved.

Maureen finally looked back at Laura.

"It's a competent work, a mature style already well developed. But he was making a strong personal statement too, I think. He was painting something he knew well, of course, but it must have held a lot of emotional depth for him. There's a mood he wanted to convey . . . his choice of colours, for instance. Look down there, in the lower left, and again, up there. See how the sky dominates with that deep blue-tone - but the church is challenging the sky with that blackish-blue shade?"

"Uh-huh . . . y-e-s."

Laura responded, at a loss to offer a stronger

endorsement and careful to avoid anything that might
be deemed critical.

Maureen stepped away, and then turned to
move along the aisle and look at the canvas beside it.
Laura watched the expression of pure delight it caused.

"O-h-h . . . it's the view from the Gianicolo
Hill!"

Then as the full import of the subject registered
a look of wonder lit her eyes. He could have painted
so many other scenes of the city. He probably had, it
was where he lived, but - she remembered then that
Tim Fenway had said there were six presentations.

How strange that this one had been selected
when Cesare had . . .

Well, perhaps not. Each city has favoured views
that are copied by every artist down the ages. The
Thames before Westminster Abbey and the Houses of
Parliament; the Bay of Naples from the Tyrrenhian
Belvedere; the skyline of Manhattan from the Hudson
River.

Laura rather liked this one. It was much
prettier, and with a lighter mood. But she was mysti-
fied that Maureen had so readily named it. For the life
of her she couldn't recall it from the tours. Such a
lovely prospect of Rome from across the Tiber. Strange
she had missed it.

"You have prints of both of these paintings that
I could order, don't you?" Maureen looked at Mr.
Fenway, who had been busy making some notes. He
quickly put the pen and notepad away and straightened
up.

"Ah. Now that is something I can't tell right off
the cuff. It's probable that extra prints exist - we seem
to have them for those that aren't . . . well, famous. I

mean popular ones. But I have to find out from the
Print Department, and that could take more time."

"How long?" Maureen said. "And should I
make an independent request?"

"I have the forms to give you. It's quite automatic, and I can tell you the cost."

"The price doesn't matter. I want one of each -
but especially this one, the Piazza Santa Emiliana."

Chapter 20

Rome basked in late October sunshine again. There had been several days of showers that brought a wintery chill to the air, and the librarian wore her new wool suit. Taking a look from Cesare's window at the street below, where women strolled with bare arms once more, she sighed and gave a diffident Latin shrug.

It had taken six weeks to secure the old Army records but she was glad, as she placed the folder on the desk, they had not been destroyed. So many were lost.

When Cesare came in half-an-hour later and spotted the red-tagged folder, he dropped on the desk the graphs he had brought back from the laboratory.

He opened the file and ran a finger down the first page. A sustained exhalation of breath came from between his teeth and he slowly nodded.

Gabi was conscripted into the Army in late March, 1939, and, as with military personnel the world over, his blood-type had been assessed on entry. To the Clinic's student trainees, Cesare always emphasised that the large wars of this century had accelerated the knowledge of blood composition and analysis.

Tuornovici, G. S., had been typed an O-positive.

Cesare went around the desk to retrieve the file and gazed at the graph, then sat down and picked up a pen to inscribe a neat O alongside the name. Just one space still remained empty, and there had been no communication from her.

If Maureen proved to be an A or a B then no positive conclusion was possible. Either Luigi or Gabi might have been her father. But if she proved to be an O type then he would know that Luigi could not have been her father.

As he sat drumming his fingers on the desk he studied the telephone, then glanced at his watch. He leaned back in his chair, rubbed his eyes, and thought for several minutes. Then he picked up the folder and removed the contents, giving a quick glance to see what other information it contained.

From the wrinkled army picture two dark eyes stared out at him. A drab black-and-white snapshot had frozen the smooth round features of youth. The serious gentle Gabi, always with a sketchpad nearby, who so adored the flamboyant society girl, Marinella.

Cesare lifted an eyebrow when he noted his rank and the name of the famous battalion to which he had been attached. That humble artist from the Trastevere, who must have died before he could learn of the child - the living portrait he had created and left behind. The presumed heir to his talent, but not his memory.

With staunch optimism he convinced himself it was true. But he knew at least that the next thought that came to him was valid. Gabi would have been ecstatic, would have sketched and painted the child in endless pride, and later on, with infinite patience, guided the crayon he would have placed in a chubby little hand.

Tuornovici had been consigned to an unremem-
bered limbo until now. These records might be the
only small memory left, but Cesare determined to find
out where and in what way he died.

April 6th, 1939

The troop carrier finally cast off her ropes and
sailed out of Brindisi harbour. The noise and confusion on board, his entire world the past few days, was
of minor concern now he had learned the news.

First Sergeant Salvatore Pastora, with whom a
sort of uneven friendship had formed, had caused his
spirits to soar. They had taken on a mail sack before
leaving, and in the pre-sorting two letters for
Tuornovici were spotted, but no distribution would
happen till night.

In a matter of weeks, the artist Gabi had become
First Officer Gabriele Salvatore Tuornovici, Interpreter
Specialist, San Marcos Battalion.

There had been no time to think about the title
and he cared little that he was attached to one of Italy's
proud and famous regiments, founded in 1873. He was
here because his mother had been born in Albania. It
had secured him the dubious honour of his present
commission. Her son could still understand the
language.

Tomorrow, he would be one of the 30,000
soldiers to 'enter' that hapless country. The lead contingent, General Guzzoni had stated, would not have
to fight. A military presence only, to bolster those
Albanians who wished to oust their discredited King
Zog. Guzzoni had said their show of force was 'a peace-

keeping exercise', and as 'liberators' they would be received 'with open arms'.

The rumour among seasoned regulars had it as
a walk-in, walk-over, and then a long rest until
Mussolini felt Greece and Yugoslavia could taste Italy's
might. A Balkan offensive would prove to be a real
battle, they were quick to inform the newcomers.

For a moment Gabi wanted to forget all that.
The thought of the letters excited him; one of them
must be from Marinella. At last! The other would be
his mother's, who exhorted him on leaving to
'honour' his half-heritage, and would no doubt repeat
herself, with her simple printed capitals and with
copious expressions of her love.

He forced his way through the sweating mass of
men, all in motion at once it seemed, either loud and
crude with excitement, or apathetic and sullen. He
managed to reach his bunk and crawled into the smelly
recess without bothering to remove his jacket. Closing
his eyes he was grateful for the half-hour freedom, off-
duty and cocooned in his thoughts.

Marinella's letter - it had to be from her - would
say she was returning to Rome, please God. How he
had urged her to return with him. Those stupid
English friends she liked, the rich, crazy Montagues,
had persuaded her to stay.

When he left London she promised to return in
a month. She had to come back, because now they
could get married and her snobbish family could go to
hell. He was an officer in the Italian Army, no matter
what his origins, and he would be a decorated specialist
after this little caper was over. There was even a
chance to be a cartographer in Rome with his drafting
skills. The major had promised to recommend him as
a war artist.

Gabi drifted off into a reverie about Marinella. So many experiences and silly adventures during those five months since they had fled to Switzerland together.

❈

At 'Federico's' it was past midnight and, for November, unusually hot and muggy, which was why so many chairs were still occupied. The latest government orders, to get home and off the streets at night, were paid little heed by the older restaurants, or their regulars, though it became harder to afford more than one coffee. The food supplies grew less reliable each week and with scant variety.

As Gabi sat and exchanged comments with the fellow at the next table he decided he should think about leaving. She was unlikely to be joining him now.

In his shirt pocket he could feel the crinkled outline of his final draft notice. He had to accept that art-school offer in Switzerland soon. For two years he had managed to delay his conscription, but at twenty-three he had run out of deferrals, and of the people who could make the necessary intercession.

So he would have to get out of Italy for a while, but not before he convinced Marinella to leave too.

Not that he didn't love his country or believe in some of the grand results and future goals of Mussolini. But he just could not think of himself in the military. It was not his sort of life and he would be useless at it.

Besides, he was in love with Marinella. He would not leave her here, whether he went to Lausanne or into the army, for if he did she would miss him and become bored. Then the temptation to look around would happen, and it would not take long before someone else . . .

He yawned into the tepid night and toyed with the pencil on his sketchpad. He should get up soon and walk to the Ponte Sisto. Go back to his studio in the Trastevere. Maybe tomorrow . . .

Joy swept over him as he looked up and saw her come around the corner into the square, straight towards him. He jumped up and shook off the lethargy. His other worries could wait.

"Marinella, I almost gave up hope you would come tonight."

"Hello, Gabi. I was detained. For much longer than I expected really."

With casual grace she slid into the chair he pulled out for her. She leaned back, crossed her legs and tilted her head up, smiling at the fond light in his eyes.

But he had paused for a moment before he sat down beside her. His eyes, those vital jurors of his skill and livelihood, could not be in error. Their nuance for detail noticed the flaccid line to her shoulders, the slack angle of her neck. It was late, yes, but the relaxed slouch to her body was not caused by the warm night or the late hour.

She looked spent and . . . satisfied. Her full moist lips were slightly puffed. Those magnificent eyes had that limpid quality to them, which appeared as a luminous glow in a jade coloured sea. Dear God, he knew that look so well.

Along with the many paintings and sketches of her strewn around his rooms, were the ones that tried to capture that look. Those canvases, in classic naked sexual repose, across his bed or on the cheap Turkish mat on the floor, where she smiled, in lovely languid abandon . . . after the passion of their love-making had been exhausted.

He knew why she was late - a man had been with her. Some old goat at her father's palace, perhaps, had been allowed to have a special *dono* tonight. But the ache in his gut, and his clenched hands, were the only reactions he dared permit himself. Even among their own friends it was a firm tenet, free love was the smart way to live. Their modern generation was more sensible about that.

Except . . . he was in love with her, his beliefs had changed. Jealousy would send him insane now if he had to think of another man, sprawled on top of her. Fingers that clutched and probed, soiling her when he - Oh Christ! Her lazy smile when she spread her legs to receive . . . what only he should give.

"Gabi? Do you still want us to run away to Switzerland together?"

Nudged out of his silent anguish he searched her eyes to see if she teased.

"Tonight I came here to beg you, Marinella."

"Good. I have been thinking it might be fun for us. For a while."

After all the weeks of pleading she had suddenly agreed. The dark thought that occurred to him had one bright aspect. Whoever he was, the fortunate recipient of tonight's fucking spree, the bastard would not get another.

"We can leave right away, *carissima*. Tonight, tomorrow - whenever you want."

Marinella smiled at him. Dear Gabi. A new excitement flickered at the edges of her lassitude and she straightened herself in the chair.

"Then . . . we shall leave tomorrow night."

Her hand reached out to pull him close. She leaned forward and nuzzled his ear. Her teeth gave the tip of the lobe a little gentle bite.

Lausanne had soon bored them. They both preferred Geneva, if they could not be in Zurich, where everything exciting happened and where the young crowd were.

Teaching at the art school had been easy, tolerable, but dull, although the pay had been good. They might have stayed if Bill and Diane Montague had not monopolized their lives. They were wild ones, too rich and without purpose, but Marinella insisted they were fun.

Intrigued by her Italian upper-class background, and the amusing artist she had in tow - so Bohemian - they persuaded her to accompany them when they grew bored and wanted to return to London.

Bill Montague had stood by his promise and secured appointments for him. He had sold several canvases - minor works and a few portraits, but decent for fees. At first he had been optimistic about England. His mentor at art school had sent some of his early work there and two were bought. The year that Mussolini had pledged support for 'The Arts', the royalties he received dried up when the threat of war loomed.

It was his mother's letter, with the government's demand for his service, that reinforced his decision, along with his own desire to be back where he belonged, in Rome. He despised their life in London, the constant talk of war, and Marinella's bizarre and extravagant habits, that emulated Diane Montague's. They had fought a lot.

He yearned for her so much, longed for the day he could make her his wife.

It was two in the morning when he received them. One with a Roman postmark, his mother's, and - *grazie a Dio* - a letter from Marinella at last.

The postmark and stamp were English and the envelope showed the clumsy slitting and re-sealing of censors. Fuck the censors, and what they read.

Stuffing the Rome letter into a pocket of his battle-jacket to read later, he held onto the foreign one. Surrounded by hundreds of army personnel in one of the ship's saloons, it would be three hours till they landed in Durazzo. Field rations, ammunition and equipment had been distributed, in uproar and confusion.

He began to manoeuvre his way backwards till he was under a fan-shaped glass wall sconce, a reminder for what the ship had been designed. With a thumbnail he gently slit the envelope open and extracted two small blue pieces of notepaper.

Good news, good news! With a brief silent prayer he furtively crossed himself. An Easter gift. Today was the 7th of April, Good Friday. Carefully holding the pages up to the light he beamed as he read, "My Dearest Gabi."

The first disembarkations at dawn were a fiasco. Officers were confused and a welter of conflicting orders had the men in chaos, stressed and ineffectual.

Heavy bombardment from the Albanian guns

forced a retreat back to the ships. Another landing attempt was made, and repelled. The warships which had escorted the troop carriers continued to shell the tiny port of Durazzo, the shore and port buildings deluged with salvo after salvo.

The third assault held some ground for a while, but was met by a barrage of crossfire coming from every direction. Sporadic and uncoordinated, it was effective by its persistence and unexpected ferocity.

Gabi discovered a tenacity he had not known he was capable of until now. He was exhausted and filthy - and suddenly possessed. Even the morose mood he set out with, so many hours ago, was expunged.

They would make it this time, or be damned to hell. No more retreat. All this insanity must be finished fast and put behind him. His life now held so much more to it than this. If they had to fight a dirty fucking battle then they must win. Sweet Christ! The streets of the Trastevere had trained its own!

Rifles in position, three of them crouched where a port warehouse gave on to an area of sandy waste-land, a seashore meadow of dune and grass. Three-hundred metres away a hedge marked a boundary. They waited for a signal to cross the open space and meet up with their armoured transport on the road beyond the hedge.

Gabi studied the shapes of the small trees in the hedge. At some other time it would have made an interesting marine study to sketch. Drifts of sulphurous yellows and blacks marred the blue sky of late afternoon.

Italian fighter planes occasionally criss-crossed the panoply of blue. As his eyes scanned the far hedge he saw a patch of colour, a clump of yellow flowers that grew among the sea grass. A sudden thudding sound behind him, boots on hard ground, brought four more of their contingent, to wait for the signal to advance.

Intervals of relative quiet fell between the sound of rifle fire, cannons, and the intermittent shelling by the warships in the harbour. During a lull Gabi's thoughts returned to the letter.

> " . . . and the stupid doctors here can't rid me of it,
> so I must arrange for its adoption. But I hear
> there are many very good orphanages too. A
> nuisance to have to wait so long, until August,
> because I now prefer to return to Rome.
> So, my dear Gabi, it seems yet another one
> of your artistic creations will be left in England!
> How 'droll,' as Diane Montague would say . . ."

A baby, - *his* baby, why does she say 'it'? But she must bring it home, she *couldn't* leave it behind in England. Oh, Marinella, what . . . ?

She was obviously feeling stress, not thinking clearly, because he was not there with her. He knew that women sometimes acted strangely at such times. But it was still April - and long before August he would have everything arranged. When things settled down here he would ask for compassionate leave. He would visit her family first and insist they bring her back - or he would go and fetch her himself.

He would find a way. And his mother would care for the baby when it came. Marinella would not have to stay inside all day and tire herself. The war could not last long, and he would be back in Rome.

The baby could play in his studio and he would sing to it while he worked.

They could be married next month and then in August . . .

The shout came like an abstract disturbance, a minor intrusion on his plans, and he was slow to react.

When he did take off across the field it was with a revived purpose and drive, an impatient impulse to reach the goal. By the time they reached the hedge he was level with Salvatore and they were running hard together.

His eyes had been on the patch of yellow flowers . . . but it was the white bird, that suddenly lifted up out of the hedge, that drew his attention. It held his concentrated stare.

He followed its arcing flight into the blue sky as it turned west, and he cried out to it. It was flying home, to Italy, where his real life had just started and all his plans for the future.

"Marinella! *Marinella!*"

Four of the men had flung themselves down below the hedge. Unscathed they waited, faces pressed into the dirt, to see if the position was secure. Three more had almost managed to gain the tangled overhang of green branches.

Inching forward on his belly, Salvatore reached out an arm to the man attempting to crawl nearer, sobbing with each futile struggle. He tugged him close, noting his useless legs that were colouring the scrubby sand bright red. After another second he wriggled out again from the dubious protection of the hedge.

Relaxed and carefree, Gabi lay on his back and stared up at the sky. Salvatore could see thin shreds of blue paper in the mess of blood and fabric that was once a pocket. With gentle fingers he closed the eyelids and scuffled back to the men still crouched under the hedge.

"What the hell was he yelling at?"

Salvatore rubbed the cuff of his jacket across his face.

"I didn't hear. Maybe God did. Or his bastard of a saint," he muttered.

Chapter 21

Maureen was engrossed with the watercolour that was about finished. This one pleased her and she was aware it had gone faster. There was more economy with greater control to her hand. The others she had made were satisfactory, but this one was special.

The telephone rang several times before she put the brush down, rubbed her hands on her shirt, and turned to run down the stairs. She would take it in the hall, ignore the extension in the bedroom because of her paint-smeared clothes, and then make some tea. It was almost four. In elated spirits she thought about a glass of wine instead. A little private celebration.

Breathless after the three flights she grabbed the receiver on the next ring.

"Hello?"

The sound of his voice brought on a sudden weakness and she sank to the floor to sit cross-legged.

"Maureen . . . is it a convenient hour for you?"

"It's all right." She steadied her breathing.

"I can call later if you wish."

"No, I'm alone - I mean . . . oh Cesare, it's really you. Where are you?"

He laughed and his face came at once into her vision. When she had tried to do that a week ago it had been difficult.

"I am in Rome. Are you well - your life, the family?"

He sounded so close it was as though he were with her.

"Yes, I am. They are." She laughed.

In Rome it was probably sunny and she was glad now that she could picture him in his office and at his desk.

"I am happy to hear it."

So many things she wanted to say, to ask, but they had all fled from her mind.

"Remember that I told you I would be in London?"

"Yes . . . "

"I am calling to tell you when. On the 5th of November I shall fly there, but late. Could we meet the next day?"

A little dazed she reached for a pencil, then hastily dropped it.

"Yes, I think so. But -"

"You are sure? If not, then I will make some changes and - "

"No! That's all right. On the fifth - no the sixth of the month."

His voice altered and became low and serious.

"Would you consider coming with me to New York, my love? I could arrange the tickets now - we would be together."

"Cesare! That's . . . impossible."

"Not impossible." He paused. "But perhaps the

next time, next year when I go there again."

A heavy sense of reality made her stop and think about what he had asked. New York . . . what was he thinking, that she could just drop everything and leave with him?   But the prospect lit her imagination. It was out of the question.   Then why did it suddenly appeal?   She would be moving to Birmingham instead.

"And . . . I won't be coming to Rome with you either. I must tell you now, before you come. You can change - "

There was only a brief silence.

No, no - not yet, I know that. But we will talk. That isn't why I called, *carissima*, or even why I come. There is much I have to tell you.   About Gabi Tuornovici and what I have found out.   And I so much want to see you again, even for a brief time."

He had said 'Gabi', and Maureen realized he meant Gabriele. It was the first time she had heard the familiar diminutive and she liked it.

A strange feeling that was warm and desirable stole over her. Rome, and the people she had met there - Cesare and Luigi - they were like a sort of family now. They actually had known her mother, and her father . . . Gabi.

"Do you not wish to see me at this time, Maureen? Would you prefer - ?"

"I do want to see you! Very much. There are so many new things I have to tell you. Oh! I almost forgot - I did find out my blood-type."

There was silence for a few seconds, then in a quiet voice he inquired.

"And - what were you told, *cara*?"

"I'm an O-positive. Is that good?"

She could hear him exclaim something in

Italian, then a word that ended in '*stasi*'. His laughter seemed to flow around her like sunlight and she felt herself relax.

"It is wonderful - and you are wonderful."

She felt the glow from his voice. Then a stab of realism hit her.

"But Cesare, I still intend - "

"When I have arranged the hotel that I will stay - then I let you know, yes?"

"Yes. Good. I will . . . wait to hear from you."

"*Ti amo*, Maureen. *Ciao, mia cara.*"

"*Ciao . . . te amo*, Cesare."

It was early afternoon in Rome and the staff were at their desks, a bit drowsy still after lunch. On the third floor of the Clinica Ematologica, in the office of Dottore Cesare Bracci, his secretary lifted her head and looked across at the chemistry assistant who sat at the desk next to her.

From inside the office they heard him exclaim.

"Tuornovici , I love you. She *is* an O."

Bemused smiles were exchanged. They looked down at their work again with broad grins. From inside there was now a loud, and somewhat off-key, whistling to be heard. It was the overture to Rossini's '*La Gazzella Ladra*'.

They both loved the Italian restaurant they had discovered on Elizabeth Street. Small, friendly, and elegant, it was a perfect place for lunch together. Laura had insisted that they treat themselves again.

After meeting-up outside the Sloane Square Underground they briefly toured the Peter Jones store, and then walked south along the trim streets of Chelsea.

The news had taken Laura by surprise. She felt almost as unhappy about it as Maureen obviously was. When they were led to their table, she didn't like the sad look of resignation in her eyes and felt a strong empathy for her.

It was very unfortunate that John's planned transition into teaching had met with such early success. The uprooting of the family was bad enough, but Birmingham was hardly a place to inspire a sense of excitement. However, it could all be viewed in a better light, she thought, later on. The best attempt right now was to placate and defer, and put it into perspective.

"You know it could still fall through, Mo. These things often do."

But she was just as aware as her friend that John would eventually achieve what he had embarked on. Laura had already assessed the single-minded determination he possessed. A hard trait to live with if their aims differed.

"Well, if it has to happen, you can still come down to London whenever you want. You could stay with us."

She had temporized, but suspected it was the thought of giving up the house that Maureen found more traumatic than leaving London.

"And think how close Stratford-on-Avon is. The summer theatre season - Michael and I would love to join you. We could have regular family get-togethers!"

Their meals appeared and the restaurateur followed the waiter to their table. His urbane and exact attention was what made the restaurant a popular one. All of the tables were filled and as the noise level rose Laura diverted Maureen onto other subjects.

By the time the coffee arrived and the restaurant had thinned of its diners, Maureen had introduced the event in November, a few weeks away. The news that Cesare was arriving had been the second surprise today.

"November the 5th? Strange timing - hasn't he heard about Guy Fawkes?"

"I won't see him till the next day."

Laura finally realized that it had not been just a romantic interlude after all. The evidence sat before her. Summer was gone but there was that glow in Maureen's eyes. All along she had assumed it was an attraction that had come about because of - well, very unusual circumstances.

Was Cesare serious in his continued involvement, or simply opportunistic? No way to assess right now, but what bothered Laura most was the way Maureen's face came alive when she said his name.

"Laura, is it possible to love two people at the same time?"

"That's a very old question, Mo."

Laura sat back and thought hard. There was more at stake here than idle speculation, and for the first time she wondered if she could be out of her depth, but she had to try.

"Of course it's possible. Don't we do it all the time? What you're really asking is, do we love everyone in the same way? And the answer to that is simple. No, we don't."

Maureen toyed with the coffee spoon on the tablecloth.

"I keep telling myself I only want to hear what he has learned about my father. But I know I want to see him again."

Laura leaned forward and folded her arms on the table. It was no good skirting the issue. The woman was obviously in love, or thought she was. This was more serious than she suspected.

"Mo, can you remember when we were younger? How every half-way decent male we met - or just caught sight of - had us madly 'in love'. But we were all being manipulated, by our biological urge - acting like programmed robots. Find a male, fall in love, start nest building!"

Laura paused, sipped her coffee, and warmed to the subject.

"We said 'we're in love'. And so we were. Each and every time. As many times as it took. But something else was going on - and the name of the game was 'procreation of the species'. Old Mother Nature making sure we pursued her sacred mission, all the way to the altar. Or whichever alternative presented itself."

"But we were in love. Weren't we?"

"Love? My dear girl, it's such a dandy little catch-all word we humans have invented. To soften raw natural impulse I suspect, and with some very strange results - if you read the Sunday papers."

"But why doesn't it last?"

Most of the time we do manage to make it work, but only by constant effort, and heartbreak. We 'love' our husbands, our children, our parents and even dear old Aunt Mabel. What we are really about is preserving the lovely illusion the word 'love' represents -

so that the clan, our species, continues.

Maureen stared at her thoughtfully.

"But that's young love. I'm not that anymore - and I've fulfilled the reproductive urge. So why - ?"

"So back to your original question," Laura said. "You think you love someone else. Which is entirely possible, and right now it probably feels real. Good old John is all wrapped up in his high-flying plans. But here's another question for you. What if that new love becomes ordinary and familiar, over time? Something you have to work at to keep alive? Just as before."

"I hadn't thought about it that way."

"There are no guarantees, Mo. And there's no way to tell, in the beginning."

Laura reached across the table and patted Maureen's hand.

"Look, there was a major upheaval in your life this summer. Rome, and your past, and being attracted to someone . . . try not to confuse separate issues. And now you're facing another upheaval. Wait. Don't make any decisions about anything now. Take the time to get your priorities straight."

Maureen gave her a weak smile. "I will. I intend to."

"Good. Maybe Cesare coming here will be good for you. Think how different he'll look bundled up in woollies, all sniffly and out of sorts, with a red shiny nose from a cold!"

Maureen looked at her aghast and then started to laugh too.

"That's better. Why don't we plan to do Christmas shopping early this year? Say, on the 7th of November? God, the suspense you bring to my life is amazing."

"Laura, I promise to call you right after and let you know. Who else can I talk to but you?"

Maureen looked around as she picked up her purse. They were almost the last to be leaving, and she saw the owner start to head their way.

"Ladies, you look so serious with what you were talking about. Here, have some chocolate truffles to bring back your smiles."

Laura looked up at him with a quizzical expression.

"We were discussing a serious subject, Mimmo, . . . Love."

"Aagh - now you've made me unhappy too. Please, take an extra truffle and forget it. Love can be as gloomy as the weather!"

The three of them walked to the door laughing. Laura and Maureen put up their umbrellas, as the rain turned from a shower into a downpour.

Chapter 22

A taxi would have been the simple choice, but Maureen wanted distraction, delay, and some familiar, ordinary activity to damp the little stabs of excitement that tried to pierce her superficial composure.

Among post-rush-hour travellers on the city's ageing Underground, she was surrounded by people - and isolated.

When Cesare's message had finally arrived last week, there had been a confused swirl of emotions that veered from elation to anti-climax. Surprise at the method, amusement for how she was addressed, let-down by its brevity. And then, appreciation for his discretion.

Later she shook with a mad laughter when she thought how very self-involved John was these days, not even to have bothered to pause - and play indignant husband.

A uniformed motor-cyclist had arrived at her door mid-morning with a to-be-signed-for envelope. Addressed to, 'Signora M. Catalbi,' a note inside read:

'Brown's Hotel, Dover Street, ten a.m.
Thursday, 6th November. Leave message there
if necessary. Alternative time and day possible.
C. B.'

Then had come a surge of intense happiness, which she fought to suppress. After so many days had passed since his telephone call from Rome, she imagined his plans had after all been changed. She had as good as implied this would have to be their very last meeting. To mask her disappointment she assumed a protective attitude of indifference, which made it easier to busy herself in all the many new plans for her life she had devised.

❀

Maureen had timed her arrival with precision. Not too early - and not one minute late. Exactly at the specified hour. As she walked along Piccadilly the cold air on her face felt good. November was its typically dull and blustery self, but no rain had been forecast.

When she turned north into Bond Street her careful facade began to slide. The idea that he waited, just moments away from her, uncurled itself inside with a little flame that warmed. But before she turned the corner, where the hotel would be in her sight, some new doubts began.

How would he look to her now, in this different setting? Too polished, a bit exotic and out of place? Too - Italian? Would the old desire she had felt be altered? Or worse, have disappeared?

It had been Rome that caused her to lose herself, to revel in a sensuality that cast aside all inhibitions. Perhaps it had really been the place and not the person.

What if he now entertained similar doubts?　He would see her as just another English matron, who blended so well into this grey northern city.　The summer romance had amused, but he was only here to keep a promise, make a courteous stop-over en route to New York.　He must already anticipate that journey.

❀

Without any pause she walked through the entrance and into the foyer . . . and there he was.

In the gracious old lobby he stood by a mahogany desk and leafed through the pages of a magazine.　At ease and formally elegant, he at once evoked the memory she had retained from when he had looked at her across the salon of the Palazzo d'Orinici.

Maureen stopped and all the nebulous cobwebs of worry vanished in the rush of endearing love for him.

Cesare looked up and his expression reflected back what her own conveyed.　Two months fell away from them in seconds.

This place - another scene of the same play, second act about to commence.　As the principals moved stage centre to the circle of light, residual bit players exited their stage.

His smile put crinkles around his eyes as they gave her an inclusive proprietorial survey.

"Maureen.　I wondered so much how it would be, when at last . . . "

"And I too, Cesare."

For another moment they appraised each other; then he put the magazine aside.

"The room is just a floor above.　We can take the stairs, I think, yes?"

With a slow, measured pace they crossed the foyer without further words, to walk up the carpeted staircase.

At the reception desk, the cashier murmured to a colleague as she laid down a receipt.

"His wife has arrived, I see."

"Mmm. Attractive couple."

Calm and unhurried they reached his room and Maureen saw it was one of the suites. Chairs and a sofa were grouped around a table, on which a bowl was filled with lovely old-fashioned roses in a melange of soft colours. She guessed he had specially ordered them.

"Let me take your wrap, *carissima*."

As she unfastened the moss green cape he shook his head in admiration of her paisley dress, in muted shades of green and amber. Then he noticed the bracelet on her wrist and smiled as he walked over to the wardrobe.

"I do so enjoy these London hotels. The English are amazing - everywhere they create the Formal Sitting Room."

They both laughed, the day ahead theirs to explore in a contented and slow progression of pleasures. No haste or premature move allowed to mar any of its moments, and this one to embrace each other, with their eyes.

A simple truth had been acknowledged without words. Their love, the summer passion, remained and would always be there for them. A new maturity revealed. Whatever the obstacles, the long lonely interludes apart, the bond endured.

"I can arrange to have coffee sent up, but I warn you, it is not very good. Not even with the hot milk."

She smiled. "English coffee is awful, isn't it?

But I don't want any, thank you."

"Good! Because I have something else that is much more suitable."

He went over to the sideboard where a champagne bucket held a foil-necked bottle, and lifted it out. Folding a napkin around it he unwound the lacy wire.

"Champagne - so early in the day?"

But her voice revealed her delight at the prospect. Cascades of golden bubbles matched her spirits, which rose in sunny bursts of pure happiness. She bent down to remove from her purse the blue tissue-wrapped square and placed it on the table near the roses.

"Did you order this bouquet, Cesare, or did the hotel put them here?"

"I ordered the roses for you, the Dom Perignon for us - and told the rest of the world to leave us in peace. But I will order lunch to be sent up later, of course."

"Of course!"

He turned to look at her and they both laughed.

"We have a lot to talk about, Cesare - I have so much to explain."

"Indeed, we do have much to discuss, *tesoro mio*. And this we will do. But first . . . "

He poured the wine into tulip glasses and brought them over to where she stood beside the low table.

"It is not too early to drink champagne." He held her eyes, his own intent and serious now. "And not too late. For us, it is exactly the right time."

He gently tipped his glass against hers.

"To this moment . . . for as long as we live."

They each sipped and exchanged the look of

adoration all lovers wear. Then he reached out to take the glass from her hand and placed it on the table beside his own. When he lifted his arms she moved into them, and the past rushed back. With all its mysteries solved.

This was the other world that had always waited, after she stepped into the frame. To enter the place the poster had called her to discover.

❀

Some time later she gave him the package and watched his smile of delight after he unwrapped it.

"A watercolour . . . yours . . . of course it is - and the Gianicolo. But Maureen, it is lovely! You did inherit his talent. You are a fine artist."

He kissed her and returned to study it. When he found the initial M encircled with a C in the corner, he looked up with a new joy in his eyes.

"Then this does mean - ?"

"No - no it doesn't mean that, Cesare. I know what you are thinking." Her smile was gentle.

"This is where I have to explain about . . . all the things that have happened."

With a sigh he nodded and lay back on the pillow, his arms behind his head. The serious attention he gave her now made her pause, to put her phrases in sequence.

She told him of her decision and the time she had spent to reach it, the many changes she was about to make in her life. For herself, as well as her family. Because he was Cesare, not John, she was able to tell him about her own needs. In thoughtful silence he avoided any comment. But when she described the new direction in John's career, with the upheaval it would create, his eyes held a gleam.

"No Cesare, you mustn't think - "

"Maureen, I have said nothing. But of course I am thinking."

"It would be foolish to imagine - well . . . what you are imagining."

Her plans were stated with firm intent, but she found it difficult to let his optimism be dashed, so she reminded him that Christmas was a special time for children and families. She would need to be here, this year especially.

"I understand, Maureen, of course. And I do agree. But after . . . then a new year will begin. And which of us can know what it will bring?"

Later still, as they lay together, she thought of all he had told her about Gabi. His effort to locate the church in the Trastevere where the remains were interred, the inquiries begun for extant works that might remain at the art school.

There was an odd comfort to know of the locations where the short passage through life of her parents was marked. They were made firm in her imagination now, instead of ephemeral shadows. It drew a line below all the other strange events, that led here.

The hours slipped away and when the time came to part there was no sadness, as before. He held her close, and told her their lives were so entwined, some future happiness they could not see might still be waiting. If, when, she desired.

❀

A glance at her wristwatch showed she was
ahead of Mark and Sara, so Maureen had the cabby let
her out at the corner. She wanted to savour her return
to Elmsmere Road. To walk slowly to No. 22 and feel
the pleasure she always had on her return.

Thin wintery sunlight broke through the clouds
and the narrow tree-lined street of unassuming
terraced houses looked serene. Chelsea Green, a ham-
let within the village of Chelsea, had a good mix of
residents - older singles, middle-aged couples, some
children, and a few young professionals. A good place
to raise children. She would hate to leave.

It was not unlike those self-contained streets of
Rome. London too was but a collection of villages, as
all cities were. Small communes of support and
sanctuary.

At the wrought iron gate, separated from the
front door by a few feet of paving stones and potted
shrubs, she looked up at her little house. Stability
required sacrifice too.

The quick movement above caused her to look
up suddenly.

From behind the chimney a white bird took
flight but she was at a loss to readily identify it. A large
gull, perhaps, driven upriver by bad weather on the
coast, but she missed seeing the usual grey on its wings.

As she watched it soar upwards, arcing toward
the rays of sun, she thought of Cesare. He too would
soon be flying away from her, and with the bird she
sent her silent blessing.

When she bent to gather the letters, after
unlocking the front door, she saw a cardboard tube
propped up against the brickwork. One of the prints

surely, and she hoped it was the scene of the Piazza.

She filled the kettle for tea and ran upstairs to change then carried the tube up to her workroom. Breaking the seal at one end, she carefully extracted the print, unfurled it on the table, and set a weight at each corner.

Maureen pored over the whole scene then ran her fingers over the artist's signature, G. Tuornovici, in a dashed scrawl of chrome yellow. Then bemused, she saw the other small detail for the first time.

The original canvas at the London Transport Museum had been framed, so must have çovered it. On the dark cobbles of the square the shape of a white bird appeared below the signature. Some artists used special designs, she knew, and this could be his. When the other print came she would find out.

The slam of the front door and voices meant that Sara and Mark were home. She turned away and called out to them, then with a smile ran down the stairs to kiss the cold rosy cheeks.

"Mummy, can we go round to the Green before tea and see if Mr. Hobbs has that book I ordered? Please, please?"

Sara's voice asserted her ability with the plea for latitude.

"Not yet, darling. Change your clothes and have tea first. Then, if you finish half your homework before dinner, we'll see. Mr. Hobbs stays open till seven on Thursdays, remember?"

"I want to go too!" put in Mark.

"We'll all go."

Maureen arranged tea things on the table and poured water in the pot.

After they left for their rooms she checked the books on their desks, and saw Mark might soon need help this term with advanced maths. Then she returned to her workroom.

She switched on lights and studied her own version of the poster scene taped to the wall. Soon after she got back from Italy she had tried to recapture it, along with others scenes, on a morning when remembrance was filled with yearning.

Her watercolours were both softer and brighter than his oils but the medium was not the main difference. Gabi's work had a solemn brooding quality. His surer brushstrokes conveyed layers of emotion too that were hard to define.

The slam of the front door again surprised her. Maureen looked at the wallclock and saw John was home early. When his voice hailed all occupants, it was followed by the clatter and thud of Mark and Sara, joyous for the interruption.

"Where are you, Maureen?"

"Up here, in my room."

In minutes she heard them troop up stairs and through the open door. Mark grabbed the cardboard tube and brandished it about.

"What's this? Can I have it?"

"It's a mailing tube, stupid. Don't you know anything?"

"Yes, you can have it, Mark." And before Sara could exclaim, "There will be another one for you in a few days."

Sara spotted the poster first.

"Hey, is that what was in it?"

All of them came to look at it and John was first to comment.

"When did you get this? It's not something that I'd choose to remind me of Rome." Then after he saw the watercolour on the wall. "Your little daub's a bit brighter - but I don't like the subject."

Mark traced the black letters at the top with his finger, 'London Transport Authority' - a familiar slogan.

"Well I like it. When can we go to Rome too?"

Maureen smiled. He was at the charming age that supported his mother and cautiously challenged his father idol.

"I think next summer, young Mark, we can all go abroad on holiday."

Maureen heard the excited conviction in his voice. Well, hello change - which had already started, of course.

"Goody! That awful Heather in my class goes on and on about Paris - the fat pig!" Sara said.

Maureen was about to reproach her, when Sara deftly steered away.

"Are you going to frame it, or what?"

"Yes . . . I'm going to frame it. And the time has come to tell you all why it's so special to me. You see, it was my real father who - "

"Oh you're not going to waste money on a frame, are you?" John scoffed. "I don't want that hanging on my walls!"

Both children roared with delight and moved off, already bored and in pursuit of another diversion.

She gave him a steady look.

"John, I've waited a long time to tell you something important. Can we spend some time alone - a drink before dinner?"

Mark and Sara chorused their objections and John began to leave.

"Not right now, luv - can it wait? I have to go and call Dad." He looked back at her with a broad smile. "I've taken up the option on the grant - that should make you happy!"

Maureen nodded slowly. He hadn't heard a word she said. But then, even had he listened, her news would have failed to be of interest.

They had all left before she started to smile. Her eyes lit up with sparkles of happiness. Alone in the room she laughed and began to talk aloud.

"Of course it can wait. After all these years it can certainly wait a while longer. There are a few other things waiting, too. But there's plenty of time!"

She looked at the calendar on the wall, the sort that had next year's months printed below, and made a quick calculation. Then she smiled to think it might coincide with her birthday.

The memory of the circular plaster pattern returned. Those cherubic images on the hotel ceiling above the bed, when she lay with Cesare's arms around her and thought, how very appropriate they were.

It was when they made love for the last time, and she looked up at the angels at the precise instant it had happened. That tiny cosmic collision within, resonant but silent - a shower of stars, a meteor that streaked across the heavens.

Her intuition knew she had conceived. Their love had led them on to another destiny. She had lain there in blissful wonder, instead of concern and desperate guilt.

She was certain that she carried Cesare's child, and felt content. The gift of his love would be her own secret treasure, for a while.

Oh, there was plenty of time still. Mark and Sara were about the right age to be intrigued by the novelty of new life. John would be horrified, resentful of the disruption and expense of baby-raising again, with his life headed in a new direction, and his new career. And Cesare?

Maureen looked down and touched the white bird, and another idea started to take shape. As her finger traced the image she made a vow. This child should know its true father, who had created it with his love. Somehow, she would work it all out the right way. Lots of time yet.

Now she looked forward to all the changes ahead with confidence. Thanks to Laura's introduction through a cousin, the advertising agency she had applied to had accepted her for freelance work.

The children would remain at school in London. She had just committed herself to do stage sets for both the Christmas and Spring school plays.

Right now she had to let John know the house would not be sold, that she would help with the mortgage. He could rent a single flat in Birmingham, which would be better for his studies, and visit them on weekends when possible.

And next year . . .

Tomorrow she would call Laura. Her friend through all the preceding events, should certainly be first to learn how the sequel was going to shape up.

How strange, she mused, that we always believe we control our own destiny. Surely there were times when other forces were at work. Life could confuse, but it was important to have the courage to love, and always to accept the gifts of the gods.

She heard John's voice float up to her from the stairwell.

"Are you coming down soon, Maureen?"

Mark's voice quickly followed.

"We want dinner mummy! . . . *Stop dreaming!*"